P9-CJJ-100

REC'D MAR 3 0 2019

NO LONGER PROPERTY OF
SEATTLE PUBLIC LIBRARY

Praise for

SPLINTER

"An absolute page-turner that uses well-paced suspense
instead of graphic violence to craft an edgy tale."
—*Booklist*

"Detailed and suspenseful."
—*Kirkus Reviews*

"An engrossing thriller . . ."
—*Publishers Weekly*

"A wonderfully written suspense novel that both
young adult readers and adults will enjoy."
—*VOYA*

"A gripping thriller whose plot kept me turning pages,
written with such skill and nuance that I couldn't help going
back to re-read some passages simply for their beauty."
—Jessica Warman, author of
The Last Good Day of the Year and *Between*

Praise for

OBLIVION

★ "Readers will feel unmoored until the last few pages of this novel, and that's all right—so does the story's narrator, Callie."
—starred, *Booklist*

"Thoroughly compelling."
—*Kirkus Reviews*

"An exciting page-turner."
—*School Library Journal*

"[A] gripping, psychologically intense mystery . . ."
—*VOYA*

"I could see the tension rippling through every scene. A fabulous book that readers are going to inhale."
—Jessica Warman, author of
The Last Good Day of the Year and *Between*

A New York Public Library Best Book for Teens 2014

A 2016 Illinois Reads selection

BLINK

SASHA DAWN

carolrhoda LAB
MINNEAPOLIS

Text copyright © 2018 by Sasha Dawn

Carolrhoda Lab™ is a trademark of Lerner Publishing Group, Inc.

All rights reserved. International copyright secured. No part of this book may be reproduced, stor ed in a retrieval system, or transmitted in any form or by any means—electronic, mechanical, photocopying, recording, or otherwise—without the prior written permission of Lerner Publishing Group, Inc., except for the inclusion of brief quotations in an acknowledged review.

Carolrhoda Lab™
An imprint of Carolrhoda Books
A division of Lerner Publishing Group, Inc.
241 First Avenue North
Minneapolis, MN 55401 USA

For reading levels and more information, look up this title at www.lernerbooks.com.

Cover and interior mages: iStock.com/stevanovicigor (screen); iStock.com/iwanara-MC (angles); iStock.com/wundervisuals (face); iStock.com/Juanmonino (tiles); iStock.com/Panptys (shamrock).

Main body text set in Janson Text LT Std 10.5/15.
Typeface provided by Linotype AG.

Library of Congress Cataloging-in-Publication Data

Names: Dawn, Sasha, author.
Title: Blink / by Sasha Dawn.
Description: Minneapolis : Carolrhoda Lab, [2018] | Summary: Sixteen-year-old Josh falls in love with newcomer Chatham Claiborne, who has come to town to find her missing sister, but when Chatham suddenly disappears Josh unearths a web of lies and secrecy surrounding her life, and in doing so unwittingly discovers vital clues to the town's longest unsolved mystery.
Identifiers: LCCN 2017010258 (print) | LCCN 2017043303 (ebook) | ISBN 9781512498547 (eb pdf) | ISBN 9781512439779 (th : alk. paper)
Subjects: | CYAC: Missing children—Fiction. | Sisters—Fiction. | Mystery and detective stories.
Classification: LCC PZ7.D32178 (ebook) | LCC PZ7.D32178 Bl 2018 (print) | DDC [Fic]—dc23

LC record available at https://lccn.loc.gov/2017010258

Manufactured in the United States of America
1-42213-25775-8/31/2017

For my very own #14 and the girls who are the copious amounts of sprinkles on our ice cream sundaes

"Let me think. Was I the same when I got up this morning? I almost think I can remember feeling a little different. But if I'm not the same, the next question is 'Who in the world am I?' Ah, that's the great puzzle!"

—Lewis Carroll, *Alice's Adventures in Wonderland*

CASTLES IN THE SAND

I wasn't here the day it happened.

My mother didn't make much a habit of taking me to the beach, or anywhere, really, but it happened just down the shore from where I've laid out a blanket for my four-year-old sisters and me. Call me crazy—I mean, I didn't even know the girl—but I've been thinking about her a lot lately. She was my sisters' age when she was abducted, and she would be about sixteen, my age, now.

Rachel Bachton.

She was plucked away from this place, near the lighthouse on the north shore, where they hold the farmers' market in the summertime. One minute, she was there and the next, she was gone. A witnessed stranger abduction, they called it.

The kidnapper could've been anyone, based on the description of witnesses: thirty to forty-five years old, five-ten to six-two, nondescript dirty-brown hair on the longer side.

He could've taken her anywhere.

Did he kill her? Probably. That's usually what happens to kidnapped children, isn't it? When they don't turn up in a few days, it's usually because they're dead.

1

One thing's for sure: if she's still alive, she's been hidden well. There's been no sign of her since the supposed sightings in the days following her disappearance.

This past week, her case has been in the news again. That's probably why I'm thinking of her now. Some bones recently turned up, and while they're a far cry from this beach, authorities estimate the remains belong to a three- to five-year-old female . . . and they've been buried in the red soil of coastal Georgia nearly as long as Rachel's been gone.

It adds up. I hate to think of her meeting an end so terrifyingly raw . . . and lonely.

I didn't know her—she lived in a neighborhood on the other side of the lighthouse, up Sheridan Road, where the rich kids live—but because what happened to her happened here, on this beach, she's part of everyone who roots down in this town, no matter what neighborhood we're from. She's the reason kids in Sugar Creek grow up looking over their shoulders.

Sugar Creek. Sounds sweet, doesn't it? Trust me, it's anything but. Just a dusty and withered old burg that's on the lake but too many miles from Chicago to be a real resort destination. Vacationers realize there are trendier places to stretch out their tired legs and plant their umbrellas and fold-out chairs in the sand.

"Excuse me."

The voice is like a tinkling of wind chimes cutting through my sisters' nonstop chattering.

I look up at an hourglass of a girl, who's standing in the soft, drenched sand at the shoreline, about five feet away from where we're planted. She's wearing cutoff denim and a dark red tank top—that much I can tell—but the sun is reflecting off the water, and I have to shade my eyes. I can't see her face. She's no more than a golden outline of a girl, but staring up at her, I feel a sort of flutter in my gut.

The water washes up over her feet. "Fourteen?"

"Huh?"

She nods toward my chest. "You have the number fourteen . . ." Her voice lilts with a slight southern accent.

"Oh. Yeah." I brush sand from the tattooed number on my left pec. "Long story."

"Need help." One of my sisters tugs at the hem of my board shorts.

I take the juice box from whichever sister's sandy hand extends it toward me. I punch the straw through the top of the cardboard box and hand it back without taking my eyes off the girl.

"Would you mind?" She sloughs a backpack off her right shoulder. "I was hoping to take a dip, but . . . Could you watch my bag?"

Another juice box is pushed into my hand, and I take it without looking. I don't want to take my eyes off this girl in case she disappears.

"I'd really appreciate it," she's saying. "I mean, God, who knew it would be so *hot*? It's almost fall. Everything I've ever heard about the Windy City . . ."

It *is* warmer than usual today. It's near eighty-five, and it's a deep, thick heat. The kind that pools on your skin the second you walk outside. The humidity makes it feel like well over ninety, but the lake breezes always help, which is why we're here.

"Summer's lingering this year. It happens sometimes." I stand to get a better look at this girl. "Hotter than Hades some years, but winter's colder than—" I shut up the second I look into her brown eyes.

It's like they go on for miles. Chocolate rivers veined with gold . . . like liquefied amber.

I should say something. Or at least finish what I started to say in the first place.

"Josh Michaels." I consider offering a hand for a shake, but how corny is that?

She raises her chin, semi-defiant, or maybe just confident. "Chatham Claiborne."

Of course, a girl like this would have a great name. I roll it around on the tip of my tongue, can't wait to drink it down. "Where are you from, Chatham Claiborne?"

"Moon River. Georgia."

"Georgia? And you think it's hot *here*?"

"Well, I *expect* it to be hot back home."

"Joshy." Caroline tugs on my shorts. "*Juice.*"

Oh yeah. I put the straw into the box I'm still holding and pat my sister on the head.

"Looks like you have your hands full. I can just . . ." Chatham Claiborne moves to swing the bag back up on her shoulder, but I intercept it at the last second.

"No, I got it. Go ahead. Swim." The way I look at it, she has to come back to get the backpack if she leaves it with me, right?

She thanks me—that's what southern girls do—and before I know it, her back is to me, and she's already shin-deep in the lake. Layers of dark brown hair, the longest falling an inch or two shy of her shoulders, bounce as she plunges into the waves. In her clothes.

No dropping her shorts to the sand, or pulling off her top to reveal some cute bikini.

Interesting.

I wonder if she notices I'm pondering her sudden appearance here, if she knows I'm still looking at her, watching her ride the waves. I hope not. Don't want to be *that* guy, obviously ogling her as if she were an underwear model on the pages of a magazine.

I snap out of it and drop back to our beach blanket.

The twins are fighting over an Oreo, which is ridiculous because we have at least twelve more in the box, but while my mother would prefer I put a stop to it, I let it carry on. I give the box a nudge in my sisters' direction—let them figure things out and solve their own problems—and recline on the blanket. I prefer their bickering to silence. That way I know where they are and what they're doing. They're always into something when they're quiet.

Besides, arguing is healthy. Let them learn early: life isn't about agreeing all the time.

Out of the corner of my eye, I catch sight of Miss Claiborne again, over the silvery swells of Lake Michigan. Cutoff denim inches up her thigh, revealing the tiniest peek of cheek, and the cotton of her tank top sticks to her wet, ivory flesh like a second skin.

I wonder why she's here, at the beach, with a backpack and no swimsuit. And why *this* beach, in *this* town? If someone was vacationing for a long weekend, she wouldn't land in Sugar Creek. Like I said, this place hasn't been a destination since 1950. These days, anyone venturing to this stretch of Lake Michigan would be more apt to stick closer to other beaches than wash up on this rundown shore.

My phone alerts with a Snapchat.

Aiden: *It's on*

I reply: *Absofuckinglutely*

There's going to be a bonfire at Aiden's dad's place, near the bluffs tonight, and I'm getting out of big-brother jail in a few hours.

My mother is, as we speak, finishing the last hours of a double shift at the hospital. I've been on sister duty for nearly fifteen hours already, and I can't wait to get out of Dodge. Let loose. Blow off the steam built up courtesy of juice boxes and tangled ponytails and Beach Babies SPF 50.

I close my eyes but still see the glow of the sun on the backs of my eyelids. At least it's a nice day. And maybe I'm letting the girls eat too much sugar, and maybe they'll be tough to handle by bedtime, but what do I care? They'll be my mother's problem by then.

Minutes later, when cold drops of Great Lake sprinkle over me, I open my eyes to see Chatham Claiborne dropping onto the sand near us. "Thanks again." She drags her bag off the corner of our blanket and, to both my surprise and relief, doesn't bolt off but starts playing in the sand, digging down for the wettest grains and forming a mountain of the stuff.

"Do you like sand castles?"

I'm pretty sure she's talking to my sisters, but I sit up and take heed anyway. Her curls are fat with droplets of water, and her lips are tinged a bluish pink, a side effect of the frigid water. She's looking right at me.

"Who doesn't?" I fight the urge to grin.

Now addressing my sisters, she holds out a hand: "Can I borrow that pail a sec?"

Caroline hands it over.

"Make a mermaid house," Margaret says.

"*Princess* house," Caroline counters.

"You know," Chatham says, "I think I can make both."

She's comfortable with young kids, judging by her easy, casual tone. I like this about her. Her hands work the sand, molding and shaping it into a new formation.

She carves away pieces, and adds others, and in the time it would take me to make a nondescript pile, she's constructed a sand sculpture that looks like a dollhouse.

My sisters, enrapt with the process, shut up for the first time since they jumped on my bed to wake me this morning.

She keeps working, making the castle even more complex than it was a moment ago.

"Impressive," I say.

When she smiles, her eyes flash a brilliance I didn't know was possible with such dark irises. "Well, it's sort of what I do."

"You make sand castles. Like, for a living?"

"Makes life *worth* living, don't you think?"

I like this girl.

"Not just sand," she says. "Any sculpture. Clay, paper . . ."

"Metal?"

"Not my medium of choice. But sure."

"So what brings you here, Chatham Claiborne?" Is it weird that I used her last name there? "Aside from our malleable sand."

"Just enjoying the beach."

Vague. If she hadn't elected to squat here with us, if she hadn't spoken to me first, I might think I'm bothering her in striking up a conversation.

"Well, you came at a good time. Not many people come past Labor Day. Better when it's not as crowded."

She doesn't take my lead, doesn't explain what put her here this time of year. Just keeps creating.

I try again: "So you like beaches." No shit, genius. I all but slap myself for that intelligent comment. "Do you like bonfires?"

She shrugs but I catch a hint of a smile on her lips.

"A bunch of us are meeting down the shore tonight. You should come."

"Down the shore?"

"We can't very well party *here*." Party. Such an arbitrary word, and I wish I hadn't used it. Don't want her to get the wrong idea about me, about what I am . . . or what I'm not: some burnout without direction or a care in the world. I care. I do. But I'm not one of those guys who thinks a party is chips and a chessboard, either. "Beach closes at sunset," I offer by way of explanation. "County property."

"Oh." She's looking at something behind me, a blatant sign of disinterest in me.

Maybe I *am* an idiot.

I should just shut up.

I open my cooler and grab a bottle of water, but then I think it's rude not to offer her one. "Thirsty?" So much for clamming it.

"Parched, actually."

I toss the bottle to the corner of the blanket—again, she thanks me—and grab a second for myself.

When she reaches for the water, her shorts shift, and a mark on her hip reveals itself. After a quick glance upward—she's not looking at me; she's opening the water bottle and drinking—I look at it again. It's a scar. A burn, maybe. Definitely the result of some sort of trauma.

I know a little something about that. The scar on the inside of my left forearm practically sizzles when I think about it, and

8

I'm suddenly tumbling back in time to the day it happened, to the dark room, to my mother's terrifying shriek . . .

"So." Chatham's voice chimes in my ears, pulls me back to the present. "How far down the shore is this bonfire?"

I shake off the memory. "About a mile or so, past the boardwalk. On the bluffs." But she's still—again?—looking at something behind me.

"On the bluffs?" She has a hand on a strap of her backpack.

"At my friend Aiden's dad's place." I glance over my shoulder. What's she looking at?

"I'll try to come." She's getting to her feet. "Thanks for the water."

"No problem."

"And thanks for watching my bag. What time tonight?" She's already taken a few steps down the shore, in the direction of the lighthouse.

"About nine or so."

"Nice meeting you, Joshua."

Joshua. Not Josh. I like it.

"Same."

"I'll see you," she calls over her shoulder. "At the bluffs."

I focus on her as she's walking away. Commit every detail to memory. I'll probably never see her again. I mean, maybe she'll show up tonight . . . in a perfect world. But perfection doesn't exactly exist in my hemisphere.

"So pretty," Margaret's saying.

I agree. "Yeah."

"She made a porch."

Oh. The sand castle. I glance at my sisters, who are admiring all the niches and details of the sand castle between them, but quickly return my attention to the girl walking away. I can

hardly see her anymore, she's so far down the beach, blend-
ing into the hundreds of beach-goers gathered here on the last
weekend of summer.

"There's a path," Caroline says.

"And a tower," Margaret adds.

"And criss-cross windows."

I turn my attention back to my sisters, who are standing on
either side of the sand castle with open mouths. I snap a picture
of them and Chatham's creation. If I ever see Chatham again, I
want her to see the effect she's had on them.

Maybe I'll even muster the balls to tell her she's had an
effect on me, too. A girl like that . . . she'd sort of sucker-punch
you in the chest with a kiss, you know?

I search for her again on the horizon, but just when I think
I've spotted her, I realize it's just another brunette in another
scrap of red cotton.

One thing I've learned over the course of my sixteen
challenging years on this planet: it's like that with everything—
fleeting, impermanent. Nothing's more than a Cheshire cat
disappearing into hookah smoke and leaving the remnants of
its grin behind. And this girl is no different. She was here and
now she's gone. Like an illusion. You fucking blink, and she's
gone. Fucking gone.

Like Rachel Bachton.

But instead of leaving bones in a shallow grave, Chatham
Claiborne left something more impermanent: a sand sculpture
on the shore. It'll be washed away by evening.

BEAST OF BURDEN

"So hot."

"Too windy."

"So *hot*."

"Too *windy*."

My sisters argue from their booster seats in the backseat of my ancient Ford Explorer. The air conditioning hasn't worked since long before I acquired the title to this hunk of scrap metal, so even though it's too windy in the backseat for Caroline's liking, Margaret wins this fight because it's just too damn hot without the windows open.

The twins' cheeks are pink, I hope only flushed with the heat. I'll hear about it if they're sunburned, which is nearly impossible, given how often I applied the sunblock.

I roll down my window a few inches more.

"No, Josh. Too windy!"

I turn up the radio to drown out the sound of Caroline's protest. I'm almost home. My mother should be home soon. Thank the fucking lord.

The sooner she's home, the sooner I'm out.

I love my sisters, of course, but that doesn't mean I want to spend every waking second with them. I mean, it's not their fault they're here, courtesy of the wrong time of the month with the wrongest guy in the world. Still, I'm ready to let our mother take a turn at raising them for a day.

And maybe, just maybe, the possibility of seeing Chatham again increases the feeling of urgency about it.

God, I hope she comes tonight.

We exit the highway and rumble through town, past Churchill General. Circle the brick-paved roundabout. Hook a right at Second Street, where the Tiny Elvis Café has its windows open. I wave to a few of the guys on the football team, who are seated out on the patio, under the teal-and-white-striped canopy.

A request comes from the backseat: "Ice cream?"

"Not today, Maggie Lee," I say. "We gotta get home."

"Mommy said." Apparently, Caroline has rejoined Margaret's team.

"She did?"

"Uh-huh," the girls say in unison.

That sounds like something my mother would do: get the girls jazzed about spending the day with their big brother because he'll probably take them for ice cream. She's always setting me up for stuff like that. Well, two can play.

"Then she'll probably take you later." After a second, I add, "Tell her Josh said."

A few blocks later, I turn onto Carpenter Street. Our house is all the way at the end, on the left, just as Carpenter bends to become Wabash . . . the smallish raised ranch with fading gray paint and a boundary of overgrown hedges lining the lot. I'm nearing the driveway when I see it: a shiny, black truck—a new one, with a full-sized bed and larger-than-necessary tires—parked at the curb.

I'm about to turn into the driveway, next to my mother's green VW bug.

I calculate the time.

She shouldn't be home yet.

Maybe her shift was cut short. That happens sometimes.

But the truck . . . what the hell is it doing here?

The front door of the house opens, and two figures emerge.

"Oh no," Caroline says. I'm guessing she saw them, too.

I go past the house, looking in the rearview mirror, where I can see my mother standing in the doorway wearing a robe, kissing her ex-husband, my sisters' father. He's a big guy, at least six-two; she looks so small next to him. I swear under my breath, and continue driving.

"Daddy," Margaret whispers.

I don't have to look in the rearview mirror to know my sisters are shrinking in their seats, cowering, hoping not to be seen.

If I'd stopped at the Tiny E for ice cream, like my mother told the girls I would, we wouldn't be in this position.

Fuck, fuck, fuck!

What's he doing at our house?

Why the hell is she *kissing* him?

I breathe through the multitude of emotions rising within me, burning in my chest.

And why do I have the feeling she wasn't really working today?

I'll circle the block, and if they're still saying good-bye by the time we're coming around again, I'll have to interrupt them. It'd be better if the girls didn't have to witness it, but someone has to tell the guy to get lost . . . and stay lost.

He's not supposed to be here. Court ordered.

And I swear to God, if my mother did what I think she did . . .

Damn it, Rosie, I scream at her inside my head. *He's not supposed to be within five hundred feet of you! And you're doing this with him!*

By the time we round the block and pull up to our house for the second time—"No, Joshy, keep driving," Margaret says—Damien Wick, the world's largest asshole, is pulling away, oblivious to the fact that we saw him.

"It's okay," I tell the twins. "He's gone."

"Gone forever?" Caroline asks.

"At least gone for now." I pull into the driveway, kill the engine, and unclip my seatbelt.

My sisters follow suit, silent, and slip out of the car.

I drop an inflatable beach ring around each of their bodies, because I believe they should get used to carrying their own things, and I grab the cooler and sandy towels. We take our time to go around the house to the backyard, where we shake out our towels and drape them on the line, and spill the melting ice into the barren flowerbed.

We leave the cooler propped to dry out, and I stow the floaties in the shed.

The girls are quiet as we take the back porch stairs.

"It's okay," I tell them again when they turn their scared eyes up at me. "He's gone."

"Uppy," Caroline jumps into my embrace. I hold her at my hip, unlock the back door, open it, and lift Margaret in my free arm, so we enter together, a united mass.

Two beer bottles and the remnants of a meal sit atop the kitchen table.

A purple ceramic unicorn has made its way from the

storage under the stairs to the center of our table. I know what this means.

That unicorn was the only gift she'd ever received from the asshole who just left our house, and she only dusts it off and displays it when she's feeling nostalgic and hopeful. Or when she wants him to *think* she's feeling that way. She thinks I don't notice these things, but I do.

Rose Michaels-Herron-Wick—my mother doesn't hyphenate, but I remember our past—glances in the direction of the mess before meeting my gaze and plastering a smile on her face. "How are my darling girls?"

I lower them to the floor. "They need a bath, and they're probably getting hungry."

"You didn't take them to the Tiny E?" She gives me her best mom-look, but it's been ineffective for years. "I gave you money."

"I used it for lunch, and drinks and snacks to pack the cooler." And because I had the girls at the beach from ten in the morning, and it's after five now, I add: "What did you think we were going to eat all day?"

My sisters are at our mother's side for hugs and kisses.

"You smell like lake." Rosie scrunches up her nose. "You do need a bath. Go pick out your bubbles, and I'll be right there."

Margaret and Caroline scamper down the hall.

"Oh, God, what a day." Rosie holds her robe closed. "The hospital sent me home, but they just called, and they need me tonight."

A ball of fire waxes in my head. She is so not going to do this to me. Not again. Not tonight. I lean against the edge of the countertop, fold my arms over my chest, and stare her down.

But she's not making eye contact.

15

"I can't pass up the overtime, Josh, and I know you've been with them all day, but I had to come home for a nap. I was *exhausted*, okay, and I know it's not fair, but life isn't always fair, you know—"

"I hope you had the sense to use a condom," I spit out.

"What are you talking about? I just—"

She shuts up when she realizes I know what she's been doing. And whom she's been doing it with.

"I just . . ." Her words die.

I shake my head in disbelief. "I assume he paid you for services rendered."

She gives me a practiced look. "You don't talk to me that way."

"What the hell was he *doing* here, Rosie?"

"Call me Mom."

I chuckle, maybe because I know it'll piss her off. "I'll call you Mom when you start acting like one."

"You can—"

"Jesus Christ, we have a restraining order against the guy, and here you are, in a robe, *kissing him* on our doorstep."

Her mouth clamps shut.

I sweep a hand toward the two bottles and the fucking unicorn on the table. "You're sharing drinks with him—"

"I have to *work*, Josh. I wasn't drinking."

"Even better. Give the mean and nasty drunk more than one drink. That makes sense. And lie to me, say you have to work so I'll take the girls for the whole fucking day, so you can spend the afternoon in bed with this guy."

"He was only here a couple of hours. Not the whole day."

An uncomfortable silence needles between us.

"I didn't have a choice, Josh. He said he had a check for me."

"Did he?"

"I had to get you out of the house. I didn't want the girls to see him."

"Well, they saw him anyway. Zipping his fly on the front doorstep. Next time, how about I meet him at the police station to pick up the check? Or how about he *mails* it *on time*, like he's supposed to? Or ask the courts to take it out of his paycheck like every other normal person!"

She pulls her robe more tightly around her thin body.

I make a beeline for the steps—half a flight down to the foyer, half a flight down to the basement where my room is. "I'm going to be late."

"You can't go out." She's pounding down the steps behind me. "Weren't you listening? I have to work tonight. I need you to watch the girls."

"No, you needed me to watch the girls last night after my game. You needed me to watch them today. I'm off the clock, Rosie."

"Stop calling me that."

"You spend the afternoon in bed with this schmuck, and I'm supposed to drop everything to cover your ass again!"

"You live here, too, you know. You have to pull your own weight." We're in the basement now, damp and dingy.

"I had a job," I remind her. "You made me quit. You made me choose between football and work."

"And you chose football."

If I ever want to get out of this hellhole and go to college, football's my only hope for a scholarship. No one's going to give me tuition money for spreading mulch. Of *course* I chose football.

"So now you have to pony up and babysit."

"I've *been* babysitting," I say. "All fucking day. What about *me*? When's it my time? When do I get to do something for me?"

Her brow furrows, and suddenly, without makeup, in her drab, terrycloth robe, she looks much older than her thirty-four years. "When do I?"

I narrow my gaze at her, just enough so I know she's listening, so I know what I'm about to say will sink in: "I think you did a little something for yourself this afternoon."

She swings an open hand at me, but I dodge it, and her second attempt, too.

"Don't you dare judge me for what I have to do." Shaking, she eases onto the nearly threadbare sofa and drops her head into her hands. "After all I've done for you. Everyone told me to get rid of you. I was too young, they said. But I loved you, I kept you."

"I'm supposed to thank you for the fact that I exist." I lean against the wall opposite her. "For the fact that you got knocked up at seventeen by a guy who didn't give a shit about you."

"I loved you before you were born."

"If you really loved me," I say, "you might've done what's best for me." Translation: she would've given me to someone who wouldn't repeatedly put me in impossible situations.

Her lower lip quivers for a moment, then hardens into a line. "Congratulations. Not only are you not going out tonight, you're not going out for two weeks."

I shake my head, and can't help smiling at the absurdity of it all. "Great. That makes perfect sense."

"Want to make it three?"

I chuckle again. "Who do you think you're talking to? Do you think I don't remember the whole story? Do you think I don't remember what Damien's capable of? That I should ignore the potentially disastrous effect his being here could have? Not just on you? On all of us?"

She stands, and takes a step toward the stairs. "You don't talk to me that way without consequence. You're my live-in nanny for two weeks."

For life, is more like it. "For what? Speaking the truth?"

"When you've gone through everything I've gone through, you have license to judge me. But until then, respect me."

Conversation over.

She forgets that I *have* gone through everything she's gone through. The only difference is that I have no measure of control over the fucked-up decisions she makes. I'm just left dealing with the fallout.

I wonder what she'd do if I just took off. If, by the time she was ready for work, I just wasn't here.

It's too late for her to get someone to cover her shift. And there's no one to take care of the girls at short notice, not that she can afford to pay a sitter anyway.

So she'll lose her job if she doesn't go, or she'll have to ship the girls off to Damien. Which is not an option.

There's no choice about it. I have to stay home tonight.

I knock my head against the wall and listen to the creak of the steps as Rosie climbs them.

Just my luck.

If the mysterious sand sculptress shows at the bonfire and I'm not there, she's going to think I'm an ass. She probably won't go, anyway, but wouldn't this be the one night the stars aligned? And I'm stuck here playing nanny on Carpenter Street.

Now I'll never know if she cared enough to meet me or not. I'll never know if she was interested. And worse yet, she won't know that I *am*.

I close my eyes as Chatham Claiborne fades off into the distance behind me.

Unreachable.

It's better if I forget she was there at all.

'Cause if she was, she'll be leaving soon anyway. This town isn't like Key West, San Diego, or other places people visit and fall in love with. No one vacations here and decides to stay forever in a place like *this*.

MIRAGE

I lit out just as soon as Rosie returned from work this morning, and I've been with Aiden ever since. We're on the bluffs behind Aiden's dad's house, watching the sun creep down the horizon. It's one of those great nights when a deep violet sky meets a fiery tangerine of sunset.

I've been gone from Carpenter Street for over sixteen hours now.

Yeah, ground me. Go ahead, Rosie. You gotta sleep sometime, and once you're down for the count, I'm out the door.

Not that she likely got much rest, once the twins started making a ruckus around six or seven. But that's her problem.

I bring the weed to my lips, inhale, and pass it back.

Then I see her—Chatham Claiborne—do a double take, and realize she's not there. I know my mind is playing tricks on me.

"It's the weed." Aiden's always trying to explain the inexplicable. And what he can't explain, he makes up for in entertaining bullshit. "Good shit."

Yeah, but I've smoked good weed before, and never has it left me seeing things that aren't there. I have to wonder if Rachel Bachton's parents feel the same way . . . if they see their daughter in crowds of people, but only in momentary glimpses . . . if by the time they focus on what they thought they saw, she's gone.

The thought occurs to me: one of my sisters could be snatched if I'm not careful. My heart quickens with the sheer terror of it.

Could anything be more terrifying than not knowing where your kid is? Not knowing what she's had to endure at the hands of some psychopathic sicko?

Could anything be worse than knowing your kid is gone because you happened to look away for just a second?

"It's a little Purple Gorilla and a little Banana Haze," Aiden's saying. "That's why you get the aftertaste."

Purple Gorilla. Banana Haze. "Who names this shit?"

"I don't know, but I want that job." He takes a hit and passes the J to me. "I think I'd go with *motor oil hum*, or *mindjam*."

Good to know he's thinking about it. Aiden's father, a botanist, is one of those pro-legalization advocates, and he just took a job as a grower in a lab out in Colorado. This means Aiden very well *could* land a job naming pot strains if he follows in his father's footsteps.

It also means Aiden is granted a certain modicum of freedom most of the time because his dad is gone a lot. And his mom . . . well, she lives across town and doesn't pay too much attention to what he does. It's a vastly different environment than the one in which I live and breathe.

The fact that I haven't heard from Rosie since her barrage of texts around noon—which is probably when she finally decided to venture down to the basement to get me moving, but found me gone—isn't all that unusual.

There are three stages to her wrath:

First, the *vilification*. She unloads a string of insults at me. I'll never make anything of myself. I'm just as reliable as my motherfucker of a father, and she should've known better than to trust either one of us. We'll see how cute it is when I'm thirty-five and cleaning toilets for a living . . . because that's where I'm headed.

Check. Stage one complete. And because I wouldn't answer the phone when she called, she texted this round of insults, so I have it all in writing to prove it.

Phase two: *the cold shoulder*. She's sweet as anything to my sisters, but pretends I'm not there. She walks around me. Ignores anything I say or do. She heats whatever frozen concoction we're having for dinner, but makes only three portions of it. Whatever. I can live on cereal and milk.

I used to walk on eggshells during this phase, but lately, I've taken to whistling in the midst of her freeze-outs. It makes the girls feel better, and she can't stand it, which is an added bonus.

This phase is what awaits me when I return home. It used to bug me, but I actually prefer it these days. The less we speak, the better. If not for the fact that the tension eventually bothers Margaret and Caroline, I wouldn't mind hovering in stage two for a year or so.

Then, days or sometimes weeks later, Rosie will crack and fall headfirst into stage three, which I call the *self-deprecation* phase. Tears are involved—lots of tears—and an underhanded soliloquy (or three or four) about how she's sorry she's such a bad mother. Maybe she should've given me up. But then I'd be living in some group home with other orphaned kids whose mothers didn't care enough to try. Maybe then I'd realize she does the best she can, that she's the only one who loves me. My father didn't want me, my grandparents begged her to get an abortion. But she had me. So why do I blame her for everything that goes wrong in my life, when she's only trying to give me the best she has to offer?

It's worth noting here that I don't randomly blame her for shit. But everything that seems to go wrong is a direct result of some fucked-up decision she's made, so whether or not I blame her, it's still her fault.

The tears used to get to me, but I learned long ago. You don't apologize at this phase or try to make her feel better about herself because it only serves as justification for her wrath. She then spirals back to stage one, and before you know it, she's throwing things at you and reminding you you're the worst son ever, *especially* because she's done so much for you—and you've unknowingly validated her efforts with your apology, thereby proving her dedication, because you gave in and said sorry for shit you really aren't sorry for and shouldn't be held responsible for in the first place.

And overarching all this is that I know there are legitimate reasons she's like this. She's been through some shit, and sometimes it's not a matter of her *wanting* to act with her best judgment, but *not being able to*. She freezes up, gets scared, doesn't seem to know how to help herself. It's just the way things are.

I don't blame her for the *reasons* she does these things. I take issue with the fact that she does them. Period.

"So this girl." It's all Aiden says. I'm glad to stop thinking about my mother and focus instead on Chatham Claiborne. This girl.

"Yeah." I don't have to say more than that, either.

After a few beats of silence, he pipes in: "If she'd shown last night, you know I would've explained shit."

"Yeah."

"Listen, I gotta make some deliveries." Aiden takes the last hit, then crumbles the charred remains of the rolling paper on the rocks on which we're sitting. "Nothing too far. All in the neighborhood. You're welcome to hang, or come along . . ."

"Think I'll take a walk."

Aiden lets out a laugh. "Okay."

He probably knows what I'm really going to do: return to Northgate Beach. It's ridiculous, I know. She isn't going to be there.

But what else am I going to do?

"Meet you back in an hour or so?"

I nod, and as I climb down the bluffs to the grassy sand at the shore, I feel the tingle of the maryjane in my fingertips.

Definitely some good shit.

I head inland a bit, toward the boardwalk, which, in half a mile or so, after obediently framing the beach, juts out over a stretch of sand, thus morphing into a pier, and extends out over the waves.

The boardwalk is closed, but I maneuver underneath the weathered and splintered planks, where it's damp and barren, and cop a squat on the cool sand. Here, I'm at a good vantage point to see the shoreline from north to south, stretching wide open as far as it can go, like a satisfying yawn.

I like it here. This is where I used to run to . . . before. Back in the days when Rosie was pregnant with the girls and things got out of hand with Damien, I'd hop the gate and ride out the storm beneath this structure.

Right here, where someone carved **Rachel Bachton Was Here** into the underside of the planks.

From a certain point of view, it's true. She *was* here, once upon a time. Not under the pier, but on the beach.

The gorilla haze tingles in my brain.

And maybe it *is* the weed, but I see a figure—I swear, I see her—walking down the beach toward me.

I close my eyes in a hard blink, fully expecting the silhouette to have vanished by the time I open them again.

But someone's there.

I hear the splash of her steps in the water.

I scramble out from under the boardwalk and meander toward the shoreline. Not toward her, so much, but near enough that if it *is* Chatham Claiborne, I might say hello and snag some of her time.

Before I know it, she's about ten feet away, and the moonlight is just bright enough for me to determine she is who I think she is.

I keep walking south. She keeps walking north.

Any second now, we will pass each other by.

"Miss Claiborne." I didn't know I was going to say it—or anything—but I blurt it out half a second before our tracks are about to intersect. It hangs there in the sky for a second or two, like fireworks the moment before they burst.

She slows, but keeps walking. She's past me now.

Then she looks over her shoulder, and sort of pauses there on the sand. Finally: "Fourteen?"

S ' M O R E

We're perched on the huge rocks near the shore, a ways from
the boardwalk, nestled somewhere between Northgate Beach
and Aiden's dad's place. The scent of his bonfire wafts down the
bluff, and I know—because it's Aiden—that any minute now,
he's going to start roasting some sort of snack over the flames.

"Can I ask you something?" She's drawing something in the
sand with a stick—a series of connected swirls, almost hearts,
like a sort of clover without the stem. The hint of Georgia in
her voice . . . it's so subtle that I wonder if her parents dragged
her out there from somewhere else and repotted her.

I know what that feels like, even though we've never left
the county. I've been dragged to this guy's place, to that guy's,
to Rosie's next savior's. We've been living in the house we rent
now for almost two years, and it's the longest I've ever lived
anywhere.

I give her a nod, although it's pretty dark on this beach—
just a wedge of moon in the sky, presently blanketed by drift-
ing clouds, and the lampposts on the boardwalk are a hundred
feet behind us—that I wonder if she sees it, if she sees *me*, if
she's noticed my gaze lingers a little too long when I look at
her. "Sure."

27

"What's with the fourteen?"

I pause for a second. "It's my jersey number. In football." So I simplified, didn't tell her why I chose to get a tattoo of the number.

"Yeah, but it's a *tattoo*. Permanent. Probably more permanent than a jersey number, I'm guessing."

"I really like football."

"Ohhhkay."

The way she says it makes me feel like she doesn't believe me, like she can see right through me. I've been told I'm pretty transparent like that, though. I'm not good at hiding what I'm thinking.

"My sister has a tattoo," she offers. "It's a shamrock on her ankle."

I wonder if that's what she's drawing in the sand. And if so, why.

"I'm thinking I might get the same one."

I like tattoos. And the fact that she's considering one . . . Damn, I like this girl.

"How old is your sister?" I ask.

"Sixteen. Same as me."

Chatham's a twin? Maybe that's why she came up to my sisters and me on the beach. Just as I'm about to speculate, she says, "We're not biological sisters."

"Oh." There's a story there, just as there's a story inked on my chest with the number fourteen. But I don't want to pry. If she wants me to know, she'll tell me.

She doesn't. Instead, she asks, "So, you live here in Sugar Creek?"

"Unfortunately."

"Unfortunately? It seems . . . nice. Quaint."

"Yeah?"

"Yeah."

"I guess it could be." If you pull Damien Wick out of the zip code, if you hit the delete key on my last girlfriend, if you erase all the *insane* parts of my mother . . . "I suppose it's just like any small town. Kids growing up here can't wait to get out, probably because no one ever does. Not much happens here, nothing changes."

Then Rachel Bachton skips through my mind. If she's still out there somewhere, what would she give to come back?

"Predictability can be comforting," Chatham says.

I think of the notation under the boardwalk. **Rachel Bachton was here**. "Actually, I guess it's not one-hundred-percent true that *nothing* happens in Sugar Creek."

"Really? What happens?"

I consider telling her about Rachel. But I want to tone down the crazy, if *quaint* appeals to her.

"I mean," I say, "*you* showed up here, didn't you?"

"I did. Think we might be staying a while."

This makes me smile. "You should. We could cut English class together. Come down to the bluffs. Skip stones instead of analyzing *Macbeth*."

"You shouldn't cut English."

"You want me to go to English class?"

"I liked *Macbeth*." She shivers in the night breeze.

Of course she's cold. Summer's officially over now, and she's still wearing those short shorts. And sure, it was mid-seventies today, but once the sun goes down, the temperature plunges, especially near the shore.

Aiden's call echoes over the lake: "C-caw! C-caw!"

Normally, I'd answer him with my own *c-caw*—it's a system

we established once after making a break for it out of a kegger with cops in pursuit—so he knows I'm coming back, but the whole thing seems sort of goofy in Chatham's company. Would the girl who's a genius with sand sculpture and apparently doesn't mind Shakespeare think I'm unsophisticated if I let out my own *c-caw*?

Better not risk it.

"You might make this town more interesting," I say.

"I doubt that."

I can't help but pry a little now. "What brings you here, anyway?"

Chatham turns her face to the breeze off the lake, and her hair whips in the wind.

Aiden's roasting marshmallows. I smell the hint of charred spun sugar in the air. "C-caw!" His call sounds again.

She tucks a chunky curl behind her ear. It's this moment, I know: I'm going to know everything about her, and then I'll tell her everything about me. I feel that connected to her.

"You want to know why I'm here?"

What I really want to know is if she's going to stay.

She licks her lips and sort of smiles. "I really like football."

JOLT

My phone hums in my pocket. I pull it out. Text from Rosie.

I don't open it. Hey, I'm at school, and it's only minutes from the beginning of third hour. For all she knows, because she never bothers to write down my schedule, I could be in the middle of a test.

I meander my way through a crowd of people, and just before I'm about to cut down the math hall, I catch a glimpse of a long, ivory leg.

I do a double take, but she's still standing there when I glance again. In the flesh.

The girl I shared s'mores with at Aiden's, Chatham Claiborne, is occupying the same building, breathing the same air as me.

It's been my experience that when people show up in this town, they're drawn to the nearest exit ramp and quickly steer their way onto it, but if she's at school, it can only mean she's going to stay.

I walk over. "Chatham."

She doesn't acknowledge me, just stands there, against the brick wall in the commons.

She's looking down at the piece of paper in her hand, which I presume to be her class schedule.

"Chatham Claiborne."

This time, she looks up and sort of smiles. "Hey there."

My fingertips start to tingle, as if her voice has the power to trigger electrodes in my system.

I'm close enough to her now that the faint smell of her shampoo—something no-nonsense, not fruity or flowery—meets me.

"Where's one-forty-three?"

"Let's see." I take the paper from her hand and give it a look. "Hey, we have English together."

"Yeah?"

"We'll be reading *Macbeth* together after all." I show her the seventh-period assigned class.

She takes the schedule back. Dried clay rims her cuticles. It doesn't take a genius to realize she's just come from the art hall. Sculpture. And she's headed to—geez—physics. I got a D in chemistry last year, so I'm retaking it.

"Looks like you've been playing in the mud." I give a nod toward her clay-encrusted fingers.

She looks at her nails. "Oh, no matter how many times you wash your hands, the stuff sticks with you."

"So you admit it. First sand, and now mud."

"No." She giggles a little. "Clay. I'm working on a relief."

"Sounds interesting." I have no idea what a relief is, but you can bet I'm going to look it up later. "You're heading toward the science hall, so you're going to—" I point in the general direction of the labs. "You know what? I'll just walk you there."

"Thanks."

I'm going to be late for class, but I don't care. For a few feet, we walk in silence. With every step, it grows more and more awkward. I finally speak. "I didn't know you were going to be here."

"Yeah."

What else did I expect her to say? *Extremely* awkward now.

But we're almost to the science hall, and I can't let this hang there until seventh-hour English class. So I try again: "Hey, what are you doing tomorrow after school? You should come to the game."

"Oh." She hugs the strap of her backpack. "Yeah, maybe. We have to get settled into the new place."

I guess that answers my question. She's seen enough of me to know she's seen enough of me. "Okay. Well, if you change your mind—"

"Can I let you know?"

"Sure." I point down the next hallway. "One-forty-three will be on your left."

"Thanks."

"Don't mention it." I turn to hustle my ass to geometry, which I'm also repeating this year.

"Oh, I forgot. Joshua."

Joshua. Another jolt sends shockwaves to my every nerve ending. I stop.

"Wait. I also . . ." Her backpack is on the floor now, and she's unzipping the front section of it. "I got my phone hooked up, so . . ."

"Oh. Good."

"What's your number? I'll text you, so you have mine."

"Okay." I rattle off my digits.

She inputs them as I say them, then . . . "There." She hits send.

My phone buzzes.

Her message: *Hi.*

I look up at her again. "Hi."

A hint of a smile appears on her lips and then she turns to walk to her room. She doesn't see the huge grin that lights up my face.

I head toward the math hallway, and while my phone is out of my pocket, I flip to Rosie's message:

Damien was here.

An arrow of fear pierces me for a split second.

He was in our house?

But then I remember: she did this once before in the middle of one of her freeze-outs. She used Damien to lure me back to her side, and then all hell broke loose between us when I realized the fucker was still in jail and she made it up.

I text back: *call the cops.*

And let it roll off my shoulders.

Even if he *was* there, what does she expect me to do about it?

ALL SHOOK UP

The ache in my left shoulder is residual, a reminder on cool, damp days of the night Damien Wick slammed me to the concrete patio behind the house we used to live in.

It was just the three of us back then. Margaret and Caroline weren't around yet.

Rosie should've left him at that first sign. Instead, when she found him snarling atop me like a rabid dog, she'd wondered what I'd done to provoke him.

Of course it was my fault. I was eleven. A smartass. Long tired of the random men who'd come into our lives, puff up their chests in oppression, eventually to split, or kick us out of whatever hellhole they'd sucked my mother into . . . but only after they'd run her through the wringer and left her shredded, with a little less substance and a little more shadow in her soul. Imagine being rejected by losers like that. Imagine what it does to you.

And then one day she learned: sometimes you don't have to do anything to deserve a beating like that. She *hadn't* done anything to provoke him, except maybe offer him another Pabst.

He'd hit her with a closed fist that day. Both eyes swollen shut, back bleeding with the lashes of the closest stick within reach.

Nearly as soon as it started, it was over, and he'd cried and said he was sorry. And she wouldn't leave him then because she was six months pregnant. With twins, no less, so how was she was supposed to raise us on her own?

And so the pattern was established.

I wonder if Rosie feels a residual ache in all the places she'd been slammed—literally and figuratively. She, too, I'll bet, has scars no one can see.

Here's the difference: I couldn't have left if I'd wanted to. All she had to do was walk out the door, and I would've followed. But something stopped her, maybe she wanted to leave but couldn't, and she's learned along the way to stay.

It's ugly, but it made me who I am. Besides, I know how to take a hit, and that comes in handy on Friday nights.

Coach Baldecki pulls the elastic wrapping from my left shoulder, and the cold pack rolls off with it. "You good?"

"Yeah, Coach." I trot back onto the field, where our guys recovered on the twenty-two. I don't have much time—twelve-point-four seconds—but we're only down by three.

Garcia, my center, snaps.

Ball in hand, I drop back into the pocket, a sea of blue and gold rushing at me, and my wall of black and red defending.

Look to the left.

Novak's covered.

Look to the right.

No one.

Left, right.

Scramble away from the big mutha honing in on me.

A window ahead.

I take it.

Hook right.

Then home free.

Just as I'm nearing the end zone line, I feel and hear the crunch of bodies, and I'm slammed to the earth, buried beneath a mountain of muscle, sweat. I tighten my grip on the pigskin and curl my body around it.

Go ahead. Take it from me. Over my dead body.

One by one, the bodies peel off, give way to the lights illuminating the field and the buzz and roar of the crowd in the bleachers.

Whistle.

The ref's hands go up. *Touchdown.*

I look down at the turf and see the red of the end zone. I made it. I'm in.

In the locker room, later, Novak shoulders me as he passes: "I was open. Dickhead."

Whatever.

"Don't let him get to you." Jensen's a senior, one of our team captains, an offensive lineman. "He's always saying he's open when he's not."

"He wasn't."

"You coming tonight, Michaels?"

There's always a victory celebration—sometimes even when we don't win—but this was pretty big. We're three-and-one now; if we'd lost we'd be a five-hundred team, which doesn't bode well for playoffs. This was our first game with our senior starter out, and a junior classman—me—standing in as QB, up against the favored and privileged boys from the north shore. "Can't."

"Come *on*. At least come to the diner."

"Grounded." I pull a T-shirt over my damp head.

"Dude, you're always fucking grounded."

True story.

I shrug it off. "Have a good time."

On my way out, Baldecki calls me into his office.

"Close the door."

I close it.

"Yates is probably out for the season. Torn meniscus."

I bite my lip, mask my elation, and nod. "Sorry to hear."

"I'm going to need you to stay eligible."

Another nod. "Yes, sir."

"How are your grades?"

We've had homework. We've had tests. But the teachers don't enter much into the grade books the first six weeks of school, so I say, "Good."

"Last year, you struggled."

I take a breath. I should explain the turmoil of last year, the court case for the order of protection against Damien, the constant looking over our shoulders. The constant sacrificing school to cover the twins. But before I can say anything, Baldecki continues:

"You're on track this year?"

"Yes, sir."

"Stay that way."

This means I'll be playing the rest of the season. Visions of scholarships dance in my head. I can't stop the wild grin coming on. "Absolutely."

He stands, so I stand.

Our meeting appears to be over, but I don't want to leave until he dismisses me. He's looking down at his clipboard.

"Your last play," he says. "The sneak."

"Yeah."

"You've got good instincts."

"Thank you."

"But that wasn't the play you were supposed to run."

"No, sir."

"You out for your own glory?"

"No, sir. Just wanted the win. For the team. For Yates."

"You had an open receiver. Novak."

Bull*shit*. "He was covered, I thought."

"He'll catch what you throw. Gotta trust him."

"I do. Just didn't see him as open."

"I've benched players for less." He fixes me with a hard glare. "*We* call the shots out there. The *coaches*. Not you."

I feel the flames of anger rising in my chest. We fucking *won* with that play, and fucking Novak *wasn't open*. I swallow the aggression, hope I can keep a lid on it until I'm out of here.

"Good game."

I bite my lip and nod.

I don't blow my top until I'm in my Explorer, radio blaring, zipping down Washington with windows closed, so no one can hear when I slam my fist into the roof and scream.

Most of the team is still busy dressing and high-fiving by the time I'm home, but Rosie's car is running in the driveway when I pull in, and I know she's going to be pissed.

She bowls out of the front door the second I step onto the porch and aggressively brushes past me. "God *damn* it, Josh!" It's all she says, but it's more than she's said all week.

No *how was the game?* No *how's the shoulder?*

Looks like we're still in phase two.

I don't know what she expects me to do. I got here as fast as I could. Did she expect me to skip my game?

She shoots me one last death glare before she slams her Beetle door and practically squeals her way down the street.

Once inside, I close the door behind me and lean my back against it. A Disney classic blares from the television. "Hey, Maggie Lee. Miss Lina."

"Joshy!" Caroline's first on her feet.

They're already in their pajamas, but Margaret's knotted nest of hair tells me Rosie didn't fight with them to wash their hair, if they've had a bath at all.

I check my phone. The last message I got from Chatham said she couldn't come to the game. I returned with a *maybe next time*. That was at three. I was the last to message, so I can't send another without seeming too overly eager, and at this stage, I have to play it cool. Don't want to scare her back to Moon River.

It's crazy how I crave her. We hardly know each other, but she's become necessary, in a sense. It's like I want English class to last a lifetime, even though she sits clear across the room and one row behind me, so I can't even look at her most of the time. But she's always there, in the back of my mind: her hands always sporting the remnants of clay relief, the curls she tucks behind her ear when she's bent over her desk, writing.

So aside from the occasional Snap, which blips on my radar and is gone before I can convince myself to screenshot it—I can't let her know I want to preserve every word she sends, can I?—we don't have many chances or excuses to talk. I want to know everything about her, why she's here in Sugar Creek, where she's living, what her family's like.

A million times I've wanted to take her by the elbow and lead her aside for a chat against the lockers. But I never do. Maybe I'm afraid to let her know how much I *want* to talk, to get to know her.

Because really, we're not more than a conversation on the beach, and a few shared s'mores at Aiden's when she barely said anything. But I feel her pulling at me—an invisible, organic luring. Somehow I know I'm supposed to know her, that we're supposed to know each other.

I shake my head to clear it of these thoughts. If I were out with the team, at least I'd be distracted, if not having fun—despite the rod up Novak's ass, and the group of seniors who somehow blame me for Yates' fucking meniscus tear. Hey, I'm not the one who landed on him. But no, I'm stuck at home watching some cartoon princess try to tame a beast. Unless . . .

"Hey, sisters." I lift Margaret, who's already hanging on my leg anyway. "Want to go to the Tiny E?"

Caroline stops watching the television instantly. "Ice cream?"

Margaret kisses me on the nose.

"Ice cream." I wouldn't dare bring them to the after-party, but . . . "Go get dressed."

"But you're grounded," Margaret says as I put her down.

I love being reminded of that fact by a four-year-old.

"We have to eat." It's a rationalization, but it's still true. Besides, Rosie wants me to take care of the girls? That job comes with perks. I'm in charge when she's not here. How's she going to stop me from leaving the compound when she's clear across town at the hospital?

While the twins fight their way down the hallway to their room, I pull out the largest canister in the pantry and dig through the flour for the sealed plastic bag of Rosie's emergency stash. She's been hiding cash in the flour since I was ten, since Rich "Dick" Herron—husband number two, before

Damien—started pushing her around and she started saving for a way out. She thinks I don't know, and she never seems to notice when I take a little, which I rarely do anyway, as I still have some cash of my own stashed away from the job I quit when pre-season football practice began.

I pull out a twenty and bury the rest.

I fight with Margaret's hair, and manage to pull it into a ball on top of her head. Playfully, I tug on it. "You look like a cookie jar. Like, I could just"—I make a popping sound—"pull the lid right off you and eat some cookies."

It makes her laugh.

I let Caroline wear her favorite pajamas—the ones that could pass as a pink bunny costume, complete with a cotton tail—and a pink, plastic tiara. I don't care.

With the girls' music bopping through the speakers, we make our way into town.

Just as I'm maneuvering this beast of a car into a parallel spot across the street from the Tiny Elvis Café, I see her—Chatham Claiborne—exiting the very diner I'm about to enter.

Okay, so she blew off my game to hang out at the diner. Even though she said she liked football, she was probably joking. And who am I to her anyway? She shouldn't feel any obligation to go to my game. So why do I suddenly feel so hollow?

Because, that's why. Because I wanted her to come. I wanted her to *want* to come.

I put the car in park and busy myself with getting my sisters out of the backseat.

Don't look at her, don't look at her, don't look at her. It'll be awkward. Don't seem overly eager, overly happy to see her.

"Hey there."

Without a second's hesitation, I look up when I hear her voice. She's smiling. "Heard you won."

"Yeah." I remind myself to hold tight onto my sisters' hands. I'm forever distracted in this girl's company; can't have my sisters wandering off.

"I saw the first quarter, the beginning of it."

"Yeah?" So she left after half a defensive line demolished me. She didn't get to see me do my thing.

"Sorry I missed the rest." She thumbs behind her, toward the diner, where my teammates occupy nearly every table, which they've pushed together in the center of the space. "Job interview."

"At the Tiny E?"

"Yeah. Got a job."

"Congratulations."

"Well . . . actually, I don't know if I can take it."

"Jah-ah-osh." Only my sisters can turn one syllable into three. "Ice cre-e-eam."

"You're busy," she says. "We can talk about this—"

"Listen, no, I want to . . ." I shut up before I say the words that have been threatening to fall out of my mouth, arguably, since the very first second I saw her: *I want to talk to you.* "Do you, maybe, want to come with?"

"I don't want to interrupt your—"

"C'mon." I give my head a toss in the diner's direction. "You're not interrupting anything."

"You're sure?"

"Positive." I think of the twenty bucks I just horked from Rosie's stash. "My treat."

"In that case . . ." She reaches for Margaret's hand. "I'd love to."

We, a connected line of four, take a step off the curb, but I stop dead in my tracks the moment I see it—an oversized black pickup parked a few spaces behind my car.

Damien Wick, my sisters' father and the man I hate more than anyone else on the planet, is staring me down through the windshield, as if he's about to blaze tire tracks over my chest.

THE WHITE RABBIT

I don't know why Damien's here, but I have a sneaking suspicion that he's reporting to Rosie: *he took my children here, he took my children there.* He may even demand time with the girls, and pretend I put my sisters in bad situations—he'll probably lie and say I did even though I wouldn't—and bully Rosie into allowing him visitation.

If he's still here when we're leaving, I'll lead him directly to the police station. He's not supposed to be anywhere near us.

Luckily, he doesn't follow us into the diner. He'd have to be an incredible idiot to do such a thing, but as it turns out, that's exactly what he is, so you never know what he might do.

It's crowded and loud at the Tiny E. So loud that I can't even hear whichever Elvis track is playing. We make our way past the football team—a few guys offer me fist bumps along the way—and find an open table on the far side of the diner. It's one of those small booths, really meant for two, but we don't have much of a choice. Chatham slides onto the bench and pulls Margaret up onto her lap, like it's the most natural thing in the world, like it's normal for a guy and a girl to have two preschoolers as chaperones wherever they go.

Again, I wonder what her life must be like that she can fit into the chaos of mine, if tonight is any indication, so seamlessly.

"I'm told you haven't had dessert"—she reaches for a menu—"until you've eaten it at the Tiny Elvis." She looks at me over the menu and smiles. "At least that's what they said when they hired me."

I shift Caroline on my lap. "It's basically true." But I don't want to discuss unimportant subjects. I want to make the most of my time with her.

Caroline grabs the salt- and peppershakers—at this table, they're mini statues of fat Elvis—and she and Margaret treat them like Barbie dolls, instantly putting them into a scene. It's what they do every time we come here.

"So you're going to work here?" I ask.

She chews on her lip for a second, like she's not sure how to answer. "It depends. I have to make a few arrangements first."

"Hmm." Is she hoping to tell me more? Or have I already probed too much? "Well, if there's anything I can do . . ."

It almost looks like she's going to take me up on my offer to help, and maybe she's about to tell me something important, when Caroline shrieks.

"No, get away!" Caroline's salt is running away from Margaret's pepper. "I'm *allergic* to you!"

Because she hasn't watched this scene twenty times, Chatham laughs when pepper makes salt sneeze.

Got to hand it to my sisters. They know how to divert a conversation. I guess, if we're going to have a meaningful discussion, it's not going to happen here. It's okay. You practically have to shout to be heard in here tonight anyway.

I order a cookie sundae for my sisters to split, and I get the *Hunk of Burning Love*, the Tiny E's version of chocolate lava cake.

Chatham gets a single scoop of strawberry ice cream, which she carves into the shape of a rose with her spoon.

My sisters stare at her, and the rose, in awe.

This girl can make a sculpture of anything.

We eat.

I pay the tab.

Chatham takes the girls to wash their hands while I say good-bye to the team. I wait at the door and survey the street for any signs of Damien. The jerk is gone, thank God.

"All squeaky clean," Margaret says as the three of them return from the ladies' room.

As we're leaving, I glance up at the clock. Elvis's hips sway in time with the seconds passing. Twenty-two minutes. That's the long and short of the time I've just spent with the most intriguing girl I've ever met. And I don't want the night to end here, feeling as if I know no more about her than I did the moment I met her.

It's not too late. If she doesn't have overbearing parents that enforce a strict curfew . . .

"Hey, just a thought." The air is a brush colder than it was when we got here. "If you don't have to get home right away, you're welcome to come back with me for a while."

"Oh." She stops in her tracks. "Really?"

"I can drive you home later."

A beat of silence follows.

I feel like I shouldn't have asked. If a girl doesn't immediately accept, she probably doesn't want to come.

Maybe in inviting her back to my place, I'm suggesting something she's not ready to face. My mother's gone, my sisters will be in bed as soon as we're home . . . We'd be alone. But now that it's out there, the ball is in her court.

"Pleeeease?" Caroline bats her lashes and hangs on Chatham's arm. "Please come."

Chatham laughs and lifts Caroline. "Does anyone ever say no to you?"

■ ■ ■

I wonder if Chatham agreed to come here because Caroline guilted her, or because she really wanted to come. But she's here now.

Bringing her back with us is a big gamble, especially because I've yet to figure out how I'm going to leave to take her home, but—obviously—I'm willing to take the risk.

She's sitting across the coffee table from me, her back to the blazing electric fireplace, on the cheap area rug I now wish I'd vacuumed when Rosie told me to. She's setting up the Scrabble board—it's the game she chose from the few on the shelf—and doling out tiles.

"So when do you start at the Tiny E?" It's not exactly my conversation of choice, but it's a place to begin.

"Actually, I don't know if I can take the job. I can't find my license. I'm sure it's just in a box somewhere, but I need an ID to start, and frankly . . . I'm running out of places to look."

She lays out a few tiles on the board: *cape*. Then she rearranges them: *pace*. "I'm not sure I'll ever find it, and getting a birth certificate from Georgia might prove difficult at this point. We'd have to go back, and—"

"Aiden can help." Here's the thing about Aiden: he's brilliant. If he used his mind for good, he could be running the country someday. But he doesn't agree with an overarching force of power, so he's made it his mission to work against the system. This includes utilizing his graphic-art skills to ensure the underage population of this town can purchase a six-pack. Or, in my case, get a tattoo.

"Tell Aiden I'll take any help I can get," she says.

I pause a moment, and then blurt out, "Okay, how the hell do you end up *here*? Of all places?"

"Well . . ." She takes a deep breath and looks at me, as if she's weighing how much she trusts me—which could be not at all, for all I know. "We're sort of here looking for Savannah." Her look holds me in, unblinking. "My sister."

"Oh."

When she doesn't elaborate, I probe a little: "You think she's here?"

"She might be. I don't really know. She ran away." And after a pause: "She's always running away. But this time, she told me she was going. She wanted me to go with. I just thought . . . it's a crazy idea, right? Taking off for a small town you've never been to?"

"She wanted to come *here*?"

"Yeah."

It's quiet for a few beats. So quiet, in fact, that I hear the rainforest soundtrack wafting down the steps. I play it to help Caroline and Margaret fall asleep, and it's soothing, but now it's just background noise.

I play off her *c: cot.*

"Do you ever just *know* something?" she finally says. "And you don't know how you know it, but you know it?"

I know what she means. I knew I was connected to Chatham Claiborne the second I saw her, but I know I can't say that; it would sound too creepy.

She's working the zipper on her backpack. "Savannah wrote about this place. The lighthouse, the boardwalk . . ." She pulls a book out of the bag and places it on the table, next to our pool of facedown tiles.

It's one of those blank-page journal types, about half an inch thick. Its black vinyl cover with worn edges is bound with a dirty rubber band.

"She wrote about Sugar Creek?" I ask. How would anyone from Georgia know about this place? To the extent she could write about it?

"I *think* so. It's mostly vague references, but she mentions the name of the town." She opens the book and shows me a rudimentary sketch of what looks like the lighthouse at Northgate Beach.

I see the name amidst scrawlings: *Sugar Creek.*

"I told her I wasn't going to run away with her. She was always running away, like I said, but she'd never left Georgia before, and I wasn't about to follow her out to the middle of nowhere—no offense."

"None taken."

"But she took off again anyway. She left her journal. And not only did she leave it, she left it underneath the pillow on my bed. Like she wanted me to find it. Like she wanted me to *read* it."

I'm nodding like a bobblehead on a dashboard. What else can I do? I don't want to interrupt her, this first time she's really opened up to me.

"We're not biological sisters. I told you that."

"Right."

"She's adopted; I'm not."

"Okay."

"Well . . ." She sighs. "All I can say is that all my life, she's been running away, but she always comes back. And one day, a couple weeks ago, she took off, and I haven't seen her since. She *told me* to go with her. She *told me* she wasn't coming back. And life without her . . ." Her eyes redden, and they start to well with tears, but none grow big enough to roll down her cheeks. "I don't know what to do."

"I can't imagine." I wonder what any of this has to do with Sugar Creek, why Savannah would come here, of all places.

"I worry about her—"

"Of course you do."

"—which is crazy, because I know she can take of herself. But still."

"Yeah."

"So I came because this is where she said she wanted to come. This is the place she wrote about—the boardwalk, the lighthouse on the beach."

"*Lots* of towns have lighthouses. *Lots* of towns have boardwalks and beaches."

"Yeah, I know."

"If she wanted to see a beach, she probably could've stayed in Georgia." *Shut up, Josh.*

A few beats of silence ensue.

"I have this dream." She rubs an eye with a knuckle. "I've had it dozens of times. Maybe hundreds, I don't know."

Already, I'm intrigued.

"I'm running. I can't miss the train. I have to get to the station, and Savannah's always there—her voice, anyway—over my shoulder, telling me to run. Telling me we have to get back to Sugar Creek before it's too late."

An eerie chill pricks my skin.

"And then I'm just . . . gone," she says. "I'm in blackness. With nothing."

I don't know what to say. I have to say something.

She's fiddling with the Scrabble tiles on her tray, rearranging them. But when she finally looks up at me, the pressure to break the silence is suddenly like flames on the back of my neck. Intense.

I clear my throat. "Well, Sugar Creek's to hell and gone from Moon River, that's for sure, so if blackness is what you're looking for . . ."

She takes a tile from the pool of extras, sets it on her tray.

"We're to hell and gone from everywhere," I add.

"So's Moon River."

It's my turn to take a tile. I've got nothing.

"We grew up in fear of upsetting our dad. He was angry all the time, you know?"

Unfortunately, I do.

"And Savannah used to say he'd put another little girl—a bad little girl—under the floorboards in the stables."

Who *says* something like that?

"It scared me when I was little. I'd listen in the middle of the night to see if I could hear her crying, and of course I never did. But eventually I figured out Savannah said it *because* it would scare me. Because she didn't want me to step out of line and get in trouble. Because she was *always* getting in trouble and she wanted to save me from that."

Savannah had wanted to protect her from something bad. I understand that, too. I'd do the same for my sisters. I'm about to ask what she means by getting in trouble in her family, but she's speaking again.

"But the strange coincidence?" She presses her lips together. "There was this story on the news. About a girl from here."

"Rachel Bachton."

"Yeah."

"They think they found her." Again I think of her little bones, huddled in a cold and lonely grave. "Buried in—hey—Chatham County, actually."

"Right. At the confluence. Where the two rivers meet." Chatham takes another deep breath. "That girl. Rachel. She's been gone a long time, and I started thinking. Rachel was talking to another little girl at a farmers' market, right? When she disappeared?"

"Mmmhmm."

"I think . . . I don't know for sure. I mean, I *can't* know, but . . ." She shakes her head, and the look on her face lands somewhere between despair and confusion. "I don't remember this, because I was barely four. But Savannah—she's slightly older—and the girl Rachel was talking to? It could've been anyone, right?"

She doesn't say it, but she doesn't *have* to say it. She or Savannah could've been that girl. As far as I know, they never interviewed the girl supposedly seen talking to Rachel, because they never determined who the girl was.

"I don't know if we were there that day," she says. "*Here,* I mean. Why would we be here when we lived in Moon River? But I have vague memories of a farmers' market somewhere. And if you look through Savannah's journal, the things she wrote about, the things she drew . . ." She flips another page in the journal and shows me the image of a homemade swing hanging from a tree branch. Again, the words *Sugar Creek* are scribbled in the margin. "I don't know how she knows things about this place if she was never here."

"Mmmhmm." My brow furrows in concentration as I try to grasp what Chatham's saying. She thinks she knows something about Rachel Bachton? About the girl whose fate I can't stop thinking about? No wonder I'm drawn to her.

"And she'd wanted me to come with her when she came. I thought she was crazy. I mean, go to Chicago? I can kind of understand that. But go to *Sugar Creek*? *Specifically?*"

"Yeah."

"Either Savannah knows something, remembers something she can't prove, or she wants me to think she does." Quietly, she busies herself with her Scrabble tiles, and adds: "I just don't know. It's probably all in my mind. Or hers."

But I can't let it go. "What do your parents say?"

"Loretta"—her eyes roll a little—"*My mama* . . . she doesn't say anything. She never says *anything* out of turn." She says it in a tone I recognize all too well.

And maybe, if I were some other guy, with some other experiences, I wouldn't have caught on to the subtle hint she just let slip, but my past is riddled with tones like the one she just aimed at me.

A window to the past opens in my mind. Rosie's holding Margaret up in front of her, like a shield; Margaret's screaming in fear, and I'm yelling to Rosie: *You think he won't hurt a little girl?*

As soon as the memory slips in, I shove it back out into the blackness and slam the window down on it.

I clear my throat, and hope Chatham didn't notice I went a little gray and lifeless for a minute there.

"I have a theory," Chatham says. "See, Savannah started talking about this place right around the time the police connected the bones they found at the river to the little girl who went missing here. She started saying we were at that farmers' market, that we'd been there."

"Savannah thinks she witnessed the kidnapping of Rachel Bachton? Or that she was the little girl who talked to her?"

"Maybe. Or maybe she just said it to accuse Wayne, to get Wayne in trouble."

"Wayne?"

"My dad. Savannah went to the police once, told them she thought she might have been the little girl Rachel was talking to, that maybe our father was involved." She clears her throat. "She ended up getting arrested. It was a mess."

"Arrested? For what?"

"Various things. Consumption of illegal substances, mainly. Public drunkenness. They called her unreliable."

The sounds of the rainforest filtering out of the speakers upstairs do nothing to calm the rapid clamor of my heart in my chest. "Did they ever check up on what she said? Look into Wayne as a suspect?"

"He doesn't match the description of the kidnapper. He's been nearly bald all my life, for one thing, and he's large. Overweight. He also had an airtight alibi—he was in Moon River the morning of the kidnapping."

I'm nodding. "Still, Savannah must have had a good reason for accusing him."

"Does *wanting* him to be guilty qualify? He's done some pretty terrible things."

"Like what?"

She bites at her thumbnail. It takes her a while to reply. "Let's just say," she finally says, "when he's angry, you don't want to be in his way."

Oh.

"I researched the case," she says. "There were sightings of Rachel in the weeks after. On a . . ." She bites her lip, as if forcing herself to stop talking. Her brow knits, and she shakes her head. "I mean, power of suggestion . . ."

On a train. Rachel was seen on a train.

"At a train station," I finish the thought for her. "Rachel *was* seen at a train station on the East Coast. Supposedly."

"And I have a dream about running to catch the train, presumably to Sugar Creek."

Chatham has a recurring dream about a train station, running to catch a train, and Rachel was seen on a train.

Savannah apparently drew and wrote about our beach, our boardwalk, and Rachel used to live near here.

Rachel was seen talking to a little girl in the moments before she disappeared, and no one ever determined who that girl was.

Is it possible Chatham and Savannah, or Chatham *or* Savannah, witnessed Rachel Bachton's kidnapping?

"But my sister . . . sometimes I hate her for putting these things in my head." Chatham wets her lips. "She's not exactly reliable all the time, and some of the things she used to say . . . they're so outrageous, you know? Like the girl under the floorboards. It's just possible enough that Savannah hates Wayne so much that she'd make this stuff up. I mean, I hate him, too, but I hate him for the stuff he's actually done. There's plenty of it. Why invent more?"

I feel an invisible tether wrap around my hand, another way this girl and I are somehow connected. She has Wayne to my Damien. She may not even know it yet, but she's pulling me in. I'm coho salmon hooked on her line, and with every word, she's reeling me in closer.

I think I hear my mother pull up, but we're too engrossed in conversation for me to do anything about it.

"You think your sister's lying?"

Chatham shrugs. "You ever go to a rave? You know the sort of mood-altering things you can encounter at a rave?"

I've never been to a rave, but because I can imagine—pot, Ecstasy, whatever else people can find—I give her a nod. "Sure."

"Let's just say Savannah's seen her fair share. Plenty of reasons to want to alter her mood."

There it is again: a hint about what went on behind the doors at Chatham's home.

Her sister is unreliable. Always running away. Pops some G every now and then, from the sounds of it. And she thinks she saw Rachel's kidnapping. She's got Chatham thinking it too, despite the fact that their dad, who's apparently an asshole, couldn't have been in Sugar Creek the day it happened.

"I don't know," Chatham says. "It's probably not true. I guess I'm here to prove she's not crazy, or maybe to acknowledge that she is. But more than that, I just want to find her."

"Where can we look?"

"I've been asking at school. Around town. I went to the mall, and that tattoo shop on Hauser. No one's seen her."

"You say she goes to raves? Maybe we should hit one."

The door upstairs opens, and I hear the jingle of Rosie's keys. I put a finger to my lips.

Rosie's shoes—standard issue, thick-soled Skechers, manufactured for and marketed to those who spend hours on their feet every day—squeak as she walks up the stairs from the foyer to the kitchen.

Chatham freezes.

Five, four, three, two . . .

"God *damn* it, Josh."

Of course she's pissed. The kitchen remains in the same state of disarray in which she left it; I didn't do the dishes. I figured, why bother? I'm not the one dirtying them, seeing as though I haven't been afforded the privilege to eat with the family all week.

But any second she's going to come downstairs. Can't have my mother making a scene in front of my guest—especially because I'm not supposed to have guests when Rosie's not home, let alone when I'm grounded.

Quietly, I stand and wave for Chatham to follow me. A second later, we're standing at two open doors: my bedroom, and my bathroom. The first implies things I wouldn't insult her to try at this point, and the second would put her in a black hole of filth I *really* should've cleaned when Rosie told me to.

I leave the choice to her.

She chooses option one.

"Be right back," I whisper.

I go up the stairs, pausing for a second on the landing by the front door to compose myself. Then, I turn to climb the remaining half-flight to face the music.

I see Rosie, frantically scrubbing the countertop next to the sink. The water is running, but I think I hear . . .

I tune in more closely. It's hard to determine between the water and the rainforest soundtrack. But I think I hear her sniffling.

At this moment, she turns toward me. Even in the dim light, I can make out streams of mascara curbing over her cheeks. A split second later, she hurls the wet sponge at my head and charges.

I catch the sponge, and manage to dodge the open palm flying at my face.

"Stop," I say.

"You're no better than your asshole father!"

"Don't wake the girls."

She manages to catch me on my bicep. Her fingernails dig into my skin. "You're no better!"

The effect of her words is minimal—I've heard them so many times—but all this because I didn't wash the dishes?

"Let go of me," I say.

For a few seconds, we're locked there.

But eventually, she loosens her grip and backs off, sniffling and violently hiccupping over her tears.

"I loved you." Her back meets the pantry door; her face is in her hands. She slides to the floor. "Before you were even born, I loved you."

Here it comes: phase three.

I shake my head.

"I always do my best. You got that? You think you've got it bad?" Her knuckles are white, and her hair is knotted between her fingers. "Try being *me*."

"It's always gotta be about you," I say.

She meets my glare with one of her own.

I step over the sponge and leave her there, in a puddle of her overly dramatic tears.

I detour down the hallway to the girls' room. They're both sound asleep—Margaret in the twin bed, Caroline on the trundle—with their rainforest CD and their butterfly night-light that sends light-images of butterflies chasing around the walls of their room.

It's a serene image, compared to the one I just left. And I still hear Rosie's bawling all the way down the hall. I close their door.

I pad down the steps, but when I get there, my room is empty.

I check my closet, under my bed.

I peek in the bathroom, sure to pull back the shower curtain just in case.

Chatham's gone. Probably shimmied out the window, like I've done so many times myself.

I go back into the den. I lower myself to the sofa and stare at the fireplace, its electric flames licking at the ceramic wood inside.

Like the fake fire, this whole place is an illusion. A façade constructed to mask the fucked-up people who live here.

I glance down at the Scrabble board, at the game Chatham and I hardly began.

She played off my *t*.

Later.

S C A R   T I S S U E

Later.

How am I supposed to take that? Is it the ultimate kiss-off? *I was getting real with you. You left to fight with the bitch upstairs. You're not worth it. Later.*

I guess I can't blame her. If I was in the middle of telling someone the things she started telling me—and of everyone in town, she chose *me*—and she asked me to hide in the closet so she could go talk to her mother, I probably wouldn't be too happy about it.

Or did she mean *later.* Like we'll talk about it later?

Either way, I'll make it up to her.

I text Aiden: *Favor.*

A few minutes later, he returns: *All ears.*

Me: *It's for Chatham.*

Aiden: *Door one?*

(Translation: weed.)

Me: *Door two.*

(Translation: ID.)

Aiden: *No problem.*

He's such a fucking criminal.

I'm drained like usual after one of Rosie's episodes, but

this one is amplified because it cost me precious time with Chatham. Worse, we were talking about *Rachel Bachton*. And while Chatham probably *doesn't* know anything about her kidnapping—what would be the odds of that?—it's obvious her life is as chaotic as mine.

The scar on the inside of my left forearm feels like it's throbbing, which is obviously a trick of my imagination because it healed a long time ago. But when I'm feeling this bruised and raw from an emotional standpoint, it's like the scar buzzes. I looked it up. It happens to veterans, too. It's post-traumatic stress. Phantom pain.

When I'm thinking clearly, I know the pain is not real, not really there. I'm just haunted by its memory.

Still, I feel the slice of it even now, hear the scream.

I close my eyes and rest my head against the back of the sofa. Take it all in. Let the event play out again—it's on a continuous loop in my mind—and wait.

I got a little dizzy when I saw all the blood. It soaked through a dish towel in a matter of seconds.

The sting of air in open flesh . . .

The vibrant scarlet dripping from my arm . . .

Pinching my skin together while Rosie used superglue and surgical tape to close the slice. *That's what they're going to do at the ER*, she'd said. *No one uses stitches anymore.*

I give the coffee table a shove with my foot and force myself to stop thinking about it. The Scrabble board jostles a bit, but the words remain, shifted just a touch from their original squares.

I leave the board and tiles where they are—I think I'll leave them there in testament to someday finishing the game with her—and head to my bedroom. I have a paper due on Monday. Maybe it'll be a nice distraction from the whirlwind of tonight.

I pull my school-issued Chromebook from my backpack and yank out a spiral notebook I actually took notes in (last year, I hardly took notes at all).

My phone buzzes with a Snap.

It's from Chatham! It's a picture of a signpost. She's just a few blocks away, at the corner of Barron and Wise.

Is it a hint to meet her?

Just as I'm pulling a sweatshirt over my head, another Snap comes through—a picture of the next signpost, at Barron and Heath.

I could trace her steps, follow her.

I'm already tying my shoes.

It's not like Rosie will come down looking for me, not after our altercation in the kitchen. And I hate the thought of Chatham walking all the way home—wherever home might be—at night.

The next Snap is a picture of the stone wall at the entrance to the Palisades, a subdivision of posh, luxury homes built up in the boom of the late nineties, before Rachel Bachton happened, before the safety of this town was ever called into question.

Is that where Chatham lives? The Palisades?

Damn, she had to be so-not-impressed with the dark and dingy paneled walls of my lair. Still, there are perks to living in the dank basement of a 1970s raised ranch: I open my window and climb out of it, head to Barron Boulevard.

I pick up the pace, and I'm in a full-out, fast-paced jog by the time the next picture comes in: it's the boardwalk.

I'm gaining on her. I'm only a few minutes behind her now.

And she doesn't live in the Palisades, if she's already past it. Not that it should matter, but what would a girl from that neighborhood ever see in a guy like me?

Then with another buzz of my phone, a picture of the Tiny Elvis Café comes through.

Perfect. The diner is closed by now—what time is it, anyway?—but we could sit out front on the sidewalk and finish the conversation my mother interrupted.

I hook a right onto Second Street. Almost there.

But my phone alerts again, this time with a picture of the Churchill Room & Board with the commentary *Home sweet home.*

I slow my pace.

She lives at the *Churchill?* They rent rooms there by the week. I suppose it makes sense. They dropped into town unexpectedly, and they don't know how long they're staying.

I feel my heartbeat in my feet, hear it in my ears.

Wait.

That means they could leave at any time. As soon as they realize Savannah's not here, they're gone.

I'm an idiot.

And—it occurs to me—I'm sort of stalking her because I don't turn around and head back home.

I slow to a trot but finish the jog to the boarding house, situated above Churchill General, Sugar Creek's version of a dollar store. From the curb, I study the windows, looking for her silhouette.

A flash in my mind takes me back to the beach, where I watched her plunge into Lake Michigan—those sexy shorts, the fringe of the denim framing her cute ass. I can see her silhouette any time I want, if I close my eyes and think about her.

My gaze trips along the front of the Churchill, from window to window, desperate for a glimpse of her. Frantic now, I give all the windows another pass, which is ridiculous, because she could be in a room facing the back alley, for all I know.

Jesus, Josh. She's home. Safe. Stop the disturbia and go home. Write your paper.

I move on, but only after running around the block and cutting down the back alley, rationalizing that it is a way home and if I happen to see Chatham, so be it. Seeing her would be a bonus to my route home, but not the reason for taking it: cherry on top of a sundae.

Eventually, I'm near passing the Churchill altogether. But there's no proverbial cherry visible from the street. I slow my pace until I'm jogging in place. And then I see her: second floor up, third window from the left. Accessible via fire escape, which might come in handy someday, if she ever decides to sneak out and meet me again.

Just knowing where she is calms me. I'm sure that makes me sound creepy, but after everything Damien's put me through, I know bad things happen to good people. I feel better actually seeing *proof* that she's home safe after her walk in the dark. And now that I have, I can go.

But I can't force my feet to move. I send a snap of the fire escape and caption it: *Say goodnight?*

A second later, she parts the curtains and opens the window. She's smiling, climbing out, but whispers, "Are you crazy?"

I jump to grab the ladder and climb the fire escape.

But now that we're both out here—she's shivering, I'm sweating—I don't know what I expected to happen. I take her hand.

"We're going to find your sister," I say.

She leans in, brushes a heavenly kiss over my cheek.

A rush of electricity darts through me.

"Good night, Joshua."

"Good night, Chatham."

She ducks back through the window, and I make my descent.

My muscles are tired by the time I hit Carpenter Street. I ran at least four miles.

I shower.

Put on a Blackhawks sweatshirt and flannel pants.

My laptop is already open and on my bed where I left it. I pull it closer and type *Chatham Claiborne* into a search engine.

Links to stories pop onto the screen, but none have to do with the girl I can't stop thinking about. I add *Moon River, Georgia* to the search.

Chatham County. It's in Georgia. So is the city of Savannah. Interesting.

But that's as far as the Internet will take me. She doesn't have a Facebook page, or an Instagram. Unless . . . I suppose it's possible she doesn't use her last name on her accounts. It's probably safer not to. Or she might have one of those clever handles for social media. Something like *SculptorGirl456*. Except her Snapchat is a straightforward *Chatham1009*.

I try something else. I type in *Savannah Claiborne*.

All sorts of profiles flash on the screen, most with variations of the name, but it essentially gets me nowhere. I don't know what Chatham's sister looks like, so I wouldn't know whose pages to open or lurk on.

I try a search on her parents, *Loretta and Wayne Claiborne*, both individually and collectively, in Georgia.

Nothing.

I close out of social media and type in the search engine: *Savannah missing runaway Moon River, Georgia*.

Nothing.

If your kid was missing, even if she left of her own volition because she was whacked out on some mood-altering substance, wouldn't you report it? Wouldn't you do anything in your power to find her?

But in this case, there are no websites dedicated to locating her.

Chatham said this wasn't the first time her sister had run away. She'd said Savannah was *always running away*. Maybe they're used to her coming back when she's ready to come back. But even then . . . wouldn't there be a record, at least, of the first time she took off? An Amber Alert issued when the family didn't know for certain where she was, if she'd come back, if she'd even run away rather than been kidnapped?

There's no report of Savannah's going missing. Yet the family is here, a third of the way across the country, looking for her. Renting by the week, so they can zip out of town as quickly as they came in if they find her—or don't.

And what appeal would Sugar Creek hold for Savannah? Why would she want to come here? It doesn't add up, unless they really do know something about Rachel.

I do another search, this time for Rachel Bachton updates, but there's not much new. Definitely nothing since the discovery of the bones at the meeting of two rivers. Just for good measure, though, I scan through some articles I've already read—some of them I've maybe read several times—to see if anything Chatham said tonight clicks with anything already printed.

There's very little catalogued about the girl Rachel was talking to before she was snatched. Beyond mentioning that Rachel was in line waiting for a balloon animal with her younger brother, amongst any number of children, there is no description of the child witness, even though there's a call for any little girl to come forward and tell what or who she saw.

When Rachel was last seen, she was wearing blue-jean leggings and a white T-shirt with a screen-printed kitten on it, and a pink sweatshirt. She had on a gold necklace with a single charm: a red-stone heart, set in gold. Her shoes were white sneakers from Stride Rite.

Mrs. Bachton has appealed to Rachel in interviews and press conferences to come forward. She says she'll know her daughter before DNA testing is even complete, because her daughter will be able to describe the charm on her necklace. It was a gift from her Nana, and Rachel loved it.

She was there, and then she wasn't. Reports of her seen on a train on the East Coast were unsubstantiated.

It occurs to me: if Savannah is really as troubled as Chatham let on tonight, could she have fabricated a connection to this case to feel important? To feel as if she has purpose? Maybe, in Savannah's mind, she really *was* there, but now that I think about it, I wonder if she hasn't simply convinced herself that it happened, that she talked to Rachel, or witnessed her abduction, even if she didn't. Wouldn't that make more sense, considering Chatham doesn't remember it? Wouldn't it stand to reason that if their father Wayne was really that much of a jerk, that Savannah would try to get him into trouble by accusing him of taking Rachel?

Was that what Chatham was hinting at when she said Savannah wasn't reliable? I can't very well sit her down, cut through all the bullshit, and jump ahead months in advance to the time in our relationship—assuming it develops—she'd tell me every thought that crosses her mind. If I expect her to trust me with these things, I have to give her time. I just wish I knew more about what she's thinking.

At this point, she isn't obligated to tell me her life story. We hardly know each other.

I'm going to change that. I *have* to.

She fills in blank parts of me somehow, makes me feel like my life isn't all that unusual, or maybe like everyone's life is a little fucked up—just like mine. It's like the skin growing over the slash on my arm. When you look at it, you still see the wound beneath the surface, and it's still ugly. And I can't forget why it's there, but it's different now. The scar healed in a few weeks' time following the incident, and now, years later, it's a reminder of how far I've come.

I text her: *Trip out to Northgate Lighthouse soon?*

She returns: *Yes!*

WHITECAPS

"Where do you think you're going?" Rosie appears at the top of the stairs with a spatula in her hand. The smell of slightly over-grilled cheese wafts down to where I'm standing on the small landing at the front door. "You're grounded."

"Library. I have a paper due. Bandwidth in this place sucks." It isn't exactly a lie. I do have to finish my paper. I even have my backpack with me. And the bandwidth *does* suck. While the twins are streaming a movie, there's no chance in hell I'll get fast Internet.

"You think I don't know when you're lying to me?"

"You gonna have me followed again? Because you'll be disappointed when your Neanderthal ex only follows me to the library."

"My *what*? Josh, I have no idea—"

"I'll be back in plenty of time before you have to work tonight. Library's only open until four on Sundays."

"I'm *exhausted*. I barely slept last night after the shit you pulled."

"You mean the tantrum you threw? For no good reason? That was *two* nights ago, Rosie."

"*Mom*. You call me *Mom*. And I'm talking about you leaving in the middle of the night and not coming back until sunrise."

70

Oh. So she knew about that. "I just went for a run." To the boardwalk. To meet Chatham, who sneaked out, too. There's something about a girl leaning her head on your shoulder as the sun comes up. A girl you'd give anything to kiss standing right there on the sand, but a girl with whom you just can't risk fucking things up to try kissing this early on.

"I was worried sick," Rosie says. "Up pacing until I heard you come back. If I'm expected to pull a double tonight—and we need the money, so I *have* to—I'm going to need a nap, and your sisters . . ."

My sisters . . . what? It's like she doesn't even have a valid reason they might need her. When they fall and scrape their knees, when they're scared in the middle of the night, when they need anything at all, who do you think they look for?

Not Rosie.

Me.

"I'll be back in an hour or two."

"I need to *sleep*. What do you expect me to do with your sisters?"

"Find some duct tape and sheet metal."

"What? What am I going to do with—"

"Build a time machine, and go back to the night it all happened and decide to say no this time."

Before she has time to process and react, I leave and slide into my car, and turn the key in the ignition. She pounds on the driver's window, and her face is all screwed up in this vicious expression.

"I hate you!" she yells. "I hate you, I hate you, I hate you!"

I give her a nod. *Mutual.*

It doesn't hit me until I'm halfway to the Churchill: my mother said she hated me.

What kind of a mother hates her own kid?

What kind of kid deserves to be hated?

Maybe I do deserve it. I mean, I love my sisters, and a few minutes ago, I all but said I wished they hadn't been conceived.

I roll down the windows, let the early autumn breeze, still calm and somewhat warm, wash away all the ugliness I feel around me. It's practically clinging to my clothes. It's like the air around my mother is a toxic cloud, and because I breathe it, I'm polluted, too.

Air it out. Can't have that pollution contaminating the space.

God, I hope Margaret and Caroline didn't get what I was saying. And I hope my mother has the sense not to explain it to them if they have questions. Can I ever forgive myself for wishing they weren't here?

Chatham's waiting on the front steps of the room-and-board when I pull up to the curb. Today she's wearing cut-off shorts—black ones this time—and a vintage-looking T-shirt—white with a black-rimmed collar—that says *Van Halen OU812* on it beneath a gray hoodie she hasn't zipped, the sleeves of which she cut off at the cuffs. She's wearing flip-flops and, on her left ankle, a black anklet that looks like it's made of rubber.

Her hair is curlier than usual, and she might be wearing makeup. Maybe a little gloss on her lips, a little mascara on her lashes.

"Hey." She's sitting next to me now, pulling the seat belt across her body. Then a second later: "Is something wrong?"

I shrug a shoulder, and just as I tell myself to let it all go, tell myself to just leave it all behind us when I pull away from the curb, I start blurting it all out. It's crazy. It's not like it's any big crisis. It's nothing next to Savannah's running away, or Rachel Bachton's being missing for over a decade, or anything like that. Still . . .

"My mother told me she hated me. Four times."

"She doesn't really hate you."

"You know, I never used to think so. But lately, I think she might."

"She doesn't." Chatham touches me on the elbow. "Mothers just don't always make the best decisions. I would know."

"Yeah?" I glance at her.

The way she's looking at me—as if the world beneath her feet is about to split and swallow us whole—tells me she really *would* know. But a beat later, she's smiling this great smile and turning up the radio. "I *love* this song!"

It's some old tune—Clapton, maybe—about things that happen late at night, when you're ready to have some fun and throw your cares to the wind. I like it, too.

For the rest of the drive out to Northgate, we don't speak. But we share the space the same as we shared the sunrise this morning. It's a moment just for us.

And when we approach the lighthouse, there's a small crowd on the lawn, which is cluttered with long, fold-out tables. It's a bazaar, or something. A craft fair, with quilts and hand-blown glass and macramé.

"This is amazing." She's a few steps ahead of me, eager, like my sisters when we're going out for ice cream.

I follow her lead. We snake through tables, and she touches the handmade wares. She's delicate about it, appreciative of artistic processes and materials, and it's clear she values the time, effort, and years of knowledge and practice that went into each piece.

"This is great, man!" Her backpack lands on the ground at her feet. She slips out of her hoodie and hands it to me, like it's the most natural thing in the world—me, holding her discarded clothing—and shrugs into a knit cardigan she found on one of the artists' tables.

It's a sage-and-beige thing, made with that kind of yarn that's dyed a different color every few inches, and it's long and soft. She looks so happy wearing it, her eyes practically sparkle. This isn't why we came here, but there's something to be said about serendipity, about the universe laying things out in your path.

She buys it on the spot, with a wad of cash she pulls from the pocket in her shorts. This place is teeming with other people like her, people who find things made with hands more special than the things you consume in mass market.

We meander through the fair, manage to make it to the end without her purchasing anything else, and find ourselves standing at a weathered, but always present, memorial to Rachel Bachton. This is where it happened. Right here, by this lamp-post, around which passersby have tied pink ribbons over the course of the twelve years that have passed since it happened. At the base of the post, the empathetic people of this world have placed now-ratty and rain-soaked and sun-dried teddy bears and withered flowers. Pictures of her frozen in time, some in frames on the ground, some bolted to the post, stare me in the face. Pleading for resolution. Praying for answers.

No one will ever throw any of this stuff away, I suspect, until she's found. And maybe not even then. God, it's been such a long time!

I don't want to think about the things that might have happened to her.

We stand there, with the lake stretching out before us.

"Nothing's familiar," she says. "If I was ever here, I don't remember it."

I feel my eyes prick with tears. I wish I'd known Rachel Bachton. "I wish I'd been here that day," I say.

"Why?" She tucks a wild curl behind her ear. "What could you have done?"

"Nothing." I know it's true. I was only four years old at the time. "But as crazy as it sounds, I wish I knew something. Something that could help save her. If not then, now."

"Maybe that's how Savannah feels, too."

I don't know if Chatham reaches for my hand, or if I grasp hers, but the moment my fingers close around hers, it doesn't matter that I wasn't here that day and couldn't possibly make a difference, that I'm probably stuck in Sugar Creek until my bones disintegrate, that I'm maybe a guy his own mother hates.

She faces the breeze tumbling in off the lake. Whitecaps today.

"You know," she says, "I don't think I've ever been here before."

And even though I've been here a million times, I know exactly how she feels.

Because I don't know if I've ever felt the way I feel around her, and it makes this place feel completely new and unfamiliar.

START ME UP

Chatham. This girl is *everywhere*. It's been five days since we went out to Northgate, and I've hardly seen her since, but she's constantly with me. Even when I don't see her, or hear from her, she's there, in the back of my mind. A preoccupation, more than a distraction: thinking about her gives me purpose, rather than taking me away from whatever it is I should be doing. She's the reason I haven't cut English. She's the reason I've been studying my ass off . . . because I want to prove to her that she can rely on me.

"Michaels."

Although I suppose she's stealing my focus now. I wipe sweat from my eyes.

Coach Baldecki is standing clear across the weight room, arms folded over his chest. He makes a show of turning to look at the clock.

Yeah, yeah. I'm late, but I'm hardly the last to arrive to early morning practice. "I had to drop off my sisters at school," I say by way of explanation, although he doesn't give a shit about the circumstances. Late is late.

It's only half true, as excuses go. While I *did* have to drop Margaret and Caroline at their preschool this morning, Chatham Claiborne is partly to blame. I swung past Aiden's place to pick up his artwork, because he may or may not come to school today. You never know. It's Friday, and it's Aiden.

Aiden: *I've never made one of these declaring someone sixteen. What's she going to do with it? Drive?*

Me: *Long story, dude.*

Some of the guys—the guys on the D-line—are still running their warm-up laps, but they have different rules, different expectations. It's like I have to prove myself a hundred times an hour if I want to keep the starting QB position.

"You warm up?" Coach asks.

"Ran three loops." I'm dripping with sweat; he should know it's true just by looking at me, and furthermore that I practically sprinted it to catch up. I drop to the floor to stretch out.

"You study your playbook?"

"Yes, sir."

"Ninety-two, Cougar, Spread."

Please.

"I'm looking for a receiver, long," I say.

This seems to satisfy him. He leans in a bit closer. "Listen to me. We have scouts from Northwestern coming tonight."

At this, I do a double take. Scouts. Scholarships. A Big Ten school. Nothing like pressure.

"You need to connect. With as many seniors as possible. With Novak. With Girard."

I squint through the glare of a fluorescent bar behind him. Does he mean to say he wants me to pause and *think* about who I'm throwing to? And to make sure it's a senior? Recipe for a sack.

"I want you to connect. Period."

That's his official position, but I heard him loud and clear. I know what he wants me to do. Think first.

Fuck that.

"I'll connect, coach."

Friday morning practices are more for team bonding than intense workouts. The coaches don't want to exhaust us before the game. But I've been here less than fifteen minutes, and already I'm dog-tired.

I'm pretty sure Rosie went out to meet Damien last night. I heard her car start around three, and found a note on my bathroom mirror, telling me she had to go in early and asking me to drop the girls off.

But her note was gone and she was there at five, when I woke up, acting like nothing was amiss, as if she'd never left a note, as if she'd never left the house.

I'll call her on it. Eventually.

But now is time for the team. I have to put Rosie's lies in a box and store them on a shelf in my mind until a later time.

Most of us are just fucking around this morning.

We do some curls, eat some bagels and cream cheese, which the football moms—minus mine, of course—take turns dropping off. Play a game of catch.

Coach tells us to walk proud today.

All in all, it's a pretty easy team meeting.

We head to the locker room, shower, pull our jerseys over our heads—we're wearing them to promote unity, and to hype up the rest of the school so maybe they'll come to the away game—and get ready to hit the halls.

"Hey. Fourteen." Novak whips his dirty towel at me.

I know he's calling me by number as a sort of insult, as if I don't have a name worth remembering. So I do it, too. "'Sup, twenty-six?"

"You gonna look for me tonight, dickhead? I'll be the one in the end zone."

I keep it simple. "If you're open." I toss his towel back to him, even though the bin of dirty towels is closer to me than he is—I'm not his fucking laundry boy—and head out the door.

I detour to the art hallway, where Chatham is in open studio during what we call zero hour before school officially begins. It's still about fifteen minutes before classes start, so I peek in. She's leaning over a slab of clay, about twelve inches square, cutting into it with a small, thin blade and carving away some of the base. In other places, she's built up the surface. It looks like she's working on a topographical map.

I did look up what a clay relief is. It's an artist's medium: clay of any sort rolled to a thick slab, and embellished. Some of the slab is carved away into valleys, some is built up to bumps and shapes. She carves bays and gashes in the wake of her X-acto blade. And like a plastic surgeon, leaves something stunningly beautiful in its place.

A few seconds pass before she looks up and sees me.

I see it first in her eyes: a smile. A moment later, she's wiping her hands on a towel and making her way toward me. "Hi."

"So that's clay relief."

"Yeah." She glances over her shoulder, back at her work. "It's just a little . . ." And now's she's looking back at me. "You have *dimples*."

"Oh." I feel the warmth of embarrassment spread up the back of my neck. I must be smiling. *Of course* I'm smiling, considering who's standing in front of me. "Yeah, I guess I do."

She wipes a knuckle high on her cheekbone, leaves a smudge of clay there. "No, I just never noticed. Could it be you've *never* smiled in my company before? How is that possible?"

"I, uh . . ." I'm looking into her eyes, and for a split second,

I forget what I'm here for. I start over. "As promised . . ." I reach into the back pocket of my jeans and pull out a genuine-Aiden, fake Illinois ID. And in case anyone's listening, I add, "You must have left it at my house the other night."

She looks it over, the same way I did when he first handed it to me. There's something about seeing her name in print, let alone on a driver's license, that gives me a jolt. It's like suddenly, she's permanent.

"What do I . . ." she raises a brow, but lowers her voice. "You know."

"Oh. Nothing. On the house."

"I couldn't . . . You have no idea how much easier this makes things for me. I've been through every box—"

"Don't mention it."

"Sure?"

"Yeah. If you feel like it sometime, you could hook me up with a piece of cake at the Tiny Elvis."

"Done." She slides her identification into the pocket of her hoodie, then turns back toward the studio.

"So," I say, when I really should've just shut up and walked away now that our business dealings are done.

Inside, I panic. Is that why we've been talking every day? Because I'm acting as middle-man to get her something she needs? And now there's no reason to talk?

She looks over her shoulder, waiting.

Now I *have* to say something.

"Maybe after the game . . ."

"Smile," she says.

"What?"

"I said *smile*. You should smile more often," she says. "The dimples."

I couldn't stop myself if I tried now, but I back off, lower my gaze so she can't see how absolutely transparent I am.

"I think, if I'm lucky, I'll be working tonight," she says. "But if you can, drop in after the game with the rest of your team. Bring your sisters."

I shouldn't have to bring Margaret and Caroline. Rosie won't be working until way-late. But I say, "Okay."

Every part of me hums as she returns to her relief, and I watch as she diligently digs into the slab of clay on her table.

It's happening. I'm going to learn more about her. Maybe not tonight, but soon I'm going to be close to her, hold her hand again, feel her head on my shoulder again.

I can feel it now, if I concentrate.

DESSERT FIRST

Think about attending our open house. You've got good instincts out there.

The guy gave me his card. Every now and then, I slip a finger into the back pocket of my jeans just to feel the edge of it.

I'm sitting in a booth with a couple of other guys on my team, the overflow table. I know my place, and as there aren't enough seats at the tables pushed together in the middle of the diner, some of us have to sit on the side.

Besides, I have to keep an eye on the time, and I have a perfect view of the clock. I have to be back by ten. I glance up at the clock, which is, of course, Elvis-themed. The seconds tick by with the sway of his hips. And oddly enough, his hips keep time with every song that comes on. Presently, it's "Blue Suede Shoes."

I still have forty-five minutes.

"And here you go." Chatham slides an enormous piece of cake in front of me, as she's passing me. Sort of nonchalant. "As promised."

I didn't order the cake. I haven't even ordered a burger yet.

She glances at me over her shoulder and winks.

"Nice throw, dickweed." Novak shoulders his way into our

booth across from me and treats me to a hard stare. "You know how important this game was? You know what chances you fucking blew for me with that fucking throw?"

I shrug a shoulder. Keep cool. "Maybe you should've caught it."

"Maybe I should've . . . *what* did you say?"

"I *said*, you should've caught it. You were open. I hit you in the numbers. I did my job."

"I had no problem when it was Yates in the pocket."

"Any receiver worth his salt," I say, "would've caught that pass."

"Are you saying I'm not worth my . . ." He raises his voice a few decibels. "Worth my *what*?"

"Hey, guys." Jensen turns around in his seat. "We're all on the same team. All share the same goals." Always the mediator. That's why he's a good captain.

"I hit you in the numbers," I say. "Can't get more accurate than that. Listen, I can appreciate that you grew up playing catch with Yates, and you're pissed he's out, but—"

Novak's on his feet now, his finger in my face. "You've got some fucking nerve, *rookie*."

Jensen: "*Guys!*"

"Excuse me." Suddenly, Chatham is there, working her way between us, armed with another plate of chocolate cake. "You're getting a little loud, and there are a few families with kids here, so . . ." She offers Novak the plate. "Truce?"

Novak backs off a bit, but doesn't break eye contact. His hands are balled into fists, and if he could manage it, steam would be coming out of his ears.

I lift my chin. *Bring it.* After all I've been through, I can handle whatever he throws at me.

"My treat," Chatham says. "I'd appreciate it."

At first, Novak doesn't move. But a second later, he takes the cake, and looks away, but only for a breath. "We'll talk about this later."

"Any time." I watch him walk back to his seat.

"Calm down," I hear Jensen say to the bastard. "We won, all right? You had a decent game."

I take a forkful of cake. Glance at the clock. Then I happen to see Damien's truck parked at the curb across the street, where it was last week.

He isn't in the truck this time, so I keep an eye out for him to return.

What the hell is he doing here?

Could be he's bellied up to the bar at the Cannery, down the road, at the intersection at Suffolk—pretty likely, actually—but it's weird that he would park here, then walk four blocks.

He probably knows I had a game tonight, and half the town knows the team congregates at the Tiny Elvis after we play. I wonder if he's looking for me.

I have half a mind to investigate, to go right up to him and ask him what the hell he thinks he's doing stalking me, what the fuck he's thinking worming his way back into my mother's life, but that would be in violation of the order of protection. And if I leave the diner, it'll look like I'm going because of what just happened with Novak, and I can't let him think he affected me. Because he didn't.

I eat my cake.

Shovel in a burger.

Relive some awesome moments of the game with the guys sharing my table.

Catch a glimpse of Chatham every now and again. Is it possible for a girl to get hotter every time you look at her?

But I never go more than a minute or two without checking Damien's truck. And suddenly, he's there, walking down the sidewalk, smoke in hand. He climbs into the cab, rolls down the window, and settles in. He's staring into the windows of the Tiny E, as if he's waiting for me to emerge.

He *wouldn't*. I mean, we have a restraining order. It's a coincidence. He's out drinking, wants a smoke. Can't smoke in bars in this county, so he's having one in his truck. That's all.

But it's not unbearably cold out, so why wouldn't he just smoke outside the bar on the sidewalk like everyone else instead of walking four blocks?

I still have a few minutes by the time the rest of the team is ordering dessert, but I pay my portion of the tab, making a point of waiting for Chatham to be up at the register so I can say good-bye.

"Hey," she says. "Everything all right?"

"Yeah."

"So smile."

It's involuntary after she asks. "What time are you done tonight?"

"I work till close."

"Around ten-thirty or so?"

"Yes, sir."

Sir. What a southern thing to say. "Want a ride home?"

"I live just . . ." She points with her pen, but stops. She knows I know where the Churchill is. "Of course you know that." She licks her lips. "If you want to see me later, you could ask."

"I'm asking."

She's smiling.

"If you don't mind hanging out at my place," I add. It's only fair she knows what she's getting into. "I have my sisters."

"I don't mind."

"I mean, they'll be in bed. Asleep. I know it's not as exciting as seeing a movie, or going to a party, but—"

"I don't mind."

"I'll come get you then." I figure I can get them to bed late, after we get Chatham. What Rosie doesn't know can't hurt.

"All right. I'll text you when we're done cleaning up."

I stand there stupidly for a second. What would she do if I just leaned over this counter and kissed her? I'd like to, and I kind of guess she knows it.

I snap out of it. "See you soon then."

"I guess you will."

I walk out into the night.

Damien's watching me.

I have to walk right past his truck to get to where I parked.

I stay on my side of the street, and feel his eyes on me the whole time.

I guess that's to be expected. He's sizing me up, preparing for what kind of barricade I might be if he decides to come after my mother again. I'm a lot bigger than I was the last time.

When I start my SUV and pull away from the curb, I see that his headlights are suddenly on. He's pulling away, too.

Coincidence, I tell myself.

But two turns later, I'm pretty certain he's following me. If I know Damien, I know he's keeping a measured distance, too, so that if I call the cops, he can truthfully say that he was farther than the mandatory five hundred feet from me. I wouldn't put it past the asshole to have measured the lengths of the town blocks just to be sure.

When I turn onto Carpenter Street, I pull over and wait a few seconds. Sure enough, Damien appears around the curve half a minute later, idling several car lengths behind me.

I inch along.

So does he.

K N O C K I N G

I reach for my phone. I'm not taking any chances.

When you're Rosie Michaels-Herron-Wick's son, when you've been dealing your entire life with idiot after idiot, all of whom your mother falls for hook, line, and sinker, you know the number to the police station by heart. Furthermore, you know that in a town like Sugar Creek, there's little else for the cops to do if they aren't answering calls like the one I'm making—save arresting the occasional spray-paint graffiti artist, or busting the rare beach kegger out at the bluffs—so you know they'll get to you faster than if you go through the emergency dispatch.

"This is Joshua Michaels," I say when the department picks up. "I'm almost to my house. Forty-four twenty-one Carpenter Street. My mother's ex-husband is following me home, and we have an order of protection against him."

There.

It's that easy, isn't it?

Why my mother can't manage to do such a thing is beyond me.

I stay on the line and answer questions for the police: what kind of automobile is he in; how long has he been tailing me . . . that sort of thing.

I pull into the driveway.

Damien parks on the street, directly across from our house.

I'm sure he's waiting for me to get out of the car, or maybe he's even waiting for Rosie to leave for her shift at the hospital.

I keep the dispatcher on the line while I kill the engine, while I approach my front door, while Damien dares to bullet out at me. My key is already in the door, and I'm inside and barricading us in by the time he reaches the house.

"He's coming to the door," I tell the dispatcher.

The twins are up the half-flight of stairs watching a movie and giggling like crazy. That's good. They *should* be happy. I'd rather they live an existence much more carefree than mine. But I hear them gasp when Damien pounds on the door.

"Joshy?" They're at the railing suddenly, their baby-fat hands grasping the spindles while they press their cheeks through the divides.

Still holding my phone to my ear, I put a finger to my lips.

Expressions of terror cross their little faces.

"You're late." Rosie glides to the top of the stairs, piercing a simple, round earring through the lobe of her left ear.

I'm five minutes early, actually. "Damien's outside."

Her eyes roll, as if he's a mere inconvenience, instead of potentially dangerous, and she lets out a dramatic sigh.

"I'm on the phone with the police," I say. "They're on their way."

The door vibrates against my back with his pounding.

Her eyes widen, and she bolts down the stairs, and before I have a second to prevent it, she pulls my phone away from me and terminates the call.

"What are you doing?" I ask.

She shoves the phone back at me, then reaches around me for the doorknob, like she's going to go out there and actually *talk* to him, but I'm too quick for her.

"Listen to me." Her voice is low, something between a hiss and a whisper. "If the police come and make trouble for him, he may go to jail."

"Good."

"At least for a little while."

"Good."

"And that means he won't be working. And that means no child support."

Is she kidding? "He rarely pays you anyway."

"No, he's paid twice now. In a row."

Which means he's had her in bed at least twice since the order of protection was granted. This isn't good from a legal standpoint, let alone a personal one.

He pounds again. "Open the fucking door! I'll teach your fucking ass!"

I glare at my mother, silently plead with her not to do what I know she's going to do anyway. "If he comes in this house . . ." I don't have to finish my sentence. We all know what could happen if he comes in. "I'm sure he's been drinking." I can tell by the inflection of his voice. "The cops are on their way," I say a little louder.

The pounding stops. Maybe he gave up and left. Maybe he heard my warning.

The twins are now huddled, arms around each other, in the corner.

"Move," Rosie says.

"No."

"*Move.*"

We stare at each other for what seems like an eternity, a silent, stoic battle of wills.

Then something catches my eye up the half-flight of stairs, at the back door in the kitchen. Damien walked around the house. He's turning the knob. The door isn't locked.

Rosie follows my gaze, then darts up the stairs to the kitchen.

He's already one foot in the door by the time she reaches him.

"You!" He points around her, as if his finger can poke me between the eyes from a distance. "When you gonna fuckin' learn you're not in fuckin' charge of every fuckin' thing?"

My mother's hands are splayed against his chest. "Honey, listen."

But despite her efforts to distract him, he's still crossing the room—she's between us, walking backward—halfway to the stairs now.

I stand my ground. "You shouldn't be here."

"You can't keep a man from his family." He grins, reaches around my mother's body, gives her ass a squeeze.

Maybe I can't, but the courts can. "The police are on their way," I say.

"Honey, it's true." Rosie's against the pantry door now, with fistfuls of Damien's collar, but he's still staring at me. "He called before I could stop him. You should go, okay? What if I come over later? After my shift? Okay?" She puckers her lips, and rises up on her tiptoes to peck a kiss onto his lips. "Do you see? I still have the unicorn."

With open eyes, and a stare directed at me, one that might very well burn into my soul, he returns her kiss. Their lips part, tongues thrash. He cups her between the legs, palms a breast. Taunting me. Showing me he can do whatever he damn well pleases to my mother, which means he can do whatever he wants to the rest of us.

Their kiss breaks.

Rosie's hands are on his face now. "You should go." With a hand on his cheek, she coaxes his stare back to hers. "Honey? I'll deal with him, but before the police come—"

"You don't meet me later," he says, "I'm coming right back."

"I'll be there, honey. I promise."

He backs off.

My mother's shoulders slump, and her body goes sort of limp against the pantry door.

"And you!" He jabs that finger in my direction again. "I'll deal with you later."

Margaret lets out a little whimper.

"Is that one of my daughters I hear?"

I cough, in case one of them lets out another noise. Out of the corner of my eye, I see them, still arm-in-arm, stiff like statues, their brown eyes wide with fear.

"They're in bed," Rosie bluffs.

"Well then, I'll just go check on them. Maybe they want to come spend the night with their daddy. Hell, if mommy can't take care of them tonight . . . why not?"

The first hint of sirens sounds in the distance.

"Some other time. You should go." Rosie plants her hands on his chest again, but she must have put on too much pressure because he gives her a little shove backward.

"I'll teach your fucking ass, you fucking punk." He points at me one last time, and ducks out the back door. "You don't come to my place later"—now, the finger points at my mother—"I'll be back."

The door clicks shut.

Half a second after, Rosie's throwing the deadbolt, bawling.

"Mom." I make my way from the foyer up the stairs, give my sisters a glance that I hope reassures them. It's all okay now.

"God *damn* it, Josh!"

"Listen." Before I get another word out, she's on me, smacking me with open palms, arms flailing, chest heaving with sobs. *Smack, smack, smack.*

I catch her wrists. "Rosie. Stop."

Her shoulders hunch, and violent tears send tremors through her system.

I let go of her.

She wipes her nose with the back of her hand and turns away from me. "God, now I have to . . . I have to go over there, and I have to—"

"Just let the cops do their thing," I tell her.

"Why do you have to make trouble?"

"Make trouble?"

"You can't ever just let something go, can you?"

"I was just coming home. He followed me."

"For no reason?"

"Yes!"

"Why would he do that? What did you do?"

"Nothing. He's fucking crazy. Remember that dog? Remember what he did to the dog, Rosie?"

I know she's thinking of the black lab, the only pet we ever had. She gets quiet with this somber expression whenever he crosses her mind. But she quickly shakes herself free from the memory. "I have to go to work. *You* did this." She grabs her jacket and the salad she packed, and gives me a look that could turn me to stone. "*You* deal with it." Not bothering to kiss my sisters, she slips down the stairs and out the door, muttering about things she *has to do* now after her shift.

"Joshy?" Caroline tugs at my jeans. "Is Mommy okay?"

I bend to pick her up. "It's okay now." I tousle Margaret's hair when she snuggles up to me, too.

The sirens grow louder.

LOOKING GLASS

As insane as tonight was, it was hardly the worst thing I'd ever endured.

At fourteen, I stepped between Damien and my mother, who'd lifted then-two-year-old Margaret in front of her like a human shield. His knife sliced into my arm.

I now run my fingers over the silvery-white line on my flesh. No longer tender to the touch, no longer an ugly, stamped memento of an even uglier night, it's just part of me, part of my past. Any lower, and the scar would look like a ragged suicide attempt.

I spring up from my prone position on the couch upstairs, where I'm resting just down the hall from where my sisters sleep, and stare at the wall. Everything is still and quiet. I watch a spider crawl from one end of the room to the other.

I'd talked to the police tonight, and my little sisters backed up my story, even if my mother, when the cops called her cell phone while she was on her way to the hospital, pretended not to know anything about a visit from her drunken ex.

"It couldn't have happened." Her voice had come through on the speakerphone. "I was at home until a few minutes ago. I just passed you on Carpenter Street. You were going to my house? I drive a VW bug. Do any of you remember seeing me?"

One of the officers had nodded in agreement, in verification.

"I'm sorry my son wasted your time," Rosie had said. "And my daughters . . . well, they idolize their brother. They'd say anything he asked them to. He'll be dealt with, I assure you, when I get home."

I stuck to the truth; Rosie flat-out lied. She threw me under the bus. Told the cops I was prone to causing drama if I didn't get my way, and that I was pissed because I'd hoped to go out with a girlfriend and was stuck at home watching my sisters. This phony report, she guessed, was my way of retaliating, my way of trying to convince her to miss her shift and come back home.

Needless to say, when Chatham texted that she was ready, and the cops asked about it, they pretty much closed their notebooks and stopped taking me seriously.

"We have your account on record," one of them said, lingering at the doorway. "Let us know if anything else happens."

Yeah, yeah.

So I had to cancel with Chatham.

With no guarantee that Damien won't be out there somewhere, waiting for us—and now that there's no chance he'll be in a cell overnight, he'll only stalk me again—I'm not going to take my sisters out of the house, not even to rush them out to the car and back. So now it's after midnight, and I'm alone in a house that's deadly quiet, except for the rainforest tracks sifting out from the girls' room.

I'm so pissed I could start breaking shit. And maybe I would be throwing Rosie's stupid ceramic unicorn against the wall, if I didn't just get the girls tucked in about an hour ago, freshly bathed and smelling like lavender baby shampoo. It's always hard to calm them down after a dramatic scene like the one they witnessed tonight. I can't stir things up for them again, so the ceramic unicorn stays put.

My phone buzzes with a text.

My mother's name, accompanied by the middle-finger emoji—which is how I programmed her in—stares up at me from the screen.

I almost don't want to look at her message. It's either a rant about my decision to involve the police, or considering we're still somewhat in stage three, a bleak explanation of why she'd lie to the cops, which might include any of the following:

Child support is hard to collect from a man in jail.

Better to let sleeping dogs lie, or don't mess with the bull, or *insert cliché here*.

Or some bullshit about the no-contact portion of the order of protection works both ways, and she's in violation of it, too, because she slept with the guy last week.

Yeah, well, whose fault is that?

Her message: *Sorry. I'll explain later.*

I delete it.

I hear something. A scratching, or maybe a tapping, coming from downstairs.

Instantly, I'm on my feet. I tune my ears into the creaks and the ticks of the house.

Am I imagining it?

I hear the scratch again, and this time, it's followed by a thump.

I grab my phone. If I call the police again, and again they can't substantiate my report, it won't go over well. Still, I can't be too careful. I can hold my own against a drunk, even if he is a beast of a man, but I have to think about my sisters.

My phone buzzes again, its vibration sending a humming sensation through my nerves.

Geez, I get it, Rosie. You screwed up. Again. I've got bigger problems right now.

I go to swipe away the message, still contemplating calling the police, when I see Chatham's name on the screen. I tap on it.

Let me in?

I glance at the back door in the kitchen. The porch is empty.

I walk down the half-flight of steps to the landing and peek through the window next to the front door. No one's on that porch, either.

And there it is again: the tapping/scratching. Another thump.

I leap down the second half-flight, even skip a few stairs, and round the corner to my bedroom, where I see her—Chatham Claiborne—kneeling outside my window.

My fingers fumble nervously over the lock, but I manage to shove it clear of the latch.

I meet her gaze in the seconds before I push the window open.

She smiles at me.

My heart quickens.

"Hey." She hands me a carry-out container through the window. "You seemed to really enjoy that cake, so . . ."

"I did." I take it and put it aside. "Thank you."

For a second, we just stare at each other.

"Well, I know you're busy with your sisters, so I'm just going to"—she thumbs toward my backyard—"you know, get out of your hair." And she actually starts to get to her feet.

The scar on her hip is eye-level to me now, peeking out at me above the waistline of the shorts that have become signature to Chatham Claiborne.

I reach for her, and land a hand on her cold hip and cover the marring with my palm, as if hiding it could possibly make it, and the memories it carries with it, go away. I tighten my fingers against her skin. "Stay."

And before I know it, her backpack lands on the floor at my feet, and she's sliding through my window, guided by my hands, and we're standing there, practically belly-to-belly, in my room.

"Hi," she says. Her hands are at the front of my shoulders. The base of her left palm is touching me in the location of my tattooed fourteen.

I chew on my lip and look down at her. She's so fucking pretty.

And I'm so happy to see her that without thinking about whether I should, I brush my lips over hers, then second-guess my confidence.

Just as I'm about to pull away, her lips part in the tiniest of invitations, and we're *kissing*.

I pull her closer. Trace her cheek with a fingertip. Sigh along with her when my hands find their way into her wavy hair.

"I want to tell you something," I whisper between kisses.

"What?" she asks.

I feel the heat of her breath on my lips. "Everything."

BONES

"That shouldn't have happened to you." That's all Chatham says when I tell her about Damien, about the scar on my arm. She doesn't try to explain it, or rationalize, or even let my mother off the hook. There's no judgment implied at all beyond *it's wrong.*

We're in the den now. I'm on the couch, and she's on the floor across the coffee table from me. She's wearing my football sweatshirt and a pair of my sports socks because a girl from Georgia doesn't understand the fickle whims of autumn in Chicago. She looks good in my clothes. Small. She's rolled the sleeves up a few times.

"You can't pick your parents." She sips from the glass of water I brought her, and I see something in her expression—resignation, maybe, or a sense of survival—that bonds us through past experiences we haven't yet verbalized. "I didn't pick either set."

Either set? I do a double take, try not to stare too expectantly, but it's obvious I have to know what she's talking about.

"It's kind of a crazy story," she says.

"Crazier than the one I just told you?"

"No comparison . . . it's a different kind of crazy. Loretta and Wayne." She takes another drink of water—I watch her, the bob of her swallow in a perfect peach neck—and follows it up with a sweep of her tongue over her lips.

Lips I've kissed, thank you very much.

Savannah's adopted, I know that.

And Chatham's told me that they weren't biological sisters.

But I assumed that Loretta and Wayne were Chatham's biological parents.

"They didn't adopt me because I have parents. A mom, anyway. My father's dead." She says it so matter-of-factly.

And I can't help but think maybe *this* is why I'm drawn to her. I have a mom. I have a father, but he isn't even in the periphery of my life. He's never even seen me.

"So technically, I'm a foster. My biological mother. She's sort of . . . I don't know . . . ever hear the term *unfit?*"

"Are you kidding? I *live* with unfit."

She laughs a little, but then her voice goes quiet. "My mother left me in a hot car on a ninety-degree day when she ran an errand." She uses air-quotes with the last word. "I mean, if you can call a drug run an errand . . ."

"God."

"I was little. I don't really remember it beyond the sensation of loss." She blinks, meets my gaze, then redirects to the Scrabble board that I never put away. "I was the only one who survived."

"The only one?"

"I had a baby brother."

"He died?"

"Yeah."

"I'm sorry. I can't imagine losing my sisters. How do you . . . how do you forgive something like that? Do you still, you know, *see* her?"

"I used to see her sometimes. Supervised visits. Every couple years, she'd request a visit. Not often. Last time, about five years ago, she basically told me I wasn't her daughter anymore, so . . . yeah. That was the end of that."

"I can't even imagine." Rosie may hate me from time to time, but she's never actually disowned me. "That shouldn't have happened to you." I know it's her line, but it's still true.

"Do you ever think about the ripple effect?" she finally asks. "Something seemingly insignificant you do one day could affect you years down the road?"

"Like watching a girl's backpack so she can take a swim?"

"Exactly." A nervous kind of giggle escapes her. "It's like whatever happened to make my mother leave us in that car that day, it led me to Savannah. It led me here." She takes a breath like she's about to explain to me why, or how, we so naturally seem to fit together. Why she decided to trust me the first second she saw me.

It's because of this story about the hot car, maybe. The neglect, the feeling that you just don't matter enough, which is an emotion I'm more than in touch with. Or maybe it's the other hints she's dropped in my lap about Wayne, about the things he's done, versus the things Savannah has tried to pin on him. About the girl under the floorboards in the stables, about Loretta not saying anything out of turn.

"We understand each other," I say.

I wait for her to confirm it.

But instead, she says, "Wasn't it seventy-two degrees just yesterday?"

What? I let a few beats pass. I don't want to talk about the weather. Not *now*. But when she doesn't say anything else, I agree. "Yeah."

"It's freezing tonight."

"Well, you're in shorts."

"No, I mean, it happened so *quickly*. It was so nice, and pleasant, and I figured I had time to *plan* for the cold, but no. It came in like Hell's Angels. For someone who's used to a steady climate, these drastic shifts in temperature are jarring."

"That happens here sometimes."

"I don't know how you get used to it."

"You don't." I play off her *D: dent.* "Some years it'll go from eighty to forty in a week. It always sucks."

"That's messed up."

This isn't where I wanted the conversation to go. I didn't tell her about my mother, about Rosie's fucked-up second husband—Richard "The Dick" Herron—whose kid used to repeatedly ram my head into the wall in the bedroom we shared only because Dick used to beat the crap out of him, or about our recent dramas with Damien, or the night two years ago when he knifed me, so that she'd spill her guts about whatever she's been through.

But I want to keep talking about stuff that really matters. I want to know everything about her. I don't want to talk about the weather.

"I guess I'll have to get something other than shorts to wear."

Is it weird that she'd arrive at the end of summer without something other than shorts and tank tops and the occasional hoodie in her suitcase? A nervous twinge, like a twisting in my gut, makes me feel dizzy for a second. They really didn't plan on staying here, did they? After all, how long would it take them to realize Savannah was or wasn't in Sugar Creek? *Please*, I pray to whichever god will listen. *Let me have her a little bit longer.*

"I swear, I can't find *anything*. I'm going to have to hit a mall soon. But the bus schedule to get there . . . take the north line to this hub, and the west line back . . ."

"Or . . . I could take you."

"Really?" She's smiling like it's the nicest thing anyone's ever offered her. "God, that'd be great. I mean, *so* much easier."

"Not a problem. Might have two little chaperones, so we can't stay *hours*, but—"

"Thanks."

It's really not that big of a deal, but she reaches over the table and places her cool hand over mine. She's freezing. Her fingers trace my knuckles.

I'm staring into her eyes, and for the first time, I understand how someone might get lost in a gaze. "Think you might want to buy a dress? There's a dance in a couple weeks, and . . ." I shut up. Is asking her moving too fast?

"Homecoming?" she asks.

Of course she's seen the banners and all the flyers in the hallways, and heard the hype about voting for court and king and queen. I don't know why I didn't just call it what it is.

"I don't usually get that much into it, but I checked my mom's schedule," I say, even though that proves I've considered asking Chatham, and this isn't just a snap decision. "She's not supposed to work that night, and yeah, I'd like to take you."

In a flash, she's leaning over the table, kissing me. Her lips are cool from the water. And when her tongue brushes against mine, it's like all that's troubling melts away. Our bodies come together, and even if it can't last forever, in this moment, it's pure nirvana.

I lean closer, make my way around the table. My hands are planted at her hips. I graze my fingertips against the fringe of cut-off denim at her thighs; she doesn't seem to mind. And before I know it, we're on the floor in front of the fireplace. I stare down at her.

She wraps her arms a little tighter around me, and pulls me a touch closer. "See what I mean? You watched my bag on a beach, and here we are."

"I almost want to tell you to run. Everything you've already been through, all the drama with Savannah . . . You don't need to be caught up in my mess, too."

She shakes her head. "Smile. I like your smile."

I can't help it. I smile.

"It doesn't matter what happened before. All the shit you've been through . . . everything I've been through . . . it's just the bones of life. We get to flesh it out. It's structure, like the wire base of a *papier maché* sculpture. Looking at it, you won't even know what it's supposed to be until the paper goes on. We— our dreams, our actions, our decisions—are like the paper. We shape *over* the structure, see." She licks her lips. "The bones, the wire bases . . . they're important. But it's not the final product, not what anyone sees when they look at you."

"I think *some* people see it."

"Really? When you look at me, do you see one-hundred-twenty degrees in an old Nissan?"

Maybe she's right.

LET IT BLEED

It's about six at night; I've been home from practice less than fifteen minutes, and I'm already at work trimming the hedges lining the east border of our yard. Anything to avoid being with my mother. Besides, this task—fall cleanup of our yard—has been on her list of chores I'm supposed to complete for about a week. It's a big job, one that will take days to finish, and I want to get as much as possible done before next weekend, because next weekend, I've got a date for Homecoming.

I glance up at the living room windows, where Margaret and Caroline are knocking and waving every few minutes. Once I turn to acknowledge them, they hide. They crack me up with how easily they're amused.

But this time, when they knock and I turn, I see something I don't expect: my former stepfather is already halfway across the lawn and approaching the door. I don't have time to reach for my phone to call the cops because I know he's not going to ring the bell. Despite the fact that he's never lived here, he somehow feels he owns the place, like he belongs here and has every right to walk in.

I start toward him, my clippers slipping out of my hand on the way. "Can I help you?"

He doesn't even glance over his shoulder.

His hand is already on the doorknob.

He's taller than me by a couple inches, and he's all brawn, but I launch myself toward him and manage to get into the foyer alongside him.

"Look." He closes the door. "I'm sorry about the other night."

I want to look at my sisters to reassure them, but I don't want to call attention to the fact that they're up half a flight of stairs. I raise my chin toward the door. "Get out of here."

"I'm sorry. I had too much to drink, and—"

"Story of your life, isn't it?"

"I'm sober now. I'm working a program. I'm working on this disease—"

"*Disease?*"

His gaze drifts upward, and everything's put on pause for a second. He smiles. "Hey, pretty."

My mother must be at the top of the stairs now. I glance to confirm it. Caroline is at her hip, and Margaret is hiding behind her. "Josh."

I ignore her. "This isn't a disease. *Cancer* is a disease. *Lymphoma.* This is addiction. A decision he makes five, six times a week."

"That's all over now," Damien says. "Last week, after your mother's shift, we had a breakthrough. I'm working a program."

"I'll bet."

"You're too young to understand this, the love between a man and a woman. I love your mother, and she loves me. We have *children* together. I want to know my girls. I want a hand in raising them."

"Your hand in raising them is supposed to arrive by mail on the tenth of each month," I remind him.

He ignores my dig. "We're going to give this another try, all right? Now, I'd like to do it with your blessing."

"Over my dead body."

"Don't be dramatic," Rosie says.

I don't have to look at her to know she's rolling her eyes, but I don't know which of us she's accusing of drama.

"Damien," she says. "Another time, all right?"

Another time. I gauge her for a second. She's not telling him to get lost. She's telling him to come back later.

"I'm not staying." Damien pulls a small box out of the pocket of his jacket, and again addresses me. "I just wanted to give this to your mother. Now, I'm asking you, man to man. Give me a chance to show you—to show your mother and my daughters—how I can change."

He makes a move to walk around me, but I shove him by the shoulders.

He puts a hand up and appears to take a step back, but half a second later, he's inching closer again, trying to get around me.

I step to the side, blocking his access. "We have an order of protection."

"It expires in a few months."

"You're in violation right now. I could've blown your fucking head off the second you stepped inside this house, and no jury would convict me. Just turn around, Damien, and walk away. Leave us alone."

"Josh," my mother says again.

"Go!" I shove him again, knowing full well I'm provoking him, knowing the consequence could be a massive beating. But it's nothing I haven't survived before, and maybe my mother needs to see it. Maybe she needs to remember what kind of monster Damien can be.

He's looking down at me now. His nostrils flare, and his cheeks are a shade or two redder than they were a minute ago. I can tell he's about to lose it. He gives me a subtle nudge, but it's not enough. Nothing blatant enough for Rosie to see.

I give him a forearm to the chest.

He grumbles a little, breathless, through his teeth. He's about to snap.

So I give it to him again, and next I know, my back is flat against the wall, and he's got my right wrist in his hand.

"I know you need this arm." His spit sprays out at me when he hisses these words. "Big football star, huh? We'll see about that."

I harden my gaze and silently dare him. Go ahead. Do it. That's all I need, motherfucker. Break my wrist. I'll drive myself to the emergency room. It isn't up to Rosie this time.

Margaret whimpers. "Joshy."

"It's okay, Maggie Lee." But I don't take my eyes off Damien. I smile because I know it'll crawl under his skin. "He's not going to do a damn thing. He's *sober* now."

Damien lets out a yell, pulls back, and punches the wall, inches from my head.

"Joshy!"

"You missed!" I'm off the wall, in his face.

Rosie's on us now, trying to get between us. "Josh. Stop."

"I'll teach your ass," he says.

"Teach me." I blow him a kiss.

Rosie: "Damien."

"Contain this animal." He whips the small box at her, but it flies up the stairs, and as he's on his way out, he spits at me— deliberately this time.

But I dodge it. Nothing he does matters to me anyway.

He points at me. "Someday you'll learn. A man can change. I'm trying to put my life back together."

"Do it somewhere else," I say.

He's opening the door. "This isn't over."

"Oh, yes it is."

Rosie gives me a scolding glance, then follows him out the door. "Damien, wait."

Christ.

I've seen this sort of thing dozens of times—my mother begging her perpetrators to stay—and I've read enough to understand that it's a survival skill I shouldn't fault Rosie for, but it doesn't make it any easier to watch.

"You're right," she says. "He's out of control. I'm sorry. I'll work with him, okay?"

I've already dialed the police by the time my mother reaches him in the yard.

She's too far away now. I can't hear what she's saying, or how he's responding, but I see him touch her under the chin, kiss her forehead. Quite a show. If I didn't know him better, I might think a tiger just rearranged its stripes.

"Josh Michaels," I say to the dispatcher. "Forty-four twenty-one Carpenter. We have an order of protection against my stepfather, and he was just inside our house." I answer a few questions: yes, he shoved me; no, I'm not hurt; yes, he's already gone.

Margaret and Caroline are sitting at the top of the stairs, so I go up there, too, and pick up the box when I pass it. I sit on the floor between my sisters while we wait for the police. My feet rest on the stairs.

"Is Daddy coming back?" Caroline lays her blonde head in my lap.

"No," I say. "Your daddy's going to jail."

"Jail?"

"If I have anything to say about it, yes."

"Love you, Joshy," they say in unison.

"Love you, too, sisters."

Margaret pets the box Damien chucked up the steps. "What's in it?"

Caroline gives my arm a squeeze. "Daddies are supposed to be in jail."

It breaks my heart when the girls say things like that. They don't know any different. "Not really. Daddies are supposed to be good." I open the box. It's a ring. A dark stone, rather small, shaped like a teardrop, in a gold setting. I snap the box closed and shove it in the pocket of my sweatshirt. "He's not a daddy, anyway."

"He's *our* dad, but not yours," Margaret says.

"He's not a *real* dad," I say. "Daddies don't do those things."

"Then what do real daddies do?" Caroline asks.

God. What a complicated question. "Well . . . I don't know because I don't have one, but I'll tell you what I read about in a book once." Now Margaret's cuddling in close, too. I put my arm around her. "Daddies are supposed to be here in the middle of the night when you're scared. They wake up early and go to work, and make money so there's always plenty of food and clothes. They read to you and take you to the beach, and play games with you. They drive you to school so you don't have to walk. They're happy for you when you win, and sad when you lose, but somehow, they make you feel like losing is okay, too."

"That's nice."

I kiss the top of Margaret's head. Yeah, it's nice. Too bad it's not real.

111

The door opens, and Rosie walks in. "Well, that went well." She plants her hands on her hips, sighs, and stares up at me. "Why do you provoke him?"

"Don't put this on me." I pick up Caroline from my lap and stand her on her feet so I can get to mine. "The guy's not supposed to be here. Don't you remember going to court? To make sure he couldn't drop in and disrupt everything and hurt people?"

"He's *sober*, Josh."

"Yeah? Give him a minute."

"This order of protection is up at the end of February." Rosie tucks her hair behind her ear and starts up the stairs. "Let's just ride this out, and see how he does until then. If he can stay sober until February—"

"Are you kidding me?"

"He's changing."

"Do you know the girls are *terrified* of him? Do you want your little girls to grow up in fear like that?"

"I can't do this alone, Josh." She maneuvers around me. "I'm seeing real changes in him. He *loves* me."

"Yeah?" I grab her elbow. "Did you think he was loving you when he beat you with a branch when you were six months pregnant? How about the day he had you by the throat and threatened to squeeze the life out of you?"

She closes her eyes for a second, then pierces me with an angry glare. "That's all over now. And thank you for trying to make me feel as if I'm not *worthy* of love, as if no one could *possibly* love me. Just like your bastard father. Boy, the apple doesn't fall far from the tree."

"He's not capable of love, Rosie."

"*Mom*. You call me *Mom*."

"You know it's true. It's not you. It's him."

"He's *changed*! You want to know how I know? Because you *shoved* him, you practically dared him, and he walked away. He walked *away*! No cops had to come, and things are already settled. This is what happens in normal families. We make mistakes, and we get mad at each other, but then it's over."

The doorbell rings.

I look to my sisters. "Just tell the truth, okay? Tell the officers what happened."

"God, you didn't." Rosie drops her head into her hands. "Josh."

I'm already down the stairs and opening the door.

I let the officers in. Give them the gist of what happened. Show them the dent in the wall, where Damien punched it.

"Your mother's home?" they ask.

"She's right up there." I point up the half-flight of stairs, where I expect my mother to be standing, but she's gone. Only Margaret and Caroline occupy the space.

"Ms. Wick?" The officers walk up the stairs.

"Yes?" Rosie appears in the hallway, with a basket of clothes, as if she's in the midst of doing laundry. She glances at me, then glances at the police.

I hold my breath. *Tell them it's true.*

But Rosie drops the basket onto the kitchen table. "God, what did he do now?"

I release my breath. "Great. Lie to them. They won't be able to help next time he's got you on the floor, with a knee to your chest."

Rosie looks like confusion personified. What a great actress she's turning out to be. "I don't know . . . Officers, I'm sorry. My son has been acting out the past few weeks. If you look at his record, you'll see: he has a history of mishandling his anger. He's under a lot of pressure. He actually punched the wall last night." She points to the foyer.

Great. "Look at my hands." I hold them out for the officers to see. "No bruises, no scrapes, nothing dislocated. If I'd punched the wall—"

"He didn't!" Margaret interjects.

"Maggie!" Rosie says.

"Josh is telling the truth," Margaret says.

"Can you tell me what happened?" An officer crouches to my sisters' level.

Caroline reaches for Margaret's hand. Their fingers entwine.

"Joshy's right," Margaret says.

My mother lifts Caroline to her hip. "Caroline, tell Mommy. Did Josh tell you what to say?"

My sister looks at me, and nods.

"I told them to tell the truth!" I say. "Girls, what *exactly* did I—"

"Really, Josh," Rosie says. "To put your sisters in this position."

"You're a fucking liar," I say to Rosie.

"Hey!" An officer is between us instantly. "That's no language to use with your mother."

"I could walk you through this house," Rosie says, "and show you every dent he's put in these walls. I'm going to have to repair them all if I want my security deposit back."

"Are you moving, ma'am?"

"Oh, no. Josh is a typical teenage boy. He's angry, he wants his freedom . . . he has to understand that while there are good choices in this world, he doesn't make all of them."

"I'm telling you," I say. "That man was in this house. He's not supposed to be anywhere near us, and he was in this house. Again. She's lying to you because he's got her brainwashed again."

"I'm not—"

"They're counting down the months for the order of protection to expire. They're going to move in together again, and it's all going to repeat. He's going to spend all the money on booze and drugs and other women. He'll beat her, he might even beat the girls—"

"He's never *touched* the kids."

"*Never*? Want to swear to that in court?" I harden my stare on her. He's hurt me plenty. "And somehow, he's going to convince her it's all her fault."

My mother's glare could carve glass, but she doesn't take the bait. She doesn't insist he's changed. "I can appreciate that there was a time our lives were pretty chaotic, but I've got it together now, officers. I'm a good mother, I make good decisions, and I'm not afraid of my ex-husband. I haven't seen him in weeks, and he wouldn't dare come here."

"Are you kidding me?" I say.

"Let's go outside a minute, son." One of the officers heads toward the back door.

Son.

I'm not anyone's son.

I follow him out and lean against the porch railing. I shove my hands in the front pouch pocket of my sweatshirt and meet with the ring box. "I'm not lying. Talk to my sisters. They'll—"

"I'm inclined to believe that if this man *was* at your house, considering his history with your mother, considering the violence you imply, there'd be evidence of it. And we don't have any."

I'm tempted to give him the ring. I tighten my grip around it in the pocket of my hoodie. But considering the way this is going, my mother will only spin things to use it against me.

"I understand you've been through some tough times with this man, and I understand you hold your mother responsible. But she's trying to put her life back together. I suggest you let her move forward. Dredging up the past isn't going to help any of you do that."

I press my lips together, keep my mouth shut. Nothing I can say will help me now anyway.

He hands me a business card. "This is a county social worker. Most of the time, insurance covers the cost. If you need someone to talk to . . ."

I take the card because it's the only way to end the conversation.

"Call us if you need us," the officer says.

A few minutes later, when the cops are gone, I head down to my room and grab my school bag.

I wonder if this is how Savannah felt the moment she decided to leave home. Had she done all she could to make Loretta see the truth of who and what Wayne is? Had she left when she knew nothing she said mattered? When the abuses continued to stack up and year after year nothing changed?

And Chatham . . . she said Savannah wanted her to leave home with her, and she refused. Maybe if I understood more about why Chatham opted to stay, I'd consider staying here with my mother now.

I pause for a minute when I think about what my leaving might do to my sisters. Will they be missing me the way Chatham misses Savannah?

This is different. I'm leaving responsibly. I'll be back to take care of them.

Rosie appears in the doorway. "I know you don't understand this, Josh, but if the cops nab him—"

"Yeah, yeah. You won't get child support 'cause he'll be in jail." I shove a change of clothes into my bag.

"And I'll be in violation of the order of protection, too. I could be prosecuted."

I shoulder around her and head to the bathroom. "You've got things covered for the night? With the girls?" I grab my toothbrush and paste from the ledge near my sink.

"Well, yes. But—"

"See you."

"Josh, I want to talk to you."

"I *don't* want to talk to you." I make my way around her, despite her trying to keep me in the bathroom.

"Why can't you understand I have to do these things to . . . listen to me! You're *grounded*! Where do you think you're going?"

I'd like to pick up Chatham and spend the day with her, but she's working at the Tiny Elvis. So I go with option two: "Aiden's."

"You can't go to Aiden's."

"Watch me."

"And you wonder why you're in trouble all the time, why you can't have your freedom. You walk out that door, and you're done for two months."

"I need some space from you right now."

"I'm serious, Josh."

"I'll be able to get the girls from daycare tomorrow after practice. I'll be here to watch them when they need me, and in exchange, I'd like lodging and an occasional meal. Once football's over, I'll get a job, and I'll pay rent and live here."

"Oh, you think you're in charge? You think you get to tell me how it is?"

"For the sake of the girls, I think you'd want me here. You think he's going to suddenly play daddy? Be a good person? You need me here for the great possibility he's feeding you a line of bullshit right now."

She opens her mouth, but nothing comes out. She knows I'm right.

"So I'll be here for my sisters. But as far as you and me? We're done."

"You're never done with me." She's got me by the arm now. "I'm your *mother*. I'm the only mother you'll ever have."

I think about Chatham, and the mother who'd left her to die in a hot car, only to reject her years later. In leaving today, I'm escaping a sweltering situation, and I wouldn't be surprised if Rosie disowned me for daring to move on. But I have to go. I have to save myself.

"One day you'll realize that mothers—"

"*Mother*? Is that the term you use? Because I call it the world's cruelest curse, being born to you."

I think I hear her crying when I walk out the door.

WAITING FOR THE SUN

I'm in the middle of a staring contest with the tiki statue standing in Aiden's living room. It's framed by the picture window behind it, which overlooks the bluffs and the lake beyond. The statue is about four feet tall, but it sits on a pedestal, so we're eye to eye. It looks like an ancient warrior, standing in the midst of an orange sunset.

It's a pretty sweet setup. Great view. Aiden's right. This is some decent shit. I hit Aiden's Banana Diesel a few times, take just enough to start feeling the tingling in my fingertips. Just enough to numb the sharp edges.

The way I see it, I don't have to have my head on straight until practice tomorrow morning on the weight deck. Plenty of time to recover before then.

I know my problems will be there tomorrow morning when I wake up, staring me down with a vengeance—but it just feels calm, and that's something I haven't felt in a very long time. I'm always chasing after four-year-olds. Providing. Protecting. Watching. Waiting.

Still, even though I'm not physically with my sisters, I feel an obligation to be available to them. What would happen if they needed me, and I couldn't get there because I was ripped?

I also have Friday night to think about, and beyond. If I'm caught violating training rules, I may as well forget about that Northwestern scout who came to see our game last week, which means I may as well forget about going to college anywhere but Creekside Community, and that's not going to happen. I can't let Rosie be right about me.

And then there's Chatham. Despite our Homecoming plans, I don't know exactly where I stand with her. I get that she's been through some crazy shit, and maybe she doesn't want to tell me all of it, but sometimes, even when we're physically close, I feel as if she's holding me at a distance. It's like as soon as we start to dig into the stuff that really matters, she shuts down.

It occurs to me for the first time: she could have left a boyfriend back in Moon River, for all I know.

Maybe I should point-blank ask her if that's why she's vague. But if she tells me she's someone else's girlfriend, I'll have to back off. One thing I know: I don't want to back off.

I text Chatham: *See me tonight?*

She responds in the most Chathamesque way: ☺

This could mean straight-up-yes, love-to-but-can't, or even so-excited-you-asked-but-I'm-not-sure. Sometimes it's really hard to get a straight answer out of her. I try again: *Are you working?*

"Unbelievable." Aiden's still reacting to my story about Damien and the ring and the cop. He doesn't even know all the bullshit my mother's pulled lately, but this story pretty much sums it all up.

I don't usually talk about Damien, or Richard "The Dick" Herron, or any other of my mother's fucktard boyfriends, because it embarrasses me. I don't know why. It's not like anyone would've expected me, at fourteen, to kick the ass of a knife-wielding, six-foot-two drunk-slash-high imbecile. But sometimes, when I think of that night, and others like it, I find myself editing the script—things I should've said but didn't; things I could've done but was too afraid to try.

"Your mother's getting to be about as reliable as mine," he says.

I crack a smile, although I don't think his mother's situation is all that funny, either. The truth is, Aiden's mother doesn't live that far away, but she never sees him. She has all the time in the world for charity and church—and her addiction to prescription sleeping pills. But no time for Aiden. She's slept through his last three birthdays, and rarely even calls him on Christmas. It's almost like he reminds her of her life before . . . and she wants to just leave it, and him, in her rearview mirror.

Which is why he's been in business for himself since eighth grade. Her pills were the first things he started selling.

I take another hit and pass the J to Aiden.

He takes it and squints at me through his exhale. "You need any cash?"

He's not asking me if I want to borrow money. He's not offering to give it to me. He's wondering if I want to work for him tonight.

"Just one drop," he says. "Some grade-A shit to this house on Sheridan, and I'm too fucking smoked out to go there."

I used to drop for Aiden occasionally—it's not really that big a deal—but considering what's at stake—football, potential scholarships—I don't think I should. Then again, if I'm really going to make a clean break from my mother, and pay rent to stay in her house, I could probably use the cash.

"You can take my dad's car. That way, if you have any trouble, you can claim you didn't know what was in the package."

"I'm not worried about it." And this is the truth. Aiden used to peddle this shit when we were pedaling dirt bikes, you know?

"When you get back, I'll have company."

"Yeah?"

"Kai Watson. Shouldn't be a problem, right?"

Kai's a total bitch when it comes to Aiden. She's raked my buddy over the coals and back a hundred times, but it's like they're magnetic—in a different way than Chatham and me. I'm drawn to Chatham because I feel like she understands and celebrates me. I feel like we've been traveling bumpy roads, destined to intersect one day, whereas Kai's not even on the same map as Aiden. She keeps coming back to him because she wants to change him. Maybe I'm naïve, but I don't feel like Chatham wants to change me . . . despite my flaws.

Aiden offers the smoke again, but I waive the opportunity. I'm already feeling just how I need to be feeling—as if Rosie and her drama and her lies are happening on another plane of existence, just far enough from where I'm rooted down.

My phone buzzes.

Chatham: *At the Tiny E till close. Slow tonight. Might get off early.*

In that case, I'll get the job done now. "Where's this package?"

"In the trunk." He hands over his dad's keys—silver convertible Audi R8; *niiiice*—and says, "Keep it under the limit."

"Will do."

He tells me where I'm going, and I get on the road.

It's a little chilly to have the top down, but in a car like this, it's a must. And the wind in my hair only helps me savor the feeling I've been craving. Carefree. Alive. With the sunset at my back, I sing along to the tunes blasting from Aiden's dad's preset station: Lithium XM. Pearl Jam, Nirvana, Soundgarden.

I glance every now and then at the passenger seat, and imagine what it would be like to have Chatham sitting there, the wind whipping through her brown curls. In my fantasy, she's as carefree as I feel right now, arms up, dancing in her seat, belting out a tune: *Black hole sun, won't you come?*

What would it feel like to know her that way? To be with her without thinking, without second-guessing my every move in her company?

I'd put my hand on her thigh, without wondering if I should.

I'd lean over and kiss her at a red light. Just a peck on the lips. Respectful, yet intimate. A moment and memory that belongs just to us.

I downshift and slow as I approach an intersection, and glance at the empty seat beside me.

Only for a second, I swear she's there, sunglasses on, lips pursed and painted red.

I shake away the feeling. Man, this Diesel is having a crazy effect on me.

I take North Avenue all the way to the shore and turn left on Sheridan, where the scene slowly evolves from rectangular, no-nonsense architecture of Northgate Park to softer lines of Victorian-era homes.

This more affluent area is where Rachel Bachton used to live. For weeks after her disappearance, you couldn't turn on the news without seeing the sidewalk in front of her house strewn with gifts and flowers, which I've never understood. All of it seemed to be put there as if it could entice Rachel to come back home. Like it was her choice to be gone. I imagine her little brother experiencing the piling up of teddy bears and dolls at their curb, and not understanding why strangers were dropping off presents no one could play with.

I hook onto Regency Street, just to see if I can pick out her house, where the Bachtons no longer live. Just to see if people still decorate the walk with what I'm sure is meant to be kind gestures, but only serves as a reminder: *that little girl is gone.*

A few houses down, on the left, I see the Bachtons' place. There's a wrought iron fence lining the property now, and a gate at the driveway, but faded pink ribbons still circle the oak tree in the parkway. I stop for a minute and stare at the house that was supposed to be the forever in which Rachel's parents, then a young couple, were to raise their family. Maybe they thought they'd live there for all eternity. Maybe when they bought the place, they envisioned warm Christmas mornings by the fireplace, with their children and grandchildren.

Then some asshole snatched the whole dream away.

I snap a picture of the house. I don't know why. It feels a little stalker-ish, now that I've done it. But maybe it's a reminder that even the best-laid plans can go to shit.

Time to get on with things.

I circle the block and head to where I'm going.

I park at the curb, open the trunk, and find a shrink-wrapped hardcover biography of Jim Morrison. I know it's hollowed out in the center, and that's where the weed—or whatever—is stashed. I know this because one summer, Aiden and I spent more nights than I can count slicing away the center squares of pages in hardcover books he'd bought for pennies at garage sales just for this purpose. I was also there the day he bought a four-pack of commercial-grade plastic and a vacuum sealer at Costco.

I take the book and head toward the house in question, which is painted a pale green with plum and lavender ginger-bread. It cracks me up to think of someone living in a house like this rolling up a fatty of Midnight Oil weed.

The house is enormous. You could easily fit three of my houses inside this one. And like every other house on the east side of the road, it sits so high up from the road that it's practically looming over me, like a presence I can't avoid. Almost like it's looking down its nose at the town below. It's crazy that I'm feeling, suddenly, like I should put the book back in the truck and get the fuck out of here. Probably just a side effect of the Diesel I smoked. It's just a house, and I'm just delivering Morrison's biography.

I count eight steps from the curb to the sidewalk—I pause there to ping a finger against the address shingle hanging from a hook on a lamppost—and an additional eight to climb the porch. You have to consider people who live an entire story above the street have some decent money to throw around. I wonder what it's like to live like this, wonder if these people have restraining orders against ex-stepfathers, if they have to steal a twenty out of a flour canister when they want to treat themselves—or their girlfriends—to an ice cream sundae. I wonder if these people would hole up in by-the-week rentals in chase of their runaway foster sisters.

Even the bell sounds expensive, a series of clangs, like church bells.

No one comes.

I peek in the sidelight, but the place is still and quiet, like a funeral home.

I hit the bell again.

Wait a few minutes.

When nothing happens, I turn to make my way to the car.

I'm down about four steps, when I hear the door open behind me.

"Wait, wait, wait!"

Over my shoulder, I see a mass of long blonde hair catching the breeze, and bare feet with toenails painted purple.

"Hey there."

"Hi." I take in the rest of her. She's thin, wearing a long, blue flannel shirt, buttoned crookedly. Her legs are as bare as her feet, and I have to wonder if there are shorts, or even panties, under the shirt.

A funny feeling skips through my system. Like an ultra-awareness. Like I know she just got laid, and I'm excited that I know it.

"Sorry," she says. "It's a big house. I was—"

"No problem."

"—in the attic." She thumbs over her shoulder.

"Is that my guy?" The deep, male voice comes from the innards of the building.

"I don't know," she calls into the house. "But it's *a* guy."

"Yeah," I say. "Aid's got a busy schedule, so he asked me to drop this off. Says you're really into the Doors." I offer the biography.

After a second, the girl takes the book. "Who isn't? I recently read something about the Dead Presidents." She shakes my hand. I feel the bill, folded into a tight square, pressing against my palm. "You should look into it."

"Maybe I will."

She sort of scratches the toes on her right foot against her left ankle, and the ultra-awareness jolts me again. It's a *deja-vu* type of feeling.

Her male friend calls again. "You gonna invite the guy in for dinner or something? What's taking so long?"

"Want some dinner?" She tilts her head to the side and smiles, so I know it's a joke. "He's so dramatic. But listen, we're hitting a rave over on Foster tonight. It's in the basement of that old brick building with the beer sign painted on it. Know the place?"

"Sure," I say, although I don't. Already, I'm backing across the porch.

"Maybe, if you bring me another something-to-read—"

"I gotta go."

She laughs a little, like she was trying to make me uncomfortable. Mission: accomplished.

In order to prevent a tumble down the porch stairs, I take the railing.

She's heading back into the house, and I'm a few steps down now, but I see a touch of green on her ankle.

A tattoo. A clover.

"Wait."

She pauses. I zero in on the tattoo, take a snapshot of it in my mind. Then she moves away.

"I don't know," she's saying as she's entering the house. "He kept *looking* at me." I hear her laughing as she closes the door.

S M O K E

It's the weed.

Got to be the weed.

Just lingering a little longer than usual, that's all.

The tattoo. Three heart-shaped leaves scrolled together. A shamrock. Or a clover. I don't know what the difference is. But it was a tattoo. On her *ankle*.

Chatham drew something like that girl's tattoo in the sand when I first met her. She said her sister Savannah has a clover—shamrock?—on her ankle. Was it a clover? Or a shamrock?

God, does it matter?

Either way, it's close enough, right?

I have to ask Aiden who this customer is. If he has a girl-friend who might be answering the door. If she's new to the area. If her name is Savannah.

From what I know of her, Chatham's sister would certainly hang out with a guy who buys Grade-A shit from a grower's son. And Chatham has reason to believe her sister's here. In the vicinity.

Ohmygod ohmygod ohmygod.

I can't calm down. What if I just had a conversation with Chatham's sister? A flush of embarrassment crawls up my neck, and I feel warm and uncomfortable. If that was Savannah, I was thinking about her on her back, with her legs wrapped around whoever was barking at her from inside the house.

I wanted to save her from him, I realize. That's what it is. I felt sorry for her, answering the door freshly tousled like that. I mean, what kind of guy would make his girl do such a thing?

I text Chatham: *Getting off early? Important.*

By the time I roll into Sugar Creek, and I pull into Aiden's circular drive, the sky is black and the sliver of moon in the sky is hazy.

I check my phone to see if I missed a text or a snap from Chatham, but there's nothing there. An uncontrollable urge to see her slams into my chest. I want to put her in that passenger seat, drive her out to Sheridan Road, and watch her stand face-to-face with that girl in the green-and-purple house.

I'm sure lots of girls have tats on their ankles. I'm sure lots of girls have tattoos of shamrocks. It's a coincidence, more than likely. But still. What if it's not?

What if that girl was Savannah, and all the time Chatham's been combing the streets of Sugar Creek looking for her, Savannah's holed up, getting high on Sheridan Road?

I'll just drop the cash with Aiden and go to the Tiny E and wait for Chatham's shift to end.

"I'm back!" I drop the keys and the square of Benjamin on the kitchen countertop—I want to tell that girl: Franklin may be dead, but he wasn't a *president*—and help myself to a quick glass of water. "Aiden!"

The place is deadly silent.

I peek out on the patio, but there's no fire in the pit. "C-caw!" I call out into the night. Maybe he and Kai took a walk down the bluffs and along the shore. "C-caw!"

But he doesn't answer.

The faint sounds coming from upstairs register then: the subtle creak of bedsprings.

Christ.

Talk about fast work.

I fish in my pocket for my keys, grab the hundred-dollar-bill—I'll give Aiden whatever's left, but what if I need some cash?—and head back out to my car.

I park on the street, across from the diner, and see Chatham wiping down tables. The sign on the door is flipped to *closed.*

I kill the engine. Might as well wait with her while she cleans up. I have nowhere else to go.

But just when I get out of the car and I'm about to cross the road, I see Damien on the steps of the Churchill Room and Board. A too-thin woman wearing a parka, open over a baggy tee and jeans, leans a hip against the railing. She's smoking a cigarette. Damien pats her on the ass, physically displacing her a few inches, which she seems to like because she laughs.

I freeze in place, and keep my eyes on him as he descends the steps.

Within a few seconds, he sees me.

"What the fuck are you looking at?" he asks.

"I don't know. What are you?"

He touches a button on his key fob, and his truck, parked somewhere behind me, revs to life. He's never spared an expense on his car, but won't pay child support. "Thought you'd be home, standing guard at the door."

My heart tightens, and for a second, it's hard to breathe. He's going to go to Carpenter Street. He's going to try to see my mother and sisters.

I should go home and try to stop him.

"Well," Damien says. "While the cat's away . . ." He walks past me, gets in his car, and peels away—tires screeching against the pavement.

I can't help them, I tell myself. *She'll only lie again if I call the cops.* Which means I can't call the cops. And I could try to handle him on my own—I'll bet I could give him a run for his money now—but where would that get me? I'd end up either in the ICU or the clink.

I can't help someone who can't help herself.

I shove my hands into the pouch front of my sweatshirt. The ring he brought over earlier is still jammed in with the lint and pilling cheap fleece there. He's not worth my effort. But this woman . . . maybe she can help wake my mother up. If this woman is sleeping with Damien—and she's obviously something to him—maybe my mother won't let him back into our lives. I cross the street and walk up the steps.

She's stubbing out her cigarette and entering the building.

"Excuse me." I follow her footsteps across the dirty mosaic tiles on the vestibule floor.

She's heading for the second door, which she gives a tug. It's locked. "Shit."

"Ma'am?"

The glance she affords me is one of pure annoyance. She leans on the buzzer to number 2F.

The door buzzer sounds, and she flings the door open and walks in.

"Ma'am." I catch the door with my foot before it closes and follow her in. "You know Damien Wick. Obviously."

She pauses on the steps, and burns me with a stare. It's the first opportunity I get to look at her, really look at her, and she looks tired. Older than she is, probably. I recognize the same look of despair, of pure I've-given-up-long-ago that I see in my mother's face. "Not supposed to be in here," she says, "unless you're renting a room."

"Oh, I'm here to see someone who lives here. Chatham Claiborne."

The name sparks no warmth in this woman's face.

"But that man you were with . . ."

She turns away and hikes up a few steps.

"Please," I say. "It's important. Damien—"

She's past the landing now, taking the steps that hook to the left.

By the time I reach the top of the flight, she's around a corner, slamming a door shut.

I lean against the wall, and kick at the scuffed floor and utter a *fuck*. Well, what did I expect? It's okay, really. I didn't have to talk to her to get confirmation that she and my ex-stepfather are screwing around. It's obvious. I've seen him cup my mother's ass with the same sense of ownership before. It's almost as if he wants to drive home the message one more time, like he wants them to know that with one final grab, he's in charge.

And maybe this woman is the reason he's been hanging around this block lately, even if it doesn't explain why he'd follow me home.

I take the box out of my pocket, and stare at the ring inside.

It probably didn't cost much, but it's nicer than anything my mother has. When they got married, she was pregnant with the twins. He never bought her a ring because her fingers were fatter than usual. At least that's the excuse he'd used. He'd always promised her a ring later. And I wonder if this piece of jewelry is his making good on that promise.

Something aches inside of me. Regret, maybe. My mother deserves this ring, even if she doesn't deserve to put up with the guy who literally threw it at her.

And who does that anyway? Who *throws* a ring at a woman?

Too little, too late, asshole.

"Joshua?"

I look up when I hear her voice and snap the box closed. "Chatham. Hi." In a flash, all the events of my evening come tumbling forward, wrestling with my mind. I want to tell her everything—about Damien's visit with the ring, about the drop for Aiden, the girl with the shamrock tattoo . . . and I want to see her reaction.

But she's looking at me as if she can't believe I'd had the nerve to wait in the Churchill, and I have to admit it might be a breach of boundaries.

How do I tell her I'm not exactly in this building for her? On the other hand, how do I let her believe I am? I mean, here I am, outside her door, with a ring in my hand. We just started spending time together; this must look absolutely insane.

Her brow knits a little. "I was going to text you when—"

"I know, but I was out in Northgate tonight, and . . . Your sister."

"Savannah? What about her?"

I swallow hard. "I think I just saw her."

"You *saw* her?" There's a sense of urgency in her voice. She touches me on the elbow. "Where?"

"A house on Sheridan Road."

"What color hair?"

"Blonde."

"*Blonde?*"

"Yeah. About this tall." I demonstrate with my hand, hold it at about five-feet-four.

"How do you know—"

"The tattoo on her ankle."

"Wait a minute."

Another resident—a kid this time—barrels down the hallway on a scooter. I pull Chatham out of his path just in time. "Can we go in and talk?"

"You saw Savannah?" Her key dangles from her hand.

It hits me like a dagger in the gut: she isn't going to invite me in.

There could be plenty of reasons why she wouldn't. She could be embarrassed to be living in this dump, for one (and I can say it *is* a dump because Rosie and I stayed here for a week once after the-boyfriend-before-Herron started showing his true colors). Her parents could not want visitors, or she could not want me to meet them. But she could at least *say* something instead of standing here in this hallway. Someone's television is on too loud, and some baby down the hall is wailing.

"You really think it was Savannah?"

"Maybe. I mean, I'd like to see a picture of her. All I'm going on is the shamrock you drew in the sand that day."

"I'll bring one up on my phone on the way. I just want to change."

"Should I wait for you outside?"

It's at this moment, I know, we're at a crossroads, practically daring each other to either turn down the same avenue, or run in opposite directions.

"Joshua," she finally says. "It's just . . ."

I lift my chin. It's just . . . what?

She sighs, studies me, as if in silent debate with her own thoughts. After a second, she leans a shoulder against the door to 2E, inserts her key, and opens the door. "Come in."

One foot in the door, and it's like everything I thought I knew about this girl—which, granted, isn't much—was smoke and mirrors.

"Joshua." She reaches for me.

I hold tight to her hand.

SHATTERED

If I were a fragile guy, I might be in a thousand pieces when the truth bowls into me.

This place is one of the smaller units at the Churchill, about ten by fifteen feet. Just a bedroom. No kitchen or private bath. Directly across from me is an alcove without doors. A rod spans the width of it, like it's meant to be a closet, but nothing hangs from it.

There's a shelf-like surface jammed into the alcove, too, at table-height, and a rusty folding chair tucked under it.

Next to the window Chatham recently climbed out of—the night she kissed me on the cheek on the fire escape—there's a twin bed nestled in the corner; a yellow-and-green quilt is tossed over it, but there's no pillow to be seen, and I wonder if there are any sheets on the mattress.

She's sketched a mural over the wall opposite the door, and she's started to paint it. Four tubes of paint are lined up in the corner, and there are a few brushes poking out of an old mason jar.

I know there's a shared bathroom beyond the only other door in the room, and I know she shares it with the woman in 2F—the one Damien's banging.

And that alone gives me a start. I don't want him anywhere near my mother and sisters, and I don't want him anywhere close to Chatham. If he knew how I felt about her . . . how I *think* I feel about her . . . he might hone in on her just to hurt us both.

When I drop her hand, she drops her backpack to the bed. I guess she carries everything she owns around in that bag.

"Chatham?"

I don't even have to ask the obvious questions: Where are her parents? Why did she lead me to believe she was with them, if she's obviously living here alone? And frankly, it looks more like *she's* the one who ran away.

Why would she deliberately lie to me? About losing boxes, about being here with her parents in search of her sister? Is she even looking for her sister, or is that a lie too?

She looks exhausted. Any other girl, and I might have just interrogated her until she explained, or maybe I would've just walked out and let her stew in her own disasters, but it's *Chatham*, for Godsakes. I want her to talk to me. I want to understand.

"You live here alone."

"I never told you I didn't."

I guess that's true, even though she'd more than once mentioned a *we*. "You led me to believe—"

"You just assumed," she says, "and I didn't know you, and how did I know I could trust you? You don't just go around broadcasting the fact that you're alone in a place like this."

"Well, you did say . . . about the boxes . . ." I shut up. Keep it in perspective. I try again: "Are you really here looking for your sister?"

"Why would I lie about that?"

"Did you run away, too?"

"Look, I told you Savannah kept saying she wanted to come here. I told you she wanted me to come with her."

"You also said you thought it was a crazy idea."

"That was before."

"Before what?"

"Before I read her journal. Before she said she'd be waiting for me." She has the journal out of the bag again, and she's got it open to a page. She points to the scribbling. "See this?"

It's a note, scrawled on an angle. The words take up most of the page:

LAST DAY OF SUMMER
FARMERS' MARKET
NORTHGATE BEACH
SUGAR CREEK
NOON
LIGHTHOUSE
PLEASE
MUST FIND THE TRUTH
SAVE YOURSELF
BE THERE!!!

I look up at her. "This is the day I met you."

"Yeah."

"Last day of summer, on Northgate Beach. She wanted you to meet her. That's why you were on the beach that day."

She's nodding.

"Did you tell anyone you were coming? Your parents? I mean, arguably, if they're worried about Savannah, they'd want to know—"

"Wayne was already gone."

"Your mom too?"

"No. No way. I started adding things up. I started to understand what might have happened to Savannah, and—"

"What might've happened to Savannah?"

She doesn't answer me, but almost talks over me. "And there was no way. I couldn't tell my mother I was coming here."

"What might have happened to her?"

She looks at me for what feels like an eternity, and I've come to recognize this stare. She's trying to decide if she wants to let me into whatever she's pondering.

I reach for her hand and give it a squeeze.

"I can't lie to you anymore." She plops down onto the mattress.

I sink down next to her.

"We can go see this girl with the tattoo," she says, "but I don't think my sister is here."

"We'll find her."

"No." She lies across my lap. "It's been too long. She would've been there the last day of summer if she'd made it here at all."

Her hair is a silky spill of waves over my legs. Instinctually, I wade through it with my fingers. "You also said she occasionally dabbles in drugs. What if she hooked up with someone and just lost track of the days? It's possible, isn't it?"

"I guess. But let me put it to you this way." She shifts, so she's looking up at me now. "Is there anything you think Damien wouldn't do?"

I wouldn't put anything past him, and Chatham already knows that.

"I feel that way about Wayne. Because I keep going over what I remember, what Savannah wrote about, what she told me." She knots her fingers. "Don't think I'm crazy."

"I don't."

"No, *promise* me you won't think I'm crazy."

"I do."

"*Promise me.*"

"Chatham, I *promise.*"

Her hands move to her shorts. One by one, she releases the buttons at the fly of her jean shorts, and inches her shorts down her hips. I try not to stare, but she's wearing these great panties—pink plaid in some shiny material like satin—and, God . . .

Then she shifts again, and I'm staring full-on at the scar on her hip, the tip of which had peeked at me over denim at least a dozen times. But now I'm looking at all of it. It's two inches wide, maybe an inch-and-a-half long, and shaped like an X with the top left extension cut a little short. A little too *perfectly* like an X, the center of which is a tinge darker than the rest of her.

I touch the mark. Deliberately. Trace the outline of the X.

"The story goes that it was an accident," she says. "I was little, three or four, Loretta says. And I'd walked into the brand when Wayne was marking the new calves."

"Awful."

"But that's not how my sister remembers it."

I flatten my hand over the scar. *No.* I don't want her to say it.

"They never took me to the hospital. If it was an accident, you'd think they'd take me to the emergency room, right? Only what you said before—Rosie didn't take you after Damien cut you because she was worried it would get her into trouble."

"Yeah."

"It makes sense, based on what Savannah remembers. She says Loretta held me down and Wayne branded me. Like, some sort of punishment. She saw it, she says."

I nod as her words of the past haunt me now: *mothers don't always make the best decisions.*

She's up now, pulling her shorts back on, and leafing through the pages of the journal.

It falls open to a page with a snapshot of a small girl, blonde, tucked into the binding. "This isn't me," she says. "And this isn't Savannah. According to what Savannah told me, she found it under the floorboards in the stables."

Under the floorboards.

"It was with some clothes."

"Clothes?" I study the image, an old-looking photo that looks like it was captured with one of those instant-film types of cameras. It's of a little girl with ghostly eyes (not quite gray, not quite green), wearing purple shorts and a white hoodie.

"Savannah said there was also a pink T-shirt there, dirty, like it had been there a while. Little girl's size."

"Under the floorboards?"

"Mmmhmm."

"In the stables?" Where Savannah used to say their dad put a little girl to scare Chatham into being good.

"Yeah. And a pair of underwear. All this time, I thought she made it up to scare me, but what if there *was* another little girl at that farm?" She points to the picture again. "What if that little girl is Rachel Bachton?"

I consider. "Rachel *did* have light blonde hair."

"Right."

"But she was wearing blue-jean leggings and a white T-shirt with a kitten on it and a pink sweatshirt when she disappeared. Not purple shorts."

"It's possible she wore our clothes when she was with us. Or that Wayne and Loretta bought her something else to wear. Isn't it?"

"She would've been there *with* you . . . but you don't remember seeing her." I think, but don't say aloud, that maybe, if she was there, she wasn't there too long.

"I have *no recollection* of her being there, but obviously, I have this mark, so there are things I don't remember. And if Wayne could do *this* to a little girl"—she indicates toward her scar—"don't you think it's possible?"

"And Savannah remembers being at a farmers' market. Savannah remembers talking to another little girl there."

"Right."

"But you didn't remember Northgate Park when I took you there."

"I don't remember much of *anything* about my childhood."

I chew on my lower lip while I sort through it all. "You think Rachel Bachton was at your farm."

"The little girl under the floorboards . . . what if Savannah was telling the truth? And what if Wayne kept her body there until he had time to drive her out to the rivers and bury her?"

Rachel's parents' faces flash in my mind, and my heart aches for them.

"Whether Wayne took Rachel or not . . . he's been gone since just after they found the bones," Chatham says. "Since just after Savannah left. He knows something. Even Loretta thinks so."

"What does Loretta think?"

"I overheard her talking to him the night he left. She begged him to tell her where he was going, what he was up to, but he wouldn't say. And she kept saying *don't let it happen again, don't let it happen again*. And that's why I came here. Because if he had something to do with Rachel Bachton, there's no telling what he might have done to Savannah. And *this* . . . this is the place Savannah wanted to meet, if she managed to go anywhere at all."

"*If* she managed to go? You said Savannah ran away."

"Yeah, I did. Because that's what she told me. She was preparing for it. She'd been stealing some of their money. A little here, a little there. She emptied her savings account. And she put her journal under my pillow. She wanted me to read it. Like she *knew* there was a chance she wouldn't make it off the farm. And the stuff about the clothes under the floorboards? I checked the stables. I went out there and looked."

I wait a second, then probe when she doesn't get there fast enough. "What'd you find?"

"No clothes. Nothing like what Savannah said she saw. But I found this." She gives the backpack a shove in my direction.

"Your backpack?"

"*Her* backpack. If Savannah really ran away this time, she would've taken this." She yanks on the zipper of the ever-present backpack so it opens even more, and exposes its contents.

When she yanks out the sweater she just purchased at the Northgate Park bazaar last week, bundles of cash emerge from beneath it.

"If she ran away, wouldn't she have taken her money? And her license is in here. So where'd she go without her license? And this shamrock brooch . . ."

I run my thumb over the pin, which is gold, with a red

stone, like a heart, in the middle of three heart-shaped leaves in a shamrock formation.

"I found it in the front pocket."

"Where did she get it?"

"I don't know. I've never seen it before."

"You don't think . . ." I shut up until I wrap my head around what I'm about to suggest. "Rachel Bachton's mother has mentioned a couple times . . . Rachel had a charm with a heart-shaped stone on her necklace the day she disappeared. Something her grandmother gave her. This pin has a heart-shaped stone. What if this pin is that charm?"

I think about it. Would a kidnapper let her keep something like that? Probably not. But what if Wayne—despite his airtight alibi—*did* have something to do with Rachel's kidnapping? What if he kept the charm and had it made into this brooch for some reason? What if Savannah knew about it? What if Wayne decided Savannah knew too much?

"Savannah thinks she saw something," I recap aloud, "and she wanted to come to Northgate Beach . . . and when you didn't want to go with her, she left you that note, asking you to meet her. And she didn't show."

"And she didn't take her money," Chatham says. "And Wayne left, and Loretta was upset, so maybe Savannah didn't even make it off the farm."

She might be onto something.

And not that I have much faith in law enforcement these days, but . . .

"We should call the police," I say.

"I already did. I called the Rachel Bachton hotline. Right before I left."

"What happened?"

"I told them about what I overheard, about Loretta begging Wayne not to let it happen again. I told them about Savannah's plan to run away, and that I found her backpack with all
her money. I told them my name, and I hung up. I left about an
hour later. I was just too scared to stay."

"Why . . ." I'm not sure I want to know the answer to this
question. "Why were you scared?"

"I didn't know when Wayne was coming home, but I knew
I didn't want to be there when the police came to investigate
what I told them."

"You're safe now."

"I don't know about that. Ever since I got here, this guy . . .
I'm not going to say he's following me, because that would be
ridiculous. But it's like he turns up everywhere I go. That first
day I met you . . . on the beach . . . he was there."

I think of the way she was looking at something behind me
that day, the way she abruptly left. "He's following you?"

"No, it's different. If he were following me, I think he'd
actually *follow*. But sometimes, he's at places I go before I even
get there, and he leaves before I do. Like at the diner. He's there
before my shift starts sometimes, but it's not like he stays until
it's over. I just keep seeing him. It's just . . . bizarre."

"When you live in a town with only four thousand people,
you're bound to run into people on a repeat basis. But it's still
weird." I stare into her eyes, travel into them, really, as if I could
follow back on the paths of her memories and see what she may
have seen. I want to wrap her in my arms and keep her safe.
"We should call the cops. They need to know about this guy,
and they *definitely* need to know about this shamrock pin. If this
stone doesn't match the one on Rachel's necklace? Okay, fine.
But what if it does?"

"If it does, then Wayne had something to do with Rachel Bachton. And that means Savannah was right." Her eyes well with tears. "And if she was right, and Wayne found out about her plan to come here . . . Joshua, whatever he did to my sister is bad."

"If Wayne had something to do with Rachel Bachton," I say, "it's probably too late to save her now. But what if it's not too late to save Savannah? We need to go see the girl with the tattoo. We need to know if Savannah made it out of Georgia."

R A V E

Seven thousand dollars and change.

Chatham Claiborne dropped seven grand in a backpack at my feet at the beach when she didn't even know my name.

Since she arrived here, she's been carrying it around with her . . . at school, at work . . . because she says she doesn't have anything else to do with it, nowhere safe to keep it.

It's not only an issue of the cash . . . it's also that the stone in the brooch is red and heart-shaped—just like the charm on Rachel's necklace—and the fact that some guy keeps showing up wherever Chatham is heading. If there's a chance that the stone in that pin belongs to Rachel, it's evidence.

I called the Rachel Bachton hotline, just in case, and told them about the pin. I suppose we'll know if it's a piece of the puzzle if someone calls me to follow up on it.

And now, the backpack is stashed under the backseat of my SUV as we head toward Northgate. On the way, I plan to swing past the house on Sheridan before searching for the mysterious brick building with the beer sign painted on it.

"Maybe you could keep it at your house?" Chatham's brain-storming things to do with the cash.

"No good. If Damien gets a hold of it . . . hell, if *Rosie* gets a hold of it . . ." I shake my head. "Maybe get a safe deposit box."

"Here." Chatham hands me her phone at a red light, and I flip through the pictures on her sister's Instagram account, which hasn't been updated since Chatham last saw her. These pictures, in particular, focus on Savannah's tattoo. They're old images; she must have posted them shortly after she got the tattoo.

I make a mental note of the username on the page: *Farmgirl1004.*

"I don't know." I only got a glimpse of the ink, and Chatham knows this. And I've seen a few pictures of Savannah's face, but I don't remember much about the girl who answered the door beyond her cloud of blonde hair and the fact that she wasn't wearing much clothing. "But it could be."

We drive past the green-and-purple Victorian, in case the girl in that house hasn't yet left for the rave—how the hell do I know what time those things start?—but the place is dark and still, so we assume she's out.

I've been driving up and down Foster for at least twenty minutes now, but it's dark, and we haven't been able to locate a brick building with a beer sign painted on it. Rosie's texted me about a thousand times, begging me to come home, and I'm getting tired. I've been awake for almost seventeen hours, and I have to be on the weight deck at six in the morning. But this trek could answer Chatham's questions, so there's no way that I'm backing out now.

"There." Chatham points to an alleyway.

I turn into the alley and look up at the shadowed buildings lining the narrow lane. "Where?" The tires crunch over the gravel, and the car dips into well-worn potholes.

"It's too dark to see if there's a beer sign," she says, "but it's all brick, and there's a stairwell back there with a few people in line."

"So you want to walk down an alley, go into a stairwell, and—"

"I don't think we have a choice."

"No." I'm at the end of the alley now. "I guess we don't." This might not be the smartest idea I've ever had, but she's right. We don't have a choice. I kill the engine, step out of the car, and meet her on the sidewalk.

She's tight to me as we walk around the building to the alley. If I've ever had a tighter grip on someone's hand, I don't remember when. I can handle myself. I'm not worried about me. But if anything happens to Chatham tonight, I'll never forgive myself.

We edge closer to the stairwell, where five people are lined up against the railing, smoking cigarettes. They pay no attention to us, and we don't acknowledge them because it's at this moment Chatham whispers, "Kiss me."

Her chin is tilted up toward me, and her lips are in perfect position. So I kiss her.

While my lips are still on hers, she skirts around the smokers, leading the way, and begins the descent down the rickety stairs.

There's a bulk of muscle standing at the door, and for a second, I think this guy's about to ask us for IDs and the password. But instead, he says, "Arms up," and pats me down, then Chatham.

"Twenty-five," he says. "Fifteen for you, ten for your lady."

I let out the breath I didn't know I was holding, and reach for my wallet.

But Chatham's already pulling cash out of the pocket of her jean shorts; she pays our cover, and we enter into the entrails of the brick building that must have a beer sign painted somewhere on it. A few seconds after we set foot on the concrete slab, someone gives us clear plastic cups, despite my attempts to refuse them.

I'm not going to drink anything in this place—because who knows what mysterious ingredients you might be drinking in even water here—and I drop the cups in the closest garbage can.

I feel the music in my bones, in my chest, and even though I'm stone sober now, I can't help feeling light-headed among the colored lights and their strobe effect.

The room isn't all that large, maybe twenty-by-forty, but it has really high ceilings, and it's packed with people.

Chatham hooks her arm through mine.

"Stay close," I scream.

She shakes her head. She can't hear me.

There's a platform that runs the perimeter of the place, barred off with thick, metal railings, and there's an iron gate—something you might see in an institutional building to block access to certain hallways—in the far left of the room.

We walk further into the sea of sweaty bodies, all bumping into one another. It's like an orgy on the dance floor—and the whole place is a dance floor, a beehive of slaves to the bass that comes up through the soles of your shoes and consumes you.

I feel her moving next to me. And we're not here to dance, but it's almost an involuntary side effect of being in this place.

After two passes through the place, I'm ready to leave. The trip's a bust; the girl with the tattoo isn't here. But when I try to tell her, Chatham starts pulling my arm toward the rear of the room. As we get closer to the back wall, farthest from the door through which we came, I see the girl she's heading for.

The blonde hair. White blonde. Platinum. Too blonde to be the same girl I saw earlier, I think. She's dancing on a platform, wearing a scrap of something that looks like aluminum foil. Really, it's a strapless silver dress that barely covers her ass *and* her boobs. She's wearing purple vinyl boots with straps that criss-cross over her calves and go all the way up to her knees, so we can't see if she has a tattoo on her ankle.

Chatham's talking to me, but I can't hear what she's saying.

It's okay. She can tell me later.

We move toward the platform.

Out of nowhere, I feel a tug on the back of my sweatshirt, and next I know, I'm separated from Chatham and find myself in the center of a ring of dancers, torso-to-torso with a girl with long, ink-blue hair. Her lips are red and puckered, like she tied them into a bow, and her lashes are so thick and so black and rimmed with silver glitter, that I can barely see her eyes beneath them.

I try to extricate myself from the circle. I have to get back to Chatham, but there are so many people, and everyone's moving, and I'm turned around and . . .

Chatham?

I don't know where she is! I lost her!

This girl's hand is in my back pocket, and her body is pressed tight up against mine, and . . .

"Chatham!"

I know she can't hear me.

I have to find her.

This girl's lips are at my ear. "I loved that book!" Her scream at close range practically deafens me.

I lean back and look at the girl whose body is rubbing against mine. It's *her*, the girl from the purple-and-green house. Isn't it? She's wearing a wig—obviously, no one's hair is really that color—and I can't see her ankles, but . . .

I grab her by the wrist, and look for the girl in the purple boots to orient myself. If I find her, I'll find Chatham.

It takes a minute, but . . .

There.

Chatham's between two guys who don't seem to care that she isn't dancing, don't seem to notice she's not interested in being the peanut butter to their bread. Her eyes are wide, and she's sort of scanning the crowd with a deer-in-headlights glance.

Thug number one has his hands on her body. She shakes her head, but then thug number two, behind her, is at the nape of her neck with his mouth, and . . .

"Chatham!" I inch my way closer, shoving a path through a crowd and yanking tattoo girl behind me, and finally I reach her.

Number one gives me a push with his shoulder, disguised as the normal bumping on the dance floor, but I have her hand in mine now, and I give her a pull toward me; she slams into me. She's shaking her head, and pointing toward the girl in foil and purple boots. I watch her lips when she speaks: *it's not her.*

It's then she sees I've got a grip on someone else.

The two girls stand there, each holding one of my hands, and stare at each other.

I glance down at the stranger's feet.

She's wearing high-heeled strappy sandals—red patent leather—but I see it now. The tattoo.

Tattoo girl raises a brow at Chatham.

Chatham gives it right back.

Do they know each other?

Next I know, tattoo girl has Chatham in her arms, and her lips on Chatham's lips.

BLUFFS

Cheek on cheek, then lips on lips.

Chatham backs off, a look of utter confusion on her face.

Tattoo girl winks at me, and in a heartbeat, she's enveloped back into the swarm of dancers.

Chatham pulls on my hand, and soon, we're dodging bodies on our way toward the door. When we finally get there, and burst back into the night, the rush of lake-effect air wakes me up.

"What was that about?" I still hear the bass in my eardrums.

"It's not Savannah."

"She *kissed* you. I mean, why would she kiss you if she didn't know you?"

"I don't know. It's not her."

Chatham hasn't said anything since she uttered those words. She's staring out the window of my Explorer, and I'm sure a million thoughts are going through her head. I guess I can't blame her.

And I might know what she's thinking because I'm thinking it, too: First, why did that girl *kiss her*? Second, if Savannah isn't here, where is she? Furthermore, if Wayne happened to catch up with Savannah, will he eventually come looking for Chatham, too?

And what happens then?

Is Sugar Creek—is *anywhere*—far enough away from the man who deliberately burned Chatham with a cattle brand?

Adrenaline is pumping through my system, and I can't imagine going to sleep, even though it's way past late, and I have an early start tomorrow.

When I left home, hours ago, I hadn't intended to go back tonight, but given everything that's happened, I'm not sure Chatham should go back home, either. So where do we go from here?

And my mind is racing, replaying the moment the two girls laid eyes on each other: the look, the leaning in, the kiss.

Why did the girl with the tattoo kiss Chatham, if they don't know each other?

I park at Northgate Beach so we can decide what to do next.

"What did she say to you?" I ask.

"What?" Chatham snaps out of her daze. "When?"

"She said something in your ear. Right before the two of you kissed."

"I don't kiss girls," Chatham says. "Or strangers."

Technically, considering tattoo girl isn't Chatham's sister, she did both tonight. But I don't think she's in the mood for me to point this out. "Okay, fine. *She* kissed *you*. But what did she say?"

"I think she said she liked you. I don't know. It was loud."

"Why would she say that?"

"Maybe because she likes you?"

"Right."

"Have you seen yourself lately? Not too tough to imagine some girls liking you."

"So she said she liked *me*, and then kissed *you*."

"Yes."

Molly can do crazy things to people, I guess. But even still . . . why would that girl zero in on me? And why kiss *Chatham*? I don't want to accuse Chatham of lying about what the girl said, and I don't want to accuse her of not telling me the whole story, but something's not adding up.

And it's not like she's always been honest with me.

"She didn't say anything else?"

"If she did, I didn't hear her."

It wasn't like there was enough time for a conversation, but still.

"And you've never seen that girl before? She just . . . laid one on you."

"Yeah."

"Why would she—"

"How should I know?" There's an edge to her voice this time. She opens the car door and gets out, heads toward the boardwalk gate.

"Chatham, wait." I hurry to catch up with her; by the time I reach her, she's hopped the gate and is heading toward the bluffs.

"Sorry," I say when I reach her. Her hair is whipping in the breeze, and it's so dark on the beach that she's only an outline of a girl right now. I can't see her expression. "I'm just trying to understand. I mean, maybe we should take this girl out of the equation for a second, and—"

"You're the one who put her *in* the equation."

"I know, I know." And for good reason. The tattoo. I got a better look at it at the warehouse on Foster Street, and I took a good, long look at Chatham's sister's ink on Instagram. The girl at the rave's tat is a dead ringer for Savannah's.

Even if it's clip art or a typical design—and it doesn't look like either; it's too complex—I can't dismiss the coincidence of it. Especially not when I factor in the kiss.

I don't want to admit it, even to myself, but I don't think Chatham's being honest with me. If that girl wasn't Savannah . . .

Then again, why would she lie?

"Let's assume Savannah did make it to Sugar Creek," I say. "Where would she hang out?"

Chatham sighs. "Joshua, I've been everywhere I think she might be. I've hung around at all the shops she might like at the mall. I've dropped into restaurants where she might have taken a job, but no one's seen her. I've been back and forth to this beach a dozen times. Do you know I leave a sand castle here every time? Just so she knows I'm still here? So she knows I'm still looking?"

"Good idea." I keep replaying the kiss—brief as it was—in my mind. Would the girl with the tattoo kiss Chatham if she was really high on X? But in that case, wouldn't she have kissed me, too, the moment she pulled me in close to dance?

"I've been to the train station," Chatham continues. "I've ridden the train up and down the north line, just to see if anything clicks, just to see if I remember being at any of the stations."

I wait for the verdict, although I suspect I already know it.

"I was pretty convinced before I saw this girl at the rave, but now I can't deny it: I've never been here, and I don't know why Savannah would've been here, either. She wasn't here then, and she's not here now."

"But the things in the journal."

"Almost everything in that journal could've been read about online. And the rest? She made it all up. The girl under the floorboards, being here that day Rachel was taken . . . it's all lies."

"So where do you think she went? What are you going to do?"

"Well, I can't go home."

I don't know if she's talking about home to the Churchill, or home to Moon River, but I decide right then and there: I'll sneak Chatham in every single night if I have to. "You can stay with me."

She comes to me then, and presses her body to my chest. She trails a finger over the part of my shirt that covers my tattooed fourteen. It takes a moment for me to realize she's drawing the same curls and loops of the shamrock she drew in the sand the first night I hung out with her.

"Rachel Bachton's family hasn't given up hope," I say. "And it's been twelve years."

I'm leaning against one of the enormous rocks at the shoreline now, and Chatham nestles in tight to my chest. Her body feels small in my arms.

"Maybe there's a good reason she didn't come that day." I kiss the top of her head. "Don't give up."

We stand there for a while, with the cold, damp breeze whipping in off the lake. She shivers. I inhale the scent of her hair and remember the first time I saw her, just down the shore from where we're standing.

She pulls out of my arms and walks inland. I follow at a safe distance until she plops down in the sand and starts to dig.

She's building a castle.

I can't help wondering: Is she doing it because I encouraged her to keep the faith? To send a signal to Savannah in case her sister really is in Sugar Creek somewhere? Or is she doing it to pretend, to amplify the lies she might have told me tonight?

■ ■ ■

My window is locked.

Touché, Rosie. Nothing like forcing a confrontation by making me come in through the front door. I guess I can't blame her. And an unlocked window could invite Damien in.

"Maybe we should just go back to the Churchill," Chatham whispers.

"No, I have a key. Wait here." I don't want to leave her, but on the off-chance Rosie's waiting up for me, I don't want to waltz Chatham through the front door, either.

I walk around to the front of the house and quietly open the door.

The place is still and quiet.

I leave my sandy shoes in the foyer, then go to my room to let Chatham in.

She climbs in and presses a kiss to my lips. "Thank you."

"My pleasure. I'd do anything for you."

And I mean it.

BREAKFAST CLUB

At first I think it's the alarm on my phone going off, which means it's 5:30. God, it feels like I just lay down a few seconds ago.

But when I start to come to, I realize it's just my text alert buzzing. It takes a moment for me to remember where I am and how I got here. Although I swore I wouldn't come back, I'm at home on Carpenter Street, in my basement, on my couch.

I stare at the door at the end of the hallway, the door that leads to my room. Chatham's in there. God, what I wouldn't give to have slept with her body up against mine all night long, but I'm not sure she's as ready as I am for that to happen. This seemed the safer option. Besides, there's no telling what Rosie would've done, had she come down and found me in bed with a girl.

All the events of last night flood back to me in an instant.

The rave.

The girls, staring at each other.

I could've sworn there was a spark of recognition between them.

And then the kiss.

It didn't last long—a second or two—before Chatham turned and walked out, pulling me by the hand to follow her.

And she insists she doesn't know the girl.

After a bit of sleep, I have to be honest with myself: I think she's lying to me. It doesn't add up. One minute, she's telling me she doesn't think Savannah is here, and the next, she's building a sand castle so Savannah, if she's out there, will know she's still looking.

A chill darts through me when I consider Wayne could see a sand castle and know she'd been on that beach, too. Or this guy who's mysteriously following her . . . if he was on the beach the day I met her, and saw her building a sand castle, could he connect the dots and know she's still here, too?

My phone buzzes at me impatiently.

All right, already.

I look at this most recent text, which is also from my mother: *Please come home. Emergency.*

I'm not surprised she didn't hear me open my bedroom window for Chatham to slip through, but how unobservant does she have to be not to hear me come in through the front door? I sit up and rub some life into my eyes. When the Scrabble board, still set up and undisturbed on the table in front of the sofa, comes into focus, I let out a yawn and stand up.

And, damn. It's only five. I'm guessing my mother's getting called in early, so I understand she needs me, but especially after my excursion last night, I could've used the extra half hour of sleep.

I slip into my room, as quiet as I possibly can be, to grab my workout garb.

Chatham's sprawled out on my bed, one incredible, bare leg sticking out from beneath the covers.

I reach for her—my fingers graze against her ankle—and tuck the covers back around her leg. It's pretty cold in here. She shifts in the covers, but doesn't wake up.

In sleep, she looks carefree, as if the turmoil of last night had never happened.

Would I be able to sleep soundly if I was close to losing hope of finding my sister alive? Maybe the pure exhaustion of the evening is enough reason for her to fall into such a deep sleep, but I consider the alternative: Is she relieved because maybe we *did* find Savannah last night? And she just doesn't want to tell me?

The bathroom tile is freezing beneath my feet, and I can't get the water to warm up either, so I splash an icy stream against my cheeks. I change into my workout clothes, brush my teeth, and climb the stairs into the land of the living.

Rosie's scuttling about down the hall getting ready for her early shift, and I hear my sisters chattering quietly in their bedroom, too. They'll have to go to Peppermint Swirl as soon as the doors open today, which is in just under an hour. I turn on the television and pour myself a bowl of cereal.

When they hear me moving around, Margaret comes running down the hallway in her socks on her way from her room to the living room, and skids to a stop. "Joshy!" She's got a Barbie by the hair.

"Hi, sisters!"

Caroline brings up the rear, dragging a blanket behind her, and crawls up on the sofa. "I miss you."

"I missed you, too," I say.

"Mwah!" Margaret blows me a kiss from the living room, where she's gone back to playing with her Barbie. Caroline stays on the sofa, wrapped up in her blanket.

I lean a hip against the countertop and eat. I look up at the television when I hear the news anchor say, "The case of a long-missing local girl, Rachel Bachton . . ."

I stare at the television screen to see her frozen in time, smiling out at the world from the frame of a twelve-year-old preschool portrait. And then, the image morphs to what she might look like now: her hair a little darker, the bridge of her nose more pronounced.

The commentator's talking: "...leaving everyone in search for a brown sedan. The suspect: a white male, thirty to forty-five years of age, five-ten to six-two in height, with stringy hair, dishwater brown, on the longer side. Police cite a generic description, given by the only witness who got a good look at the man who snatched her, as an explanation for their lack of resolution to this case. Rachel's younger brother was only three years old at the time. Tips came in. A task force was assigned.

"But as yet, she hasn't been found."

The camera clicks to another face. "We have to remember we aren't looking for a four-year-old girl anymore." The moment Mrs. Bachton's face fills the screen, my heart aches for her. We've watched her parents age on television over the years since Nondescript Longhair snatched her. It's like the Bachtons get ten years older every time they do an interview, and today is no exception. Rachel's mother looks war-beaten and too thin as she describes watching the team of investigators dig for more of what could be her daughter's remains in rural Georgia. The commentator continues:

"An unconfirmed report says initial DNA testing *disproves* the remains have any link to Rachel Bachton, but local police have not ruled out a connection between the remains, to which investigators are referring as 'Baby A,' and 'Rachel.' Some suspect the reference to 'Baby A' *may* indicate the possibility that the dig site *may* contain the remains of more than one body.

Investigators are now following a lead in the form of an anonymous tip, northwest of the Vernon and Moon Rivers' meeting in unincorporated Catoosa County, Georgia. No details as yet, beyond the possible excavation of farmland known as the Goudy tract."

I'm rapt. That might be Chatham's tip! Despite the fact that the police all but ignored the information when Savannah offered it, they're finally taking it seriously. I have to tell her.

On television, Rachel Bachton's mother is speaking to her missing daughter: "If you're out there, and we believe you are, all you have to do is tell someone your name. Remember the charm on your necklace. It was a gift from Nana. It's okay if you lost it, or if someone took it from you. You're not a little girl anymore. You can find someone safe to tell. Tell them about the charm."

"Josh." My mother whips into the kitchen, stabs a finger against the remote control, and terminates the morning news. "Really. Your sisters."

I spoon the last of my cereal into my mouth.

"When did you get home?" she asks.

"Last night."

"You can take the girls to school?"

"Yeah. But we're leaving early. I'm going in to lift this morning."

"Do you have to?"

"If you want me to take them, we gotta shake it." And as soon as my mother is out the door, I'm going to head downstairs to tell Chatham about this morning's newscast. "Girls! Go get dressed."

"No," Margaret says. "Hunnnngrry."

My mother sighs. "Couldn't you, just this once, skip early morning practice?"

I put my bowl in the sink with just a few flakes stuck to the sides. "Not even once."

"Rinse it out." Rosie reaches over me and blasts the faucet for a second or two, filling my cereal bowl with an energetic splash of water.

Whatever. It's not like she'll be washing the dishes tonight—or any night, for that matter. If I want to scrub dried flakes from the bowl twelve hours from now, it's my business, right?

"Who wants a Pop-Tart?" I'm standing in the open pantry now.

"Pop-Tarts, Josh?" Rosie sighs an overly exasperated sigh. "Really?"

"Hey, you bought them," I remind my mother, who is packing her lunch—watercress and bamboo shoots and some other nonsense she eats because she thinks she's fat.

"Sisters!" I raise my voice.

"Joshy!" Margaret says.

"Who wants a Pop-Tart?"

"I do, I do!" Margaret squeals, and she comes running.

"Can we maybe find something a little healthier for breakfast?" My mother hoists her bag over a shoulder. "You could scramble a couple eggs . . ."

I ignore her. I don't have time for healthy. "We got chocolate, we got strawberry, we got s'mores."

"What's s'mores?" Caroline calls.

"It's the best one. Chocolate, marshmallow, and graham cracker."

"Okay." But she stays on the sofa.

I toss her a package of s'mores—it lands on the sofa cushion next to her—and dare Margaret to try something new. "What do you say, Maggie Lee?"

She chooses strawberry. She's predictable like that. She likes what she likes.

"So I'll be home in between," Mom's saying. "To sleep. Then I'm pulling the double from eleven tonight to three tomorrow afternoon. You can be here? For the girls?"

After all the drama of yesterday, she doesn't have anything else to discuss with me? I don't say anything.

"Josh."

It's not like I have a choice. I'll work around the girls.

"Text me," my mother says. "Let me know everyone's home safely this afternoon."

"You got it, Rosie."

"Help, Joshy?" Caroline's at my leg, resting her cheek against me, and she shoves the s'mores at me.

I rip open the package, then tend to Margaret's. "You're going to be late," I tell my mother.

She fills her go-cup with coffee, kisses my sisters. Then she's out the door.

I turn the television back on and watch the news anchors speculate about the bones found at the confluence, and what investigators might find on the Goudy tract.

Chatham's just downstairs, but I don't want to tear away from the news even to wake her. I text instead: *Are you up? Goudy tract on the news.*

It's still dark, but the sun is attempting to rear its impotent head over Lake Michigan. It's going to *look* like a nice, sunny day, but take one step into it, and you'll freeze your ass off.

"Joshy." Caroline tugs on the sleeve of my hooded sweatshirt. Her cheeks are flushed, and she looks sad.

"What's wrong, Miss Caroline?" I look down at her and thumb away a streak of graham cracker and sugar from her cheek. She feels warm.

"Love love," she says.

"Aww." I lift her up.

She kisses my cheek.

Her cheek is hot against mine.

I put my hand on her forehead. "Do you feel okay?"

She shakes her head. "Yucky." And a second later, she retches.

I manage to run her over the sink just in time. Only a splash of vomit lands on the floor; the rest of it lands on top of my cereal bowl.

"Done?" She looks up at me with teary eyes. But a second later, she turns back toward the sink, and more is coming up.

Margaret's crying sympathy tears, and I know it's only a matter of time before she starts hurling, too. They eat each other's food, sleep in the same room. If one's sick, the other always gets sick, too. "School?"

"No school," I say. "Not today."

Then, it hits me. If they're not going to school, and Rosie's already gone . . .

Fuck.

Once I get Caroline cleaned up and resting on the sofa with a bucket in reach, I dial my mother. While it's ringing, I walk downstairs. I don't want the girls to hear what I'm about to say. I don't want them to think they're a burden.

"Hi, Josh." This is how my mother answers, in a clipped tone.

"Caroline's sick."

"Shit. I thought she looked a little—"

"Christ, Rosie, you could've given me a heads up."

She sighs in return, as if my call is a big inconvenience for her. "Come on, Josh."

"You have to come home," I say. "I can't miss practice."

"You can miss *one* practice."

"No, I have to go to breakfast club." That's what we call the early morning team meetings. "And I have school, and if I miss school today—"

"Well, I can't miss work."

"Well, I'm leaving soon—*I have to*—so you have to come back here and take care of your daughters."

"Look, Josh. Football doesn't pay the electric bill, all right? I'm sorry, but you're going to have to stay home. You're grounded anyway."

"From *school*? I have a test in history."

"You'll make it up. I have to go. I'm sorry, but—"

"Rosie."

"My name is *Mom*."

"Come on. I have a game tomorrow, and if I don't practice today—"

"I know it's not fair, but life isn't always fair, you know."

I don't say anything in response, and this seems fine with her. The silence between us lingers on the line, indefinite, until I hang up. In a silent rage, I throw my phone against the cushions on the sofa and shove my hands through my hair. "God-fucking-dammit!" I whisper.

I pace back and forth, trying to calm myself down. But it's especially difficult because there are no options to pursue. Rosie won't come home, the school won't take Caroline in her condition, and I'm sure as hell not calling Damien to cover, which means I have to stay home. The girls are sick. It's not their fault.

Life sucks.

Missing this practice will send a message to Coach Baldecki. I can almost hear him now: *You're not committed to the team, Michaels. All these guys counted on you, and you let them down.*

I plant myself on the sofa.

God-fucking-dammit! I wouldn't miss school even if *I* was the one throwing up, but there's no way to explain my lack of control over the situation to the coach.

"Hey."

I look up.

Chatham's standing there in one of my T-shirts, which is too large for her. Her hair is a curly mess, curlier than usual, and her cheeks are especially pink.

I can't focus. It's like the world is starting to spin too fast, and I can't keep up. I'm juggling these gargantuan issues—Chatham and her sister, Rachel Bachton and the shamrock pin, Rosie and Damien and the twins, the Goudy tract—and now I can't even focus on the things I do routinely *because I have to stay home and play nursemaid.*

"What did they say on the news?" She falls onto the cushion next to me, and snuggles at my side, like my sisters do when they're cold or sleepy.

I kiss the top of her head, and try to concentrate on how it feels to have her cuddling next to me. She smells like hand soap and mint toothpaste.

"You okay?" Chatham asks. "Was it bad?"

"That girl at the rivers." I aim the remote control at the small television in the corner of the basement to turn it on. "They don't think it's Rachel."

She sits up a little more when the picture on the screen develops.

"The police are referring to the remains as 'Baby A' and they're wondering if it's more than one body," I say.

"Wayne's farm," she says when the camera pans over an aerial view of the Goudy tract, then cuts to a clip of police dogs combing the area.

"Investigators are concentrating on the area around the stables," a reporter on site says, "but are not yet ruling out the excavation of this vast tract of land."

"They're investigating your tip. And Savannah's."

"They're finally going to know." Her eyes are wide. "*I'm* finally going to know. The girl under the floorboards."

The impact of what she says hits me full force. If Savannah was telling the truth about that little girl, the dogs will sniff out the place in the stables where she was stashed.

The reporter is now talking with members of the small crowd amassing outside the gate adorned with a giant, silver X.

"This monster was raising my daughter," a woman in the crowd says. She's distraught, and looks as worn as Rachel Bachton's mother.

"Oh, God," Chatham whispers.

The woman continues: "This *man* . . . they gave a little girl to *him*. And I ask you, where is my daughter now?"

The reporter briefly faces the camera—"Channel Seven, with this exclusive"—and turns back to continue her interrogation. "Ma'am, when was the last time you *saw* your daughter?"

"Years." The woman nods. "*Years.*"

The reporter: "And she's a foster child of the family who owns this land?"

"She *was*. No telling what he did to her."

"God!" Chatham says again.

I stiffen. "The girl under the floorboards."

"No," Chatham says. "She's talking about *me*. That's my mother."

"*Loretta*?"

She shakes her head. "The one that left me for dead in a hot car."

I snap my attention back to the television. The woman on screen doesn't bother to wipe at her tearing eyes. Strings of saliva hang from her teeth when she opens her mouth with more accusations. She looks positively insane. "This woman? She's your—"

"Yeah."

On television: "Do the authorities know your daughter is missing?" The reporter shoves the microphone under the unfit mother's nose.

"They know," the mother drawls. "Just don't care."

Chatham grabs my hand. "They *know*?"

But there aren't any reports. For a second or two, neither of us says anything.

I finally break the silence: "They're looking for Rachel Bachton. They shouldn't be distracted right now."

"So you think I should call. And tell them where I am." She pauses for a second. "If I call, they'll come for me."

Will they take her away? And then what? Does she go back to living with Wayne and Loretta, assuming they're cleared of this accusation? Or does the state offer her birth mother another chance? Or do they ship her off to live with another family? A family she doesn't even know? Or even a group home?

I feel her slipping from my fingers and imagine life without her. My insides feel like they're disintegrating with the thought of it. But still. She should call.

"Joshy!" Margaret calls from upstairs. "Lina threw up again."

"Fuck." My sisters are another problem I have to solve today. What am I going to do? I'm already on my feet. "We'll talk about this, okay?"

Chatham's nodding.

"Just give me a minute to—"

"I have to think."

"Joshy!"

"We'll talk it through." I press a few knuckles to my forehead. "I have to stay home anyway, so—"

"You have a game tomorrow."

"Yeah, well . . ."

"Go to school," she says. "I'll stay here and think about things, and watch the girls."

I lean against the newel post by the stairs. "I can't ask you to do that. Caroline's sick."

"I know."

"You'll be cleaning up—"

"Listen, I've pulled a few dozen calves into this world. I think I can handle a little throw-up."

Really? Calves?

"After all you've done for me, it's the least I can do. And *this* . . ." She indicates toward the television. "Do you think I can concentrate on school with all this going on? God, what do I do? If I call to tell them my birth mother is crazy, that I'm alive and well—"

"Joshy!"

"Coming!" I call up the stairs. Then I turn to Chatham. "Listen. You have enough going on without dealing with a vomiting four-year-old."

"It's the only option that makes sense," she says. "It's settled."

I almost say it right then. I almost tell her I love her.

But how crazy is that?

You can't love someone you hardly know, but if you could . . .

RECONNAISSANCE

All day, I keep an eye on the breaking news, which isn't too difficult. It seems the whole school wants to know what's happening in rural Georgia and how it connects to the girl who was taken not five miles from here when we were all little kids.

But I'm a little more invested than most.

Instead of eating lunch with my team, I'm in the library, researching. I figure there might be a new story about the foster children living on the Goudy tract, now that there's national news happening there. And I'm right.

Police records show there might have been typical complaints and challenges of raising teenagers—no mention of Savannah's outrageous allegations about the girl kept under the floorboards—but no known formal complaints against the Goudys have been filed with Family Services until the woman Chatham identified as her birth mother recently started ranting at the Goudy gate.

As for Chatham's birth mother—identified as J. Stevenson—the list of complaints against her with the state of Georgia is extensive. It seems she's been in and out of prison as often as she's been in and out of rehab. Her testimony at the gate of the Goudy tract has been determined as nonsensical and a nuisance to the investigation.

But one investigative reporter points out: if it's nonsense, why can't the authorities comment on the whereabouts of the two foster children entrusted to Loretta and Wayne Goudy?

Furthermore, why haven't the minor children been reported missing, if not considered endangered, as no one has seen them since the investigation began?

Police neglect to comment, except to say Loretta is cooperating, and if there's reason to presume the girls are missing, reports will follow.

This is strange.

Because technically, they *are* missing . . .

Chatham is in Sugar Creek without her foster parents, and according to what she told me, they don't know she's here.

Savannah may or may not be in Northgate. *No one* knows where she is . . . unless Chatham's lies extend beyond knowing or not knowing the girl with the shamrock tattoo.

What's going on?

I send the link to Chatham, hoping she'll volunteer some information or want to clarify.

I search for information about J. Stevenson's hot Nissan and the day she left her kids inside it. Now that I know her name, it's easier to find information. There are a few old articles, but none offer much information about the children.

I look up Chatham Stevenson. Nothing of importance hits.

I try Chatham Goudy. No dice.

I text her again: *Everything okay?*

Minutes go by, and Chatham doesn't reply.

Hello?

Nothing.

Panic booms like thunder through my system.

She's with my sisters.

"Jesus." Not that she'd deliberately put my sisters in danger, but what if she's in danger, and they're with her?

My mouth goes dry.

This is all too familiar. Memories emerge from dark places:

Rosie leaves me with some guy. She has no choice. She has to work. And he's a nice guy, after all . . . who just happens to get his kicks beating the fuck out of his son, and watching his son beat the fuck out of me. How was she supposed to know? You can't see the truth about someone if you love him.

I shake off the memories. The girls are fine. They *have to be.*

I try again: *How's it going?*

I wait a few minutes, drumming my fingers against my jeans. I can't sit still.

When there's no reply, I call, but she doesn't answer.

Why wouldn't she answer?

What should I do?

Call the cops for a welfare check?

Call Rosie and admit I found a proxy to sit with the girls today?

I glance at the clock hanging above the double doors that lead out of the library. It's almost one. I'm out of here in an hour and a half.

But then I have practice. I won't be home until four thirty, the earliest.

That's too much time to wait and see.

I'm sure everything is fine.

But if it were, wouldn't Chatham be replying? Even if she was in the middle of holding a ponytail back from the bucket while one of my sisters throws up, she'd have a minute to text me back in between emergencies. And I haven't heard from her in over two hours.

Something's wrong.

I don't have a choice. I have to go.

I pack up and practically sprint out of the library.

"Mr. Michaels?"

I ignore the hall monitors and keep running through the maze of hallways, ignoring the *stop-right-there* and *where-do-you-think-you're-going*.

I burst out the back doors, by the gym—some retired guy they hired to stand guard at the door is calling after me, but I don't have time to explain—and go straight to my car.

Chatham's cell rings nonstop every time I call.

God, let them be okay.

I rip through town, and practically skid to a stop on my driveway.

I dart across the lawn and almost drop my keys at the door when I'm unlocking it.

"Chatham!"

I take the stairs two at a time.

All is quiet.

Eerily so.

Her phone is on the kitchen table.

I pick it up and see all the missed calls from my number, my number, my number. Unopened texts from me, me, me.

The floor creaks somewhere in the house.

"Chatham?"

She's standing at the end of the hallway, in front of my sisters' room, putting a finger to her lips in the universal signal to shut up. She's closing the door.

Relief gushes through me at the sight of her.

I put down her phone.

What must this look like? Me, looking through her phone?

"What are you doing here?" she asks. "School's not over."

"I've been texting. Calling. I was worried."

"I gave the girls a bath," she says. "It helps with the fever."

I'm nodding. Of course she's been busy.

"I was reading to them. They fell asleep. I didn't want to bring my phone in—"

"Sorry. It's just that . . ."

She's looking at me like I've overreacted. Like I've just made the pop of a firecracker out to be the blast of an H-bomb.

"Here." I tap on my phone to pull up the link to the story about the Goudy tract. I hand it to her to let her read it. "The police don't think you're missing. Why wouldn't they think you're gone?"

"I don't know." She scrolls through the story.

"I don't understand it."

Her brow crinkles up as she reads.

I'm growing more and more impatient. There has to be something she isn't telling me.

"I just don't get it," I say.

She shoves my phone back at me. "You think I do?"

"Explain this to me, Chatham. Please. If we're going to help each other, I have to know what you know."

"You want me to explain why the police force in Moon River hasn't declared Savannah and me missing."

"It doesn't make sense."

"Well, how should I know why they do anything? Maybe Loretta spun a great story. Maybe it's taking the police a while to put it all together. I don't know."

"But you'd think, especially with Family Services now involved—"

"What? *What* would you think? Would you think two little girls wouldn't end up in the hands of someone with a cattle brand? Because it happens all the time. People have kids who shouldn't. People trust people to be parents, when there's no way in hell they should be around kids. You *know* that, Joshua."

I guess I do.

"I don't get it, either," she says. "But if you're looking for answers, I can't give them to you. I can't explain what I don't understand."

I pull her into my arms.

With some reluctance, she eventually folds against my chest.

"I just started thinking about all the terrible things that could be happening, and nothing makes sense," I say. "I got scared. For you. For my sisters."

She's warm against me. "The girls are fine."

"I have to ask you. And I don't want you to get mad. But you can trust me, Chatham. Is there anything you know that you're not telling me? About Wayne and Loretta. About Savannah. About that girl with the tattoo at the rave."

Her lips brush over mine. "I've never told a single soul as much as I've told you."

She didn't exactly answer my question.

"And I'm trying to make sense of all this," she says. "Savannah. My foster parents. Rachel Bachton. I *want* to explain it all to you. But I don't understand it either."

"Will you call the police in Georgia? Will you tell them you're here? That you're worried something might have happened to Savannah?"

"You don't know what'll happen if I do that, Joshua. What if they bring me back?"

"Then we find a way through it. Just like with everything else." I hand her my phone. "Please."

She looks up the number, then punches it into the phone.

"My name is Chatham Claiborne," she says. "I'm calling to tell you I'm okay."

PAINTING THE ROSES RED

If Chatham's call made any difference, it isn't apparent.

The world carries on, as it usually does. Thirty-six hours after the story about the Goudy tract broke, no one, except maybe the police, knows how Baby A ended up by the rivers, or who Baby A might be. No one knows if there's a Baby B, and if there is, if her remains might match Rachel Bachton's DNA. And so far, there's no mention of bones, or the scent of them, found beneath the floorboards of a stable.

My own Babies A and B—my sisters—are feeling better today. This morning, they'd begged Rosie to bring them to my game—*we'll see*, she'd said—but they didn't show.

And Chatham . . . I can't quite get a handle on her since we went to the rave. She's preoccupied, distracted. I can't blame her, but I wish she'd let me in on whatever it is she's mulling over. Maybe she's just waiting for the authorities to swoop down and take her back into protective custody.

I'm trying not to think about that.

"Nice fucking game."

I look up from the locker room bench to see Novak standing over me. He's managed to step into some jeans, but his

181

shirt's still dangling from his hand, and he's bare-chested, as if any minute now, he's bound to emulate a silverback and pound his fists against his chest. "Yeah," I say. "It was."

It turns out the douche bag can catch a rope, after all.

"See what happens when you fucking trust me?"

I could remind him that I've hit him in the numbers before, and he literally dropped the ball. I could tell him trust has to be earned. But I don't want to get into it, so I say, "Trust isn't the issue. When you're open, I'll get it to you."

It's a good night for Novak to perform, too. Even though Coach didn't say anything about it, the scout from Northwestern was here again tonight to watch us play. The guy even gave me a nod as I walked off the field. I'm about to share this tidbit, when Novak hits me with:

"So I'm thinking I might ask that girl from the diner to wear my spare jersey next week. For Homecoming."

He's talking about Chatham.

"You know, the one who gave me cake that day."

"Yeah."

"The one you can't close the deal with."

I shrug a shoulder, even though I know what Novak doesn't seem to realize: there's more to closing the deal than getting between a girl's legs. Chatham will be wearing number fourteen on her back next Friday night, and she'll be with me all day Saturday. At the parade. At the dance. I might even take her downtown to Navy Pier after, if she doesn't have to work too early Sunday morning. "Give it a shot."

"Yeah? You don't mind?"

Wait. Is this a *courtesy*? I'd considered it sarcasm, but . . .

"She's kinda cute, you know," he says, "and she's new, so she hasn't figured out yet I'm an asshole, so . . ."

"Actually, Novak, I'm sort of—"

"I appreciate it, buddy." He claps me on the shoulder, and says, in Holden Caulfield fashion, "I really do."

"She's going with me," I blurt out.

"Oh." He takes a step back and finally shoves his arms and head through his shirt. "Well, good for you."

"Yeah."

"She's a *nice* girl."

Something in the way he says it, in the smirk on his face, makes me pause. How would he know if she's a nice girl or not? Does this mean he's *talked* to her? That he's tried something on her?

Again, he claps me on the shoulder, but this time it's with such force that I know it's not meant to be friendly, as much as it's an attempt to duel with me. He's always got to be a total jerk.

Jensen passes us on his way out of the locker room. "Going to the Tiny E?"

Novak and I don't interrupt our staring contest—which is ridiculous, right?—but I nod. "I'll be there."

"Let's see which one of us can *get there* first." Novak makes a show of air-fucking an imaginary girl.

"Whatever." I turn away. I don't want to see that shit. It's insulting to girls, both real and imaginary. And it's insulting to air, too.

Still, if he's going to be that way . . . game on. I finish dressing and get out of there as quickly as possible, which turns out to be about three hundred feet ahead of Novak. I dash through the parking lot and climb into my Explorer, but the engine doesn't turn over when I turn the key. *Great.*

I try again. And again.

Finally, after a few whinnies—and after Novak peels out of the lot in his Jetta—the engine revs to life, and I manage to catch him on Washington. I pass him on the stretch, give him a middle-finger salute.

But he cuts me off on the next curve.

Then I take the lead again, and while we arrive at the same time, I pull straight into a parallel spot. Novak has to back in like usual, so I'm first inside. A few guys are already crowded around the center table.

Chatham's at the counter, serving the customers sitting there. I catch her glance, and give her a flash of a smile.

But Novak shoves me—the idiot practically bowls into me—when he passes, and only to get to a seat at the center table, as if I mind sitting on the outskirts—and I don't. Seniors should sit at the center table.

Chatham rolls her eyes.

It's then I catch the sense of dread hanging in the air, and somehow, I know. I know before I take in the details of a guy at the counter . . .

The work boots with the broken laces on the left boot.

The patch sewn into the right elbow of the insulated, gray plaid flannel jacket.

The dingy baseball cap worn backward and sporting the trademark C, the one everyone's been wearing since the curse of the billy goat was broken.

It's Damien Wick.

I know the drill. I can't stay. If he imposes on a place I'm frequenting, he's in violation of the order of protection. But if I willingly enter a place he's occupying, all bets are off.

My heart is banging like mad, but it's not because I'm afraid. Not really. It's more that I just can't believe it. He *knows* the team comes here. He's here for one reason: to fuck up my life. He may as well be pissing his scent around the perimeter of the place, reserving it as his territory.

And this place, of all places! It's where Chatham works. If Damien starts coming here, starts chatting her up every second he gets . . . The man is poisonous. If he knew what Chatham means to me, he'd be filling her head with all sorts of stories of my weaknesses. He'd make me out to be a wuss, at best. At worst, he'd do all he could to make her feel uncomfortable, like a rabbit in the middle of a wolf pack.

A sick feeling tumbles in my gut, and sweat breaks on my forehead.

I catch Chatham's attention and mime that I'll call her later.

I don't explain; I just turn and head for the door. I don't even want him to know I'm here, so the more quietly I leave, the better. If I'm not here one day, maybe Damien will give up the territorial pissing contest.

Unfortunately, Novak realizes I'm heading out and says, "Michaels! You fucking pussy!"

I'm only halfway past the threshold, and while I don't look back, I can feel Damien's stare burning a hole into my back. I hop back into my SUV.

I pull out my phone and text Chatham: *Couldn't stay. Damien at Tiny E. Be careful.*

Then I add: *See me after?*

I know she probably doesn't even have her phone on her. I can't imagine what her boss would do if she was texting when the diner was full of customers. But when she does check her phone, she'll understand why I had to leave. Nothing will change. She's still going to wear my jersey. We're still going to the Homecoming dance. Damien can't ruin everything.

After fighting again with the engine for a few turns of the key, I slowly pull away from the curb.

When I'm far enough away to breathe more deeply, I let out a scream of rage and pound a fist against the roof of the Explorer, against the headrest on the passenger seat, on the dashboard.

I think about that slimeball, Novak, trying to weasel in on Chatham, thinking that because I left, he could have a crack at her, and maybe even assuming that I left because he intimidated me.

I think about Damien's smug smile, when he must have realized I was leaving only because he was there.

Then I think about Damien's assuming I'd left for whatever reason Novak's spewing, about Damien's taking it as confirmation that I *am* a pussy, and it fueling his urges to come over and prove it to me.

I think back to my twelfth year:

I'm not doing a god-damned thing. Just sitting on the back patio with a game of Solitaire laid out on the table in front of me, when a fist comes flying at my head.

A flash of silver.

A twinkling of stars at the periphery of my vision.

And I'm on the concrete, and this monster is on top of me, pounding on me. Jabbing me in the kidneys. Calling me a pussy. Daring me to hit back.

But I take it. I take it so Rosie doesn't have to. So he won't even *think* about shaking the babies, which he threatens to do on a daily basis.

I hear it over and over again, echoing in the dark closets of my memories: *Hit back, you fucking pussy! What? Not man enough to defend yourself? Fucking hit me back!*

I pull into the driveway and cough over tears. I lean my head against the steering wheel for a few seconds so I can catch my breath.

My hand hurts from all the pounding on my car. Maybe I've even dented the roof, but it's not like I could notice a new dent in the midst of all the old ones.

After a few more deep breaths, I pull myself together.

The house is quiet when I enter. The twins are whispering to each other in the living room. Once I close the door, Margaret peers at me through the rungs of the railing. "Joshy," she whispers.

"Hi."

The sound of a broom whisking against the floor meets my ears.

Rosie looks up then, and pauses in the midst of her sweeping. She's wearing her usual expression—one that says she's utterly disappointed in me, in life, in the world in general—but the second she really looks at me, she softens. Maybe she can sense I'm upset. Or maybe it shows I've let a few tears slip. "You're home early." Usually, she'd be in her scrubs already, but she's wearing a pair of yoga pants and a sweatshirt.

"Yeah. Damien was at the Tiny Elvis, so . . ."

She nods. "Okay."

I go to take off my shoes.

"Leave them on if you're coming up. I was wiping the table, and the cloth caught the hoof of the unicorn."

I look down at the sparkly purple shards in the dustpan. She's stepping a little gingerly as she moves, and there's a slight tremor in her voice.

"You okay?"

"I'm *fine*, Josh."

I take the broom from her hands.

"Josh." She grips the back of a chair and takes a step closer.

I narrow my glance and take a step back, so she has to follow me.

Yep. She's sort of limping. But not like something's wrong with a foot. Like she's *hurt*. I've seen this sort of walk before.

"Was he here?" I ask.

"Josh, I'm fine."

I raise my voice: "What *happened*?"

Margaret and Caroline shut up.

"It was an accident. We were joking, all right? And I lost my footing." Her glance toward the stairs tells me she fell down them. On its own, the incident is semi-believable. But toss in the broken unicorn, and it doesn't make sense.

"It doesn't have to be this way." I'm practically whispering, so the girls don't hear. I sit at the table. "You can call the cops and tell them the truth for once."

"He didn't do anything this time." She joins me, sitting across from me.

"He's seeing someone else, you know."

Her eyes widen for a split second, but she quickly controls her reaction. "He wouldn't dare—"

"I saw him come out of the Churchill. She's young, super thin. Rough around the edges."

My phone buzzes with a text alert. I glance at my phone and see it's a message from Jensen. He's probably just wondering why I left.

"I know you better than anyone on this planet," I say. "You go from man to miserable-fucking-man, but you know who's been here for you every time they drop you on your fucking head? *Me*. They come and go. Breeze in, shake us up, and leave our lives after a few months, a few years, maybe. Guess who's been here the longest?" I point my thumb at my heart. "*Me.* I've been with you longer than any man, and I'm the only man you've ever been able to count on."

She opens her mouth to reply, but I don't give her the chance.

"And I know Damien's back because you think you can't make it on your own. But Rosie, you've been *on your own* since you were knocked up at seventeen. You've been doing this *on your own* our whole lives. I can't do this anymore. It's him or me."

"God, Josh, don't make me choose. *I'm* the mother. *I* get to say who stays and who goes, and you're staying. Can't you just—"

"The funny thing is that you think I have any choice in the matter. That you think I'm *making* you *choose.* There is no choice, Rosie."

She lets out a sigh. "The ring."

"What?"

"Damien said he brought a ring. Remember, he threw a box up the stairs."

"Yeah."

"Do you have it? I want to wear it."

"I'm sorry. I don't know where it is." I look her right in the eye when I lie to her.

"Oh, God." She hides her face in her hands. "God, what am I going to do?"

Her voice catches, like she's about to cry, and I'm suddenly sorry I lied. I'm about to come clean when she says, "It's fine." She wipes a knuckle under her eyes and pushes back from the table and stands. "I'm fine. I'm sure it'll turn up." She cups a cold hand at the back of my neck and kisses the top of my head.

A rush of warm emotion courses through me. I haven't felt this sense of warmth between my mother and me since I was about nine or ten.

"Go out. See Aiden. Go be sixteen."

It's funny: I've been waiting a lifetime to hear her say those words, but now that she's spoken them, I don't feel right leaving. I'm worried about her, about the girls.

My phone buzzes again.

I glance at it. *Chatham.*

J E R S E Y

"He threw his jersey at me," Chatham says. "I mean, who *does* that?"

It's so like Novak to push his luck with Chatham, even though he knows she's with me. "Novak's an ass."

"Obviously."

"So, what'd you do? With his jersey?"

She's sitting in my passenger seat, sucking on one of those striped pink candy sticks they sell for a quarter at the Churchill General, and I'm driving aimlessly through Sugar Creek.

We can't go to my house, and Chatham's place isn't more than a bed, so going there would be sort of presumptuous. Aiden's got another date with Kai, so I'm steering clear of his house.

Chatham's feet are propped on my dashboard. She's wearing skinny jeans with the left knee blown out, and the cuffs rolled to a few inches above her ankle. Some kind of canvas kicks cover her feet, and she's wearing that sweater she bought at the Northgate bazaar. It's more clothes than her usual cutoffs and tank tops, but it's about forty-five degrees right now. She's still got to be cold, so the heat's not only on, but blasting.

"Nothing. I think he took it with him when he left."

I weigh what his reaction must have been against what it might have been had she torched the thing in front of him. Either way, it had to have been a blow to his ego.

Maybe I'm just irritable this evening because of my mother, but suddenly, it's not enough to assume Chatham's wearing my jersey for the reasons I want her to wear it—not because we've kissed a few times, and not because we're working through family messes, both hers and mine, but because we don't want to see other people. I want her to be my girlfriend, officially, and it's killing me that I'm afraid to say it.

I glance at her. "Can I ask you something?"

She raises a brow, and pops that sugary stick back into her mouth.

I take that as an invitation: "I know we're just starting to know each other, but there's something about you." It wasn't a question, I know. "I want to know you . . . I want *you* to know *me* better than anyone."

She presses her lips into this thrilling smile.

Deep breath. "What I mean is . . ." I glance away, but she's so magnetic that I return my glance to her within a breath. "I mean, I think about you. All. The. Time."

She leans over the center console in my car and rests her head on my shoulder. "You know what's funny." Her hand on my knee is cold, but sends a warm dart of electric energy through my system. "We have this enormous thing in common, you and me: we can't go home. But being with you . . . it *feels* like home, you know?"

God, do I ever know.

I pull into a lot at the county preserve, where I'll take my sisters sledding, once the world's covered in snow. The park has been closed, like all parks, since sunset, so I know we can't stay here, but I want her to experience this place. I want to feel her bundled up and tight to my body on a toboggan. I want her to come with Margaret, Caroline, and me in a month or two. I want to taste the snow in her kisses and warm her up with cocoa and big socks and blankets in front of the electric fire in my basement.

Just when my imagination starts heating up to the possibility, it goes cold. It's months away. A lot can happen in two months. Chatham could be shipped back to Georgia. Savannah could show up halfway to California for all we know, and Chatham could follow her there. And there's still a niggling doubt in the back of my mind that Chatham has been utterly transparent with me. She could have plans I don't know about.

Sometimes no matter how good your intentions may be, things just don't always work.

"You know what?" I look at her, and decide to make it happen. Tonight. Even though there's no snow, even though the park is closed, I want to share that toboggan slide with her.

We could sneak in over the gate, but the car in the lot will practically advertise we're there. I have to park somewhere else. "I've got an idea."

"I like ideas."

I laugh and reverse out of the lot, drive up the road a piece, pull off on the shoulder, and turn off the engine. I'm not supposed to park here, but I can always say I've had car trouble if we're caught coming back. We get out of the car, and I lead her toward the woods. I climb over the split-rail fence bordering the county property; she ducks under it.

The woods at night in October smell like a cold snap waiting to break. Like moss and wet leaves and freezing air. The scents mix with the smell of her strawberry candy, and I can't help but think about the way she looked at the rave the moment that girl kissed her. And the way she looked beneath me, in front of the fake fire, on the floor: hair fanned out against the rug, skin reflecting the amber light from the fireplace, lips plump and rosy from kisses.

I tighten my grip on her hand and quicken my pace.

"Where are we going?" Her whisper dances up my spine.

"I want to show you something."

"How can you even see where you're going?"

"Just trust me." I grew up in this place. I could weave my way through Sugar Creek in the dead of night with my eyes closed. We make our way through the woods, and emerge on the other side at the park grounds. The sledding hill is in the distance, washed only with the light from the fraction of moon in the sky.

And that's what I want her to see.

That's where I want to take her. I want to lay her down on the acme of that hill, the highest point in Sugar Creek, from which we can see the Northgate Lighthouse and the lake and the boardwalk . . . if it's a clear enough night.

"What *is* that?" she whispers.

I'm about to tell her it's a toboggan slide carved into a forest on a hill, but she's heading to the left, pulling on my hand.

She starts walking a little faster. "It's a *train*."

"Oh. That."

She's running now, having dropped my hand, and I'm running alongside her, toward the Soo Line caboose that's permanently planted on the grounds of the preserve. A few hundred yards later, she's pattering over the makeshift platform, then climbing up the grated steps of the car.

She steps over the threshold to the interior of the space. "What's it doing here?"

"It's always been here."

"But *why*?"

"The story is that it detached from a train and came to a stop here." It's true that's what everyone says, but I don't know if it's actually what happened.

She props a hip against a built-in bench, her brow slightly wrinkled, as if in deep concentration, or just deeply affected. "This is incredible." She sweeps her gaze around the car.

I remember playing in here as a kid, in awe that an engineer once slept in the tiny bunk, once *lived* in this tiny space as the car traveled cross-country, the last in a long line of cargo cars. And if it felt tiny when I was small, it's positively cramped now.

When I was a kid, someone had carved onto the booth-like table up in the top loft:

RACHEL BACHTON WAS HERE

And it hits me, the reverence of that statement, every time I see it plastered in some unexpected place. Rachel Bachton likely *was* here, like every other kid in the vicinity, once upon a time.

And I want to see the carving again.

I grab hold of the bars on the bunk ledge, and get a foothold in. Up I go, and in no time, I'm in the loft of the train car, a tiny box, with windows on either side and a booth-like table and bench, where the engineer used to sit. Chatham's head pops up a moment after, which makes me like her even more. I just love an adventurous girl.

I slide onto the booth bench, my ass on the back, my feet resting on the seat. She squeezes in past me, leans against the table. And right there, near her hip, carved into the table, layered in coats of dull gray paint, it is:

RACHEL BACHTON WAS HERE

Seeing it gives my heart a jolt.

"God." I say it like it's a prayer, as I trace the words with my fingers, feel the concave of the etching with my fingertips.

It's like an X on an old treasure map. The only difference is, of course, that finding this marking in no way denotes that Rachel Bachton is anywhere near. It's not like we could crack open the floor of the caboose and pull out the treasure of a girl gone so long she's become legend. Rachel isn't here.

But Chatham's here with me now, and suddenly, I'm ultra aware of the rhythm of her breath at my side.

Simultaneously, we look up from the carving.

The light from distant lampposts in the parking lot reflects off the window and illuminates her in a soft glow.

She licks her bottom lip, and the way she's looking at me . . . it's like she wants to lick *me*.

I imagine she tastes as sugary as the pink-striped stick she must have dropped in the midst of her sprint to the caboose.

I can see down the front of her v-neck tee, the curve of her breasts plunging dangerously into the depths of a lace-trimmed bra, but I keep the view in my periphery, try like hell to hold her gaze.

She smiles.

I think I've been smiling all along.

She hooks a finger into the waistband of my Adidas track pants, and yanks me closer.

My lips fall onto hers, and I reciprocate when her tongue flickers against mine like a flame.

But I don't close my eyes because she doesn't close hers.

"You're beautiful," she says against my lips, and kisses me again before I can tell her I'm nothing close.

I'm leaning over her now, conscious of the confines of this loft—how crazy would it be if one of us fell off?—and she's slowly edging her way onto her back on the table, and our bodies are so close that her chest squashes against me. Her knee grazes me at my thigh.

Before I even know I'm doing it, I palm a breast. My breath catches in my throat, and my every muscle tenses.

Every.

Muscle.

"Okay?" I whisper.

"Mmmhmm." And for a few seconds, I damn near imagine the way it might feel inside her—hot and wet and tight—but I don't want to start thinking about it.

I mean, I do, but I don't.

Because even if we were ready to take the step, we can't very well do it *here*. In an abandoned—"God."

Her hands are at my fly, fingers tucked into the elastic waistband.

Well, maybe we *could*.

I shift, anticipating she's going to yank on the drawstring of my pants any second now. She's pressing a hand against me, and as much as I want her to keep her hand *there*, I want even more to navigate my way over her body, feel her, experience every inch of her. I feather a few fingers under her T-shirt, over her stomach, and suddenly, I can't stop thinking about kissing her belly button.

But once I'm kissing a circle around it, I'm craving the flesh of her hips. God, I have to know how that scar feels under my tongue!

I pull on the button of her jeans and tug them down a few inches, and . . . intimate. That's how it feels. Uncharted. As if she doesn't trust—hasn't trusted in a long while—anyone else to roam there.

I weave a trail of kisses up her torso, and maneuver the cup of a bra over the heaven it contains. I circle a pretty, pink nipple with my tongue for only a brief moment. I've really gotten out of hand now that I've slipped a few fingers beyond the waistband of her jeans, and even dipped them into her panties—she's slick and warm—so I want to check back in with her lips, gauge her reaction to what I'm doing. Because I'm haphazardly taking charge of her body . . . as if I own it, and I don't.

"Sorry," I say at her lips.

"Don't be."

"But, God, what you do to me."

"What *you* do to *me*." She's flushed in the cheeks. I see their color even in the dim light from the moon and the lights off in the distance, but I feel it even more. Her eyes are heavy-lidded now, and a thick curl is hanging down between her eyes, and she looks sexy as all hell. And happy. Really happy.

I lower my lips to hers again, this time slowing things down. I move my fingers against the holiest parts of her, and hear her gasp a little. God, I want to be in there.

Normally, I'd keep pushing my luck, see how far she'd let me go. Normally, I'd put it on her to stop. I'd keep going until she tells me she doesn't think we should go any further. But maybe because it's Chatham, I see the hypocrisy of doing that.

For the first time, with this girl practically melting under the influence of my hands, of my mouth, I don't want to put her in this position—to stop me, to disappoint me, to take responsibility for both of us.

Say she doesn't want to stop. And we go as far as two people can go . . . before we should've gone there. And it ruins us.

I pull my hand from her pants and slide up over the smooth skin of her stomach.

The consequence, exhilarating or devastating, would be ours to share. Because I'm not like my father. Because I'm better than him.

Shouldn't taking this step be *our* decision, as well? Instead of solely hers? Instead of me attempting to get her to want it?

Maybe it's a rationalization. Maybe I've stopped because I know she's going to stop me eventually, and it's going to be easier to cool it now than it will be in five minutes. Or maybe, if she's as revved up as I am, I know she won't *want* to say no, and I like her too much to risk ruining this by going too far too fast.

"Holy hell, you're good at this," she whispers.

I laugh because I'm so rusty that my ADHD exploration of her terrain couldn't possibly be impressing her.

I want to ask her if she's done this before. Well, maybe not *this*, not lingering at the edge of the inevitable, but what I think we're about to do, or what I think we're going to do eventually, be it tonight, next week, or even next month. I want to tell her I'll wait. That we *should* wait, if we don't want to fuck this up, because we're *more* than this. I feel it. Do it too soon, and it becomes *only about fucking*.

And then it dawns on me. I have faith. I believe in something: her.

Despite the fact that she could blow out of town tomorrow, I know it's going to happen eventually. Even if I have to travel to the ends of the earth to find her again.

Still, it would be freaking *great* to do it atop this old caboose table in the black of night when we're not supposed to be here. I nudge against her, still imprisoned by the walls of fabric between us, but I feel the heat between her thighs.

I look at her, forehead to forehead.

I'm threatening to burst out of my pants.

"I want you to wear my jersey," I say.

"I'm going to." She presses a kiss to my lips.

"Not just Friday. For the rest of the season. Next season, too."

This time, when she kisses me, it's a slow, determined kiss with parted lips.

And she pulls at the drawstring on my pants until it gives way.

And she draws her delicate fingers over what she finds there.

Oh my fucking God.

DREAM ON

Her skin feels smooth and hot against mine, and the heat between us might be enough to steam up the windows of this caboose.

I lace my fingers into her hair while we kiss. "You can't leave. No matter how bad it gets, you have to stay. We'll find a way."

"If I could," she whispers against my lips, "I'd hide here forever with you."

And now, with the front clasp of her bra undone, and me memorizing the peak of the nipple beneath my thumb, and her hands stirring up magic as she draws the tips of her fingers over me, I can't remember feeling as if she was deliberately putting distance between us, purposely misleading me or lying. I can't remember anything but honesty between us because this . . . this is honest. Pure.

"We could be like those people who live in tiny houses," she whispers. "We could make a home out of this train car."

I laugh, and so does she.

"What if we could?" she asks. "Would you? I mean, assuming we could find a way to heat it."

"Are you kidding? I'd run back here at the end of every day, and we'd make our own heat."

She tenses. "Wait."

I pull my fingers over her contours.

She pulls back. "Wait."

My hands slide out from under her shirt.

"Joshua."

And she's straightening her clothing.

"I'm sorry," I say. "It's too much, right?" I silently curse myself for getting too comfortable, too fast, with her body.

"I—"

"We'll slow things down."

"What? Oh. Joshua, no. I'm just . . . you said *run back here*."

"Yeah. I would."

An awkward moment hangs between us.

"It's just that . . ." She swings back over the ledge and jumps down from the loft.

It's just that . . . *what*? From up above, I watch her. She spins in a slow circle, and appears to be studying everything inside the caboose.

Slowly, she makes her way through, touching the walls and built-in bunk. She then exits out the back.

I'm on my way down now. When I meet her on the rear grate, she's leaning against the rail, by the crank the engineers used to turn.

"Savannah was running, telling me to catch up, catch up. We had to get to the train."

"Mmmhmm."

"What if . . ." she says. "What if *this* is where we were running?"

"Do you think—"

"Are there ever lots of people here?"

"Few times a year. Fourth of July. Sugar Creek Summer Days."

"This place. There's something familiar about it."

I dare to drape an arm around her hips.

She melts against me. "It's the first time something feels familiar. Like, maybe I was here before. Maybe this is the place Savannah and I were running to."

"In your dream?"

She shrugs. "That dream . . . maybe it was there to make me remember something. And if I was here before, maybe I was here around the time someone kidnapped Rachel Bachton. It's not too crazy to think . . . maybe Savannah was right. Maybe we really did see something that day."

The flicker of light in the distance catches my attention. Something like the beam of a flashlight.

"Hey!" The call echoes up the rolling terrain of the park.

Chatham practically jumps out of her shoes when she hears the voice booming at us from a distance.

We've been found.

I grab her hand and take off, and she pounds down the grated step behind me. She stumbles a little when we hit the ground running. I feel, more than see, the security officer pursuing us, but I don't look back to confirm it. "Head for the pines," I say.

She keeps pace at my side, and we plunge into the forest.

I pull her over the pine-needled paths, dodge branches and protruding tree roots, and finally, I hook to the left, where I know there's a split-rail fence marking the edge of county property.

I step on the lower rung and hurdle the thing, and turn to help Chatham over it, too, but she's already clear.

A few steps later, our feet meet with the gravel of the roadside, and the streetlights are like a spotlight on a dark stage.

My Explorer is just up ahead.

I get Chatham in first, then settle behind the wheel.

"Hurry," she says.

Out of the corner of my eye, I see the officer emerging into the light.

I turn the key in the ignition.

The engine doesn't fire.

Try again.

No dice.

"Fuck."

"C'mon c'mon c'mon," Chatham's whispering.

I take a deep breath and try again. Third try does the trick, and I put the car in gear, and we're gone.

About a mile down the road, when repeated looks in the rearview mirror confirm no one's following us, adrenaline starts to wane.

"Guess they don't want us living there," Chatham says.

I laugh.

She laughs.

And neither of us can stop.

We go back to Carpenter Street. I go in the front door, and let her in through my window.

She pulls off my hoodie and presses ice-cold hands to my bare chest.

I look down at her. Should we dare to finish what we started in the caboose?

"We probably shouldn't," she says, as if she's reading my thoughts.

"Yeah." But I can't help it. I kiss her.

And before I know it, she's sitting on the edge of my bed.

Then, I'm leaning over her.

She nudges a knee between my thighs.

Maybe it's the rush of running away from that rent-a-cop tonight, the thrill of escape, of survival. Or maybe it's just that she's the most amazing person I ever met . . . and I can't believe, of all the people in this town, she chose me. But I'm all in. If I ever actually doubted it, the uncertainty is long past by now. I know how I feel.

Now, to garner up balls enough to tell her.

"Chatham?" I pull back to look at her.

She's smiling. "I can't believe the car almost didn't start."

"Right?"

"We were lucky."

"Well," I say. "*I* am."

And even though I know it, I can't say it. It's too soon, maybe. Or she's not quite there with me yet. But whatever the reason, something stops me.

I can't tell her I love her.

DIRTY WORK

Every time I close my eyes, I see her naked curves. I remember the way her skin felt against mine, and I imagine what it's going to be like next time we happen to have the opportunity to get a little risky.

I replay last night in my mind, like a movie on repeat in my head: from the moment she started sucking on that pink-striped candy stick to the moment she kissed me this morning and disappeared out my window.

It helps the time pass while I'm out raking.

"Josh!" Rosie's on the back porch, which is really a small deck raised a story off the ground, standing halfway out the kitchen door. "Take this trash out?"

It's not really a question, or a request, judging by the way she drops it and heads back inside before I even acknowledge that I've heard her.

I give my mother a nod through the exterior walls of the house.

I'm taking Chatham to Homecoming tonight, and the parade starts at five, so Rosie's going to have to know she's on her own with Margaret and Caroline starting at four.

It shouldn't be a problem; I checked her schedule, and

she's not due on shift until Sunday evening.

I drop my rake and make my way up the porch steps to grab two bags of trash—one for the landfill, and one full of recyclables—and retrace my steps back to the lawn. Just as I'm about to dump the landfill bag in its bin, something catches my eye through the plastic bag: an envelope with my name, typewritten, on it.

I have to tear the plastic to open the bag, but I dig out the envelope, which is soiled at the corner with spaghetti sauce, so I wipe it off in the grass.

The orange-and-green return address stares at me: Miami University. Coral Gables, Florida. The fucking U.

I tear open the envelope and scan the letter. It's an invitation to visit their website and, eventually, their campus. Enclosed is a list of the U's scholarship offerings, majors, and extracurricular campus groups.

My fingertips tingle, and I'm already plotting ways I could get myself to south Florida to visit. A train? Maybe. My insides flutter with the mere suggestion of the word. I doubt I'll ever look at a train the same way again after last night.

Definitely a Greyhound bus would get me there. How much could that cost?

I go back and carefully read the letter again, which is addressed to me personally, and signed—my heart almost stops—by the head of football recruitment.

Football.

Recruitment.

And Rosie threw this in the trash?

I bound up the porch steps and into the kitchen, where my mother is cleaning up after the pancake breakfast she offered my sisters and me—which I, of course, silently declined—and

I shove the tomato-stained letter under her nose. "You think I wouldn't have wanted to see this?"

She glances up at me, then turns her back and wipes down the same patch of countertop again.

"Rosie."

"You call me Mom."

"Do you know they might want me to play for them? Football, Rosie! In the Atlantic Coast Conference! Do you know who's come out of the U? Vinny Testaverde! Brad Kaaya! *NFL players*. And they're inviting me—"

"Don't get your hopes up. It's a form letter."

"No, it's not! It's addressed to *me*."

"Yeah, well, wait till they see your grades. They'll backpedal faster than—"

"What?"

"You can't cut it there, Josh." She looks at the letter. "And we can't afford it. I'll scrape up all I can, put your sisters and me into poverty, you'll have mountains of student loan debt anyway, and you're only going to flunk out. You *know* that."

I'm shaking my head. This is really what she thinks of me?

"*If* you go anywhere at all, and that's a big *if*, it's Creekside Community."

"No. I'm going to the U."

She smirks and keeps wiping down the dingy countertop, as if she'll someday make it sparkle. "You might be second in line to King Shit at Sugar Creek High, but when you get into a big pond like that . . . have they even seen you play?"

"I know *you* haven't."

"Oh, stop it. Do you know how many times I sat in cold, rainy weather—"

"When? At the park district when I was seven?" She hasn't been to a game in at least that long.

"My point is," she says dryly, "that you're the second-string *junior* quarterback for a high school in a fly-speck town. You think they're coming all the way up here to no-man's-land to see Josh Michaels ride the pine?"

She doesn't even know I've been starting as quarterback since the fourth week of our schedule. I want to call her on this, to tell her about everything she's missed since . . . well, since forever ago, since she's been twisting in the turmoil her life's become. But looking at her, I know it's pointless. She's too caught up in her own bullshit to notice she's way off base, or to care that she's killing me with every word she speaks.

She doesn't know anything, but still she says again, "Don't get your hopes up. They didn't even see you play."

"You know who *did* see me play? Twice?" I ask. "You know who gave me his card, and wants to talk to me about playing for them? *North*-fucking-*western*."

"North-fucking-western," Caroline parrots from the next room.

I bite my lip, instantly regretting that the girls are hearing this.

Rosie ignores my sister. "Ha! You know who comes out of *Northwestern*? Astrophysicists. Cardiovascular engineers. *Smart people.* They'll be real impressed with your one-point-nine grade point average, I'll tell you that much."

For a second I wait, give her a chance to ask how my grades have been this semester. Does she care that lots of this year's grades will nullify last year's? Just another second. She'll ask. She'll say *something.*

She gives her head a minute shake. "Northwestern."

"You know who was there at the game last night? Wisconsin-Madison! You know who was QB? Me. But you don't know because you don't care!"

I fold the letter and turn away. It doesn't matter that I see a touch of regret in Rosie's face. What matters is that she actually *said* those things to me. She doesn't believe in me. And if that's the case, I don't need her. All the rest of the bullshit she puts me through . . . okay. I understand it's post-traumatic, I get that it's defense mechanisms at work, and I can deal. But I can't deal with living with someone who doesn't believe in me.

I head to the stairs, toward my room.

"You're not finished raking!" Rosie calls after me.

Yes, I am. But I don't reply beyond the slamming of my bedroom door. "She can clean up her own damn yard from now on," I mutter to myself.

I yank my duffel bag off a shelf in my closet. I jam it full of jeans, sweatshirts, socks, boxers. Whatever I can fit. I grab my school bag, shove in my Chromebook and phone, my chargers.

I grab Chatham's bag of cash. Once I pull my jersey out of the dryer—it's not all the way dry, but close enough—I have everything I need. I head up the half-flight of stairs to the front door.

I fling Rosie's re-engagement ring—still in its box—up the second half-flight of stairs. It slides beneath the old dresser she tucked against the wall next to the kitchen table. Let her find it in a month or so when she's doing her own fucking cleaning.

I walk out the front door, laden with all my worldly possessions—when you don't have much, it's easy to carry it all on your back—and get in my beat-up Ford Explorer.

One last glance at 4421 Carpenter Street proves two little girls, with hands pressed to the glass in the living room window, might be the only ones who realize I'm leaving. I should've stopped to hug and kiss them. I should've told them everything would be all right, but the truth is that I'm not sure it will be. I don't want to lie to them. She's their mother, too, after all. Without me there to verbally shred every now and then, who's she going to turn her claws on when things don't go right? Who's going to clean up her messes in the middle of the night, when she's feeling lonely, and makes a bad decision?

"Sorry," I say, although I know my sisters can't hear me. "I wish I could take you with me."

CRASH INTO ME

I take a seat at the counter at the Tiny Elvis.

"Let Me Call You Sweetheart" is playing in the background, its casual, sweet melody a contrast to the rambunctious Saturday morning crowd—lots of kids under five, lots of tears and parental threats to *sit down or else*.

Chatham's eyes brighten when she sees me sitting there—I've noticed that about her; she smiles with her eyes—and she gives me a wink as she crosses the room, balancing plates on her hands and forearms like some sort of well-rehearsed circus performer.

I hold my breath when I realize who she's waiting on: Damien and his extracurricular woman.

When was the last time he took my mother out for a meal?

Even the day they got married, she'd fried burgers at home and dealt with the verbal barrage of his dissatisfaction at their being a little overcooked.

Yet here he is, with a woman I can't help but feel sorry for because she's with him, sipping a cup of coffee and eating eggs Benedict. Not that this place is a five-star restaurant, but it's the principle of the thing.

He hardens a stare on me.

A feeling of discomfort washes over me—dizziness with a touch of nausea—but a second later, I remember I'm not a twelve-year-old twerp anymore. I'm over six feet tall, damn near as tall as him. And while I know it would crush my mother to know I'm contemplating my fist meeting his head, and reveling in thoughts of pounding him into the pavement, he'd deserve every punch. She'd want us to get along. It'd be easier, she'd say, if we all just put our differences aside. And who's it really hurting anyway? *Her.*

Maybe it's true that she's in the middle and we're both pulling at her. But no one can get along with a man who's seldom at his best—especially when his best falls short of decent. I understand that she *wants* him to be a good man, and that things would be easier if he could be defined that way. But I can't *make* him good by playing nice.

I know I should be going. I shouldn't be here while he's here, but I have to talk to Chatham.

I give the stare right back to Damien, and I don't doubt this contest could go on for hours. But his woman must have said something because he laughs and looks toward her.

I zoom in on the scene with my phone and snap a few pictures—Damien feeding her a dollop of cream from her waffle, Damien wiping said cream from her lips with his thumb—and text them to Rosie with a message: *this is what you chose over your firstborn.*

"Hey there, cute boy." Chatham slides a piece of chocolate cake onto the counter before me.

Her voice calms me . . . the southern lilt, the phrasing like *hey there.* "Hi." I pick up a fork and start eating.

"Didn't expect to see you until later."

"Shit went down."

"Oh." She cocks her head a bit. "You okay?"

I put on my invisible armor. "I will be."

"Can I get you anything else?"

"The cake is fine."

"Okay."

"But if you don't mind . . ." I lick chocolate frosting from my lip, "I could use a place to crash."

"Lord, what happened?"

But someone's lifting a mug and she has to go fill it, so I can't get into the details.

She drops a key onto the counter and says, "Tell me later?"

"Yeah."

She's on her way to the beckoning coffee cup. "I'm off at two."

Rosie's blowing up my phone, I assume in response to the pictures I sent. But I ignore her.

I finish my cake. Drop a fin to the counter, even though I don't think I even have a tab to pay, and get out of there, under the watchful glare of my once-stepfather.

It's no surprise when he steps out onto the sidewalk a moment after I do and yells after me, "Your mother hears about this, and I'll know who spilled the beans!"

Yeah, yeah.

I want to tell him I don't care what he does, or who he does it with, as long as he leaves my sisters and me the fuck alone. Instead, I ignore him. Not responding is better than any retort I can imagine.

I don't want him to see me walking up the steps of the Churchill, because then he'll know where to find me and, worse, where to find Chatham. So I take a stroll through town, all the way to the edge of the boardwalk.

Some grassy plants sprout from the sandy soil there, and they're blooming these small, white-and-blue wildflowers. A dichotomy. The rest of the world is getting ready to hibernate, and these things choose now to unfold their petals.

I hop the gate and lean against the railing, staring out over the lake, where horizon meets sky.

It's cooler here, and the lake looks positively enormous. There's a whole other world on the other side of this great lake, and a whole other life to be lived. Why my mother finds it necessary to jam a life into this toxic box of a town, I can't comprehend.

Even if we're sandwiched between this great view and, on the other end of town, the state preserves—and the abandoned caboose—what's in between just doesn't work for us. She should have learned that long before Damien.

Rachel Bachton's family isn't here anymore. They had the sense to get the fuck out and move to the other side of Chicago after their kid disappeared. Why can't Rosie see that I'm slowly disintegrating—that *she* is, too—the longer we stay here?

Enough time has passed, so I head back. I tear a handful of the autumn wildflowers from their stalks along the way. I take the long way back to town, plucking grasses and these interesting umbrella-like flowering weeds along the way and winding the blades of grass around the stems. It won't be the most gorgeous of bouquets at the dance, but at least I'll have *something* to offer Chatham.

Rosie texts again.

Again, I don't reply.

When I get back to the Churchill, I drop the flowers in the mason jar of water, the one holding her paintbrushes. I bring everything I own into Chatham's shoebox of a place, and afterward, I sort of organize things so I'm not in her way—my bag under the bed, my jersey laid across the rusty back of the folding chair, the khakis and button-down I'm wearing tonight hung alongside what I assume is the dress she told me about, still sheathed in drycleaner's plastic. She bought it at the vintage shop in town. (This is another thing I've come to learn about her: she prefers old, unique things to the bright, shiny, and new.) From what I discern through the plastic, the dress is dark red, the same color she was wearing the very first time I saw her. I can't wait to see her in it.

But after all I've been through this morning, and my long walk in the fresh air; after the thrill of our winning streak, which continued last night, and everything that followed in the caboose, then later at home, I'm drained of energy. It's a struggle to keep my eyes open. I sit on her lumpy mattress and stare at the mural on the opposite wall.

It's amazing, of course, like every piece of art I've seen her work on. At first glance, it's an abstract mish-mash of items she's referenced: a clover, a train . . . a confluence of two rivers.

Remains of a little girl—maybe Rachel Bachton—were found at a place like that.

As my glance travels over the wall, I see a window with a teardrop shape in the glass, and a penciled-in homemade swing, the kind with a thick board and coarse rope knotted through it. Suddenly, I'm chilled; there's a swing like that down by the creek on Damien's property.

And I remember Savannah drew something like it in her journal.

Coincidence?

And then I see what I think might be Margaret and Caroline—shapes that could be blonde twins huddled in a corner.

It makes me angry to see my sisters there, or maybe I'm just worried. Why are they in the middle of this mess?

There's now a train sketched into the bottom left quarter, and while it might have been there before we shared a small slice of heaven at the caboose, I have to wonder which train she thinks about when she looks at it: the one from her early memories, the one she and Savannah ran to catch? Or the one she shared with me? Or is it the same train at all?

I replay the events of last night again, and they work their magic on me, relaxing me, plucking at strings of hope in my soul. And even though we didn't actually get around to having all-out sex in that train car, or even later at my house, there's no inch of her I haven't memorized, no patch of skin I haven't touched or kissed. I could reconstruct her with clay. That's how much I paid attention to every curve that makes her what she is.

I'm lying down now, still studying the mural, wherein she's woven hints of turmoil. I zero in on the twins in the scene— two blonde girls huddled close together. My sisters, living in fear. We've become part of the artist's life, and Chatham sees right through to the core what my mother can't see in front of her: in taking Damien back, she's agreeing to keep my sisters gripping each other in a corner for life.

Nerves tighten in my gut when I consider I've abandoned Margaret and Caroline, thrown them to the wolves. I can't go back home, but I don't know how to stay away.

Who am I kidding? Where would I live, if not on Carpenter Street? I could probably hang at Aiden's for a while. Or . . .

Could we make it work, Chatham and me, in this closet? Sharing rent and toothpaste? Maybe we could squirrel away enough to rent the room through the adjoining bathroom, too, for the twins. We'd be an unconventional family, and while this place is a dump, we'd be together. And safe, once Damien tires of the girl he's presently fucking. I hear them through the wall. They're doing it now.

I cover my ears with my sweatshirt, which I've balled beneath my head like a pillow, and imagine this town without him in it. For a brief second, my mother wanders into the scene, but I shove her back out the door, out of my mind. She can fend for herself. This place is just for the girls and me . . . and Chatham.

Would Chatham even have me in that capacity? I mean, sure, we've had some incredible times, but the scenario I'm considering . . . it's a big step even for people who've been together for years.

It's a long shot, and the odds are stacked against us, but it's nice to think about as I fall asleep: *us*.

I feel her, more than see her, when she comes in. The aroma of the Tiny Elvis—greasy fries and gravy—wafts in with her. I open my eyes and glimpse her, peeling off her clothes, yet as much as I want to watch her strip down, my eyes are so heavy that I can't keep them open.

She lifts the comforter and slides into bed next to me. Her soft, cool back against my chest triggers a need deep in my body, and because I'm not quite awake, and not all the way asleep, I just tighten my arms around her nearly-naked body.

"You awake?" she whispers.

"Hmm."

She traces the scars on my inner left arm and drops kisses there, and the next three words out of her mouth stun me and steal my breath.

My eyes snap open.

And then I see him, standing in the bathroom Chatham shares with the woman in #2F. Chatham must not have locked the door because it's open now, and he's *looking right at me.*

Damien Wick invades even this moment with his stare, with his sick and twisted grin, and even though he's about to close the door, I spring out of bed, over my girl, and launch at him.

I barrel into him, send him flying across the bathroom, and crash him against the black-and-white checkerboard of a tiled wall.

He shoves back, and comes at me swinging.

Lands a punch square on my left cheekbone.

I stumble back, and he slams me again, this time with a hook to my ribs, and another one in my face.

For a second, all I see is a wash of silvery white, so I don't even realize I've connected with his jaw until I feel the crunch of my knuckles, until I hear the thud of his bulk landing on the cracked, mosaic tile floor.

I readjust, and the blur of my vision rights itself. I blink hard and focus. There's a box from a hair color kit in the trash.

"God dammit," he mutters.

I turn my eyes to him. He's using the wall to get to his feet.

There was a day I thought I'd be halfway to Wisconsin after landing just one punch on him, but today, I just stand over him and shake the feeling back into my hand, the hand I need on Friday nights to throw. I pop a knuckle back into position. I'll be fine. I suspect he will be, too, once his lip stops bleeding.

"Looks like you grew a set after all." He laughs a little and slowly steps toward me.

We're toe-to-toe now. I'm looking up at him; he's looking down at me.

"You gonna leave so I can take a piss now?" he asks. "Or you gonna hang around to see what a real dick looks like?"

"Looking at one right now." I back my way out of the room, close the door, and this time, lock it behind me.

The thrill of victory, of confidence, infuses my system, and my heart is *pounding*. My knuckle must have hit one of his teeth because it's bleeding. I stretch and contract my hand a couple of times, and then meet Chatham's gaze.

She's sitting on the bed, with the comforter hiding all the really delicious parts of her, wearing an expression of surprise: brows raised, lips slightly parted.

I go to her, watch the comforter fall away and reveal her bra and panties. "Boundaries." It's all I can think to say by way of explanation for what just happened. I lean over her and kiss her lips. What she said before deserves a reply: "And I love you, too."

D Y E

We're back from the parade, and I'm fresh out of the shower. Chatham reaches for something on the floor. It's a permanent marker, which she uncaps. "Come here."

I lean to her, shirt still not buttoned. My hair is still damp from the shower.

She presses her lips to mine and shoves my sleeve up my left arm. The marker meets the scar on my inner arm. "It's like when you're little, at school. Or when you go to summer camp. You put your name on all your belongings."

I watch as she writes her name onto my flesh with the fine-tipped marker. But she isn't *signing* her name as much as she is *drawing* it, as if her name is the stuff of galleries and museums. The scroll in her C, the upstroke on the M . . . "So I belong to you now? Is that what you're saying?"

"Don't be ridiculous." She giggles and glances up at me. "I never went to summer camp."

When I laugh, and to be honest, even when I don't, my cheek hurts a little, high on the bone, where Damien socked me. I'm bruised, and it all-out looks like I've been in a battle, but there's no way we're staying in tonight.

Chatham's dress is this sleek little number, and it looks like it was custom-made for her, even though it's probably fifteen years older than she is. It's longer than I expected it to be—the hem hits just below her knees—but there's a slit on the left side that climbs high on her thigh. The material is like velvet, and it looks purplish from some angles and dark red from others. She looks too damn good to keep behind this door.

I finger a curl. Fuck, I'm a lucky guy.

We head into the hallway. I lock the door and pocket the key because she doesn't have a purse to put it in, and this isn't exactly a backpack sort of event. That said, I've got the backpack hanging on my shoulder so I can hide it in the car during the dance. No way in hell I'm leaving it at the Churchill with Damien one wall away.

Then, we're out the doors and heading to my SUV. Me, looking like I've gotten the sense knocked out of me, and Chatham, looking all classy.

A strange thought comes to me: if Rachel Bachton hadn't been kidnapped all those years ago, would she ever have found herself slumming with a Sugar Creek guy? Going to a dance like this?

I imagine, if she were here, she'd be just like the other Northgate girls: untouchable and sort of bitchy. Not too good for us, but too high on themselves to know we're all the same underneath it all, and that they should be nicer. It's not their fault. They've been told they were special since before they could talk.

Some of the more affluent schools in the area rent banquet halls for their dances, but Sugar Creek's events are held mostly in our gym, or in our commons. This one is in the latter, and we have to walk past the art hall to get there.

Chatham tugs on my hand and leads me to a glass showcase cabinet. In it are vases and clay pots, but it's what's spanning the back wall of it that she wants me to see: sixteen separate squares of clay relief, arranged together in four rows of four tiles in a four-by-four square.

"You finished it!" I pull her in closer, and although I have no idea what I'm looking at, what it means, or what it represents—I see streaks of red in the browns and whites, an amalgamation of different clays and varying glazes—I know it's awesome because she created it.

"Look closer."

Some portions of the squares are raised up, and others dip down. On some squares, there are shiny rivulets of blues and greens, almost like melted glass. Others are glazed off-white. It looks like the bird's-eye view of some mysterious city. In the bottom right corner of each of the squares, is one letter of her name. I gauge each and every one of them: **CHATHAM CLAIBORNE.**

And then I see it: the ribbon dangling from the upper left corner of the upper left tile. *Best in show.*

I didn't even know there *was* a show. I think she might've said something about it, but I've been so preoccupied with my own bullshit . . . I pick her up and twirl her around—the girl who says she loves me—because she's the best in the whole school. She didn't need to get a ribbon to tell *me* that.

This is what it feels like to be a normal guy . . . sans the bruise on my left cheekbone and how it got there, that is.

"Let me get a picture of you with your work."

"No pictures."

"Are you kidding? You look *amazing* tonight."

"*You* look amazing."

"*We* look amazing."

"You come in the picture, too."

So I do. I stand next to her and extend my arm for a selfie.

"Smile," she whispers.

She likes my dimples.

She likes the flowers I picked for her.

I click the picture just as she's up on her tiptoes to kiss me.

She's not much into dancing, which I suppose I learned at the rave, but that's okay, because I'm not either. It's enough just to be there together. We grab a table near the back, where the rest of the wallflowers are gathered, and watch my teammates take over the dance floor. Novak cuts a rug, like he just caught the winning pass in the end zone.

"You coming over later?" Aiden pulls up a seat. Kai sits right on his lap, despite the fact she's obviously pissed at him about something.

She crosses her arms over her hardly-contained chest and sticks her bottom lip out in a pout that could rival my sisters'. "He *smells* like weed and chocolate."

Of course he does. It's *Aiden*.

"Small gathering," he continues. "Just the four of us."

"Okay," I say.

He grins. "And about twenty other people."

"Wouldn't miss it." My phone buzzes in my pocket. I pull it out and look at the caller ID. Rosie. I decline the call.

■ ■ ■

"I'm so tired." Chatham lies across the center console of the Explorer and pulls my right arm over her.

It's an awkward angle, but the discomfort is well worth it because I'm still holding her. "If you'd rather skip Aiden's, we can."

"You wouldn't mind?"

God, is she kidding? Houseful of people smoking chronic? Or tight quarters with Chatham? I stop at a red light and glance down at her.

She isn't looking up at me, and I suspect her eyes might be closing fast. She worked early at the diner today, and it's after ten now.

I brush her hair from her forehead, amazed at the fact that she dropped to the sand at our beach blanket last month, a complete stranger, and now, she's all I think about.

A contented sigh escapes her. I could listen to sounds like that forever.

She can't see me, but I'm smiling. I'm just so happy. And I'm draping a curl behind her ear, so I can see her pretty profile, and—

Wait.

There's a patch of light hair there. At her temple.

The reflection of the red light casts it in an almost-pink glow, but I'm pretty sure . . . there's something there . . . I flip through the events of today:

The letter from the U.

Damien at the Tiny Elvis.

Damien at the Churchill.

The brawl in the bathroom.

The hair color kit in the bathroom trash.

"My God. You're *blonde*."

"What?" She jolts up.

I'm looking at her, imagining what she must look like as an all-over blonde. "Wow, I just never—"

"What do you mean, I'm—"

"I saw the hair color kit in the bathroom, but I didn't—"

"So?"

"I'm just surprised."

But it's more than a surprise. It's another question mark. Alone, the dyed hair doesn't mean much, but add to it everything else . . .

Chatham has Savannah's journal, her backpack, her money.

Savannah ran away, and even though Chatham *said* she came here looking for her sister, it's apparent Chatham is hiding out, too.

Chatham needed an ID. Who leaves home without an ID?

I can't find any information about Chatham Claiborne online. No profiles on any social media.

I can't find a Chatham Stevenson, or even a Chatham Goudy, online either.

And she called the hotline . . . *This is Chatham Claiborne.* No one came to get her. No one followed up.

Is Chatham even her name? Could it be that Chatham Claiborne is a figment of her imagination? An alias I helped her perpetuate when I provided her with a driver's license?

And the hair . . . If she'd left her hair light blonde, she might be harder to miss in a crowd. Would Chatham dye her hair to remain inconspicuous? Would she assume another name to keep herself hidden?

And then there's Savannah and the girl at the rave. They *kissed*. Would Chatham pretend not to know her sister so even I wouldn't know the truth of what they'd run away from?

I take a deep breath. "You're blonde," I say again. "I just never noticed." I try to regroup, to pull it together. "I just never pegged you for—"

226

"For *what*?" She cranes back, crosses her legs away from me, and the way she's looking at me . . . "Why does it matter what color my hair is?"

"It doesn't." My phone starts buzzing again. I don't bother to check it before silencing it.

The light turns green.

She shifts in the seat, faces front. "Maybe you should just drop me off at home and go to Aiden's, all right?"

"No. Not all right. I don't see what the big deal is. So you colored your hair."

"I *like* it dark."

"So do I."

"Just take me home, okay?"

I ease off the brake and inch ahead. I have three miles to make this right. "I don't want to drop you off."

"Of course, you want to come in."

"Of course I do, but Chatham, I . . ." I think of the condom I stashed in my back pocket *just in case* and suddenly feel like a pompous ass for doing such a thing. "I don't expect anything, all right?"

"This was a mistake. I don't even know how long I'm going to be here, and . . . I don't know what we were thinking, getting attached like this."

I feel like I can't even draw a full breath. "Chatham. What did I do?"

"Nothing, Josh."

Josh. Great. She's *never* called me what my mother calls me.

She won't look at me now. "Let's just forget it, okay?"

My phone buzzes again.

In my peripheral vision, I see it's my mother. "I want to talk about this."

"Your mother's calling. Again."

"So, she can leave a message. Again. Chatham, I want—"

She grabs the phone. "Hello."

My heart sinks. She really wants this night to be over if she's willing to answer my mother's call.

"No, honey, it's Chatham." She looks at me and puts the call on speaker. "It's Margaret. Something's wrong."

SLITHY TOVES

"Keep talking to me, Maggie Lee."

"He'll *hear*." She's whimpering, or maybe that's Caroline. "Joshy, just come."

"Almost home."

"Not *home*. *Daddy's*."

I glance at Chatham. "You're at your dad's place?"

"Just come."

The line goes dead.

I pull a U-turn, and let out a roar of frustration and pound on the steering wheel as I drive in the opposite direction. In a matter of seconds, I piece together what must have happened. Rosie had to go into work tonight after all, probably because she called in sick last week. When she couldn't reach me *because I kept ignoring her*, she called Damien and dropped the girls at his place.

But . . .

"Why would Maggie Lee have Mom's phone?" I wonder aloud.

"This isn't your fault."

"The hell it isn't! God dammit! I should've answered the phone! I should've—"

"You're scaring me."

"We have to get there."

"We can't help them if we don't get there alive."

I hadn't wanted to forfeit this night, the night that began so perfectly and turned itself upside down in the space of a few blocks. But now, Chatham's pissed for some stupid fucking reason about her hair, for God's sake, and she wants to go home, and doesn't want to invite me in, and my sisters . . . let's just hope they're okay.

"Should I call the cops?" I glance at the girl who, up until two minutes ago, I saw as my salvation.

Her eyes are rimmed with tears. Like she's really scared.

I ease up a little on the gas, and drop a hand on her thigh. She doesn't flinch away, but to my surprise, grips my hand.

"Say I call them," I say. "It's null and void, then. The order of protection. The judge can revoke it because my mother voluntarily violated it. Right?"

"I don't know." She gives my hand a squeeze. "Probably."

We need that court order of protection. I can't risk canceling it out.

We just have to get there.

Stones spin out beneath my tires on the rocky lane that leads to Damien's place, which is way off the beaten path. Memories flood back to me; I remember the last time I traveled this road, two years ago, when I thought I wouldn't ever have to travel it again. The feeling of liberty, the hope that at last we had a chance to live a normal life . . . I knew then that that chance required a certain measure of self-sacrifice on my part. I remember feeling as if I'd do anything—*anything*—not to be there, falling prey to him, anymore.

Skip school when the girls are sick?

Okay. Even though Chatham handled the most recent occurrence, it was me staying home all last year.

Stand guard throughout the night when the dirt bag threatens to come over?

Who needs sleep, anyway?

God, how could I have forgotten?

No matter what Chatham says, I'm here tonight because I forgot how important it was to put my sisters first.

Damien's shack of a house sits right along the creek for which this town is named, and it's far enough out of the way that no one can hear the turmoil erupting within it.

As I approach it now, it looks just as run-down as ever. An old, 1940s fishing cabin, with gray paint peeling from the clapboard siding, and a faded red door. One bedroom. The smallest bathroom you'll ever see, with a shower you can barely turn around in. A tiny kitchen and living area, where Damien hung on the wall the collar of our departed dog. And a loft, where the girls and I slept.

Another memory flashes in my mind: Damien, drunk and belligerent, holding two-month-old Caroline over the railing, threatening to drop her onto the floor below if we didn't all just *shut the fuck up.*

It all blares in my memory like a siren: Rosie's scream. The babies' uncontrollable wailing . . .

I pull into the gravel horseshoe driveway.

Chatham's holding my arm now. "Wait. I don't feel good about this."

"I have to go get them." If she were in my head, watching events of the past play out, she'd understand. I toss her my phone. "If I'm not out in two minutes, call the police."

I leave the car running, and approach the door. It's locked, so I pound on it.

The door opens, and the first thing I see is my mother's hair in Damien's fist.

My gut tumbles when I see her face. Her left eye is swollen shut.

God, if only I'd answered the phone five minutes earlier . . . maybe she wouldn't have taken those blows.

He's dragging her by her hair and shoving her out the door. "Take this fucking cunt home!"

My mother falls into my arms, and it's not that I don't want to hold her up, but I have to get the girls. She slips to the porch, sobbing, when I lunge through the door. I hope she has the sense to get herself safe, to go to the car, and let me get my sisters.

"Maggie Lee! Miss Lina!"

Damien has me by the throat now that I'm in his house, and he slams me into the closest wall. "All I have to do is squeeze."

I swallow over the pit of fear accumulating in my throat. "Just let me get my sisters, and—"

"They're *my* daughters."

"You don't want them here tonight. I'll take them."

"You couldn't let well enough alone, could you? You had to tell your fucking mother about what you saw."

"Seems you taught her a lesson. She knows her place now. I just want my sisters."

He tightens his grip a bit, I can barely breathe, and now I'm really starting to get scared.

"The police are on their way," I manage to get out, even though it's a lie. "Just let me go, and . . . they don't trust my reports anyway. Damien, please. They'll get here. We'll be gone. Please."

"Big man now, aren't you? Begging me."

"Please."

"You want I can do to you what I did to your fucking dog? Huh?"

"Please!"

"You ever take a swing at me again, your mother won't get up. You hear me?"

"Yeah."

"I'll teach your ass!"

"Yeah. Yeah, I got it."

He screams in my face: "Get out!" Strings of saliva hang from his teeth, his eyes are bloodshot and yellow, the vein in his forehead bulges. But ultimately, he shoves off me and lets go of my neck. "Get the brats and get out."

I cough and gasp when I draw in a full breath. And as soon as I'm able, I call their names. "Come on, girls. It's okay."

They appear a split second later, both bawling and running at me.

"Cops come around here, and I'll put your mother—better yet, I'll put *your sisters*—in traction!"

I catch both my sisters by a hand, and we're almost out the door when I feel a size twelve work boot in my back. I stumble, but manage to regain my footing and prevent a fall.

I hike Margaret up in my arms, and a second later, I go to grab Caroline, but Chatham's there, and she's already pulling her into the car. We don't bother to strap the girls in before I peel away.

"We should get your mom to the hospital." Chatham pulls the seatbelt around her and Caroline, and Rosie's working on securing Margaret in the back.

"No," Rosie says. "No hospital."

I glance at her in the rearview mirror. This isn't the worst I've seen her. There were days *both* her eyes were swollen.

"I'm sorry, babies," my mother is saying. "Mommy's sorry."

I swear, I'm holding my breath all the way down the rocky road. I don't breathe until we hit the first stoplight, and this is when I finally take it all in:

My mother has taken a few blows.

Margaret is still gripping my mother's phone.

Caroline looks so small and helpless in Chatham's lap. I reach over and wipe a tear off the tip of her nose. "It's okay now, Miss Lina."

She extends a hand toward me.

I go to take it, but instead of little-sister-hand, I find something else. "What is this?" It's an old photograph. The light turns green, but I glance at it.

It's brittle and yellowing.

Old.

I've seen one like it before. It's a picture of the same girl in the Polaroid tucked into Savannah's journal: the little blonde girl. "Chatham." I show it to her.

She gasps.

Our glances meet. She nods in confirmation.

"Where'd you get this?" I ask Caroline. "Did you get this from Chatham's bag?"

"Uh-uh. Daddy had it. In the closet."

TRUE COLORS

"You should take your girlfriend home."

I fixed a cup of tea for my mother, and I bring it to her now, at the table, where she's holding an ice pack to her swollen eye. The swelling's gone down a bit now, but the corner of her eyeball is all red and veiny where it should be white.

I can't take Chatham home. In fact, I'm wondering if she should ever go back to the Churchill again, now that Damien knows where to find her and what she means to me. He was spying on us; he saw her in bed with me.

And the whole mess with the photograph is another thing. How is it that he had a photograph of the same mysterious girl whose picture Savannah tucked into her journal? And she *is* the same girl. Chatham and I compared the two side by side.

That photograph is a direct link between whatever happened at Chatham's family farm and my ex-stepfather . . . and maybe Rachel Bachton, if Rachel happened to be the phantom girl under the floorboards in the stables.

Chatham's down the hall in the girls' room now, reading to them. And I don't know how Rosie's going to react, but I've already decided that Chatham should stay here with us until she can find another place, a safer place, to stay.

"How long have you been together?"

"Long enough."

Rosie sips the tea. "Why didn't you tell me about her?"

"Would it have mattered?"

She doesn't reply beyond the shrug of a shoulder.

Silence buzzes between us.

I hear Chatham's rendition of Dr. Seuss, and it makes me smile, despite all the turbulence in the air tonight.

"So, you going to tell me what happened?" I ask. "Or am I going to report the scene that's on repeat in my head?"

She meets my glance. "Report."

"You're not seriously considering *not* telling the police, are you?"

The look on her face tells me that's *exactly* what she's considering. "Damien called me, Josh, and offered to make dinner for the girls and me. I went willingly."

"Why would you do that? Didn't you see the pictures I texted?"

"*Yes*, Josh, but you know how Damien is. You have to let him think he's in charge. Look. If I'd started ignoring him, he would have kept coming over. I needed things to be on my terms, okay? So I had it all planned."

"Was the black eye in your plan?"

"I figured I'd go, and I'd tell him that I knew about the other girl, and if he wanted, I'd just let him have her on the side."

I shake my head. Disgusting that she'd simply look the other way.

"You don't understand," she says. "I know why he has that girl. Because it makes him feel good to be getting away with something. I took that away from him."

"So tonight was—what?—a success?"

"Do you always have to be such a smartass?"

"You shouldn't have taken the girls."

"Well, I couldn't get a hold of you. You *said* you'd be here for the girls. You *said*—"

"It's Homecoming," I remind her. "There was a dance."

"Oh."

"What'd you think? We were just out at a party, dressed up like this?"

"I'm sorry, Josh. You have to tell me these things."

"I swear I did."

"No, you didn't."

It's a pointless argument. "Back to the girls."

"When I couldn't get a hold of you, it was too late. Damien showed up to get us, I figured we could just go, have a nice dinner—"

"Because he's *changed*."

"—and I'd confront him some other time. But he knew I knew. Just by looking at me. And your sisters . . . they weren't on their best behavior, and it got to him. I gave them my phone so they could play games, but then they started fighting over the phone." She hides behind her mug when she says the next part: "He sent them to the room as punishment, and that's when it happened. That's when I couldn't take it anymore."

"You confronted him." My head is in my hands now. "You provoked him. On his turf. You went with him willingly, when you *knew* something like this was going to happen. Rosie, you have to . . . at some point, you have to realize you allow this to happen. I get that you're in a tough situation. He's their *father*. You *loved* him. But he's incapable of loving you back. He's dangerous and violent, no matter how good you want him to be. We have a restraining order against this guy, and you took your baby girls to his house. You have a black eye, and he's going to get away with it because you won't go to the hospital, and you won't call to have him arrested."

"I voluntarily violated the order of protection, Josh."

"So lie to the cops. How about this: he came here, forced you to go with him, I came to get you when Margaret called, and long story short, here you are." I shove her phone a few inches across the table. "You've lied to them every time *I've* called, so what makes tonight any different?"

She drums her fingertips against the table, and has a hard time meeting my eyes. "You know why I threw away that letter from Miami University?"

"Yeah." She was perfectly clear about that this morning.

"Do you know how far away Miami is?"

I let the question hang there, but I don't take the bait. I don't want to talk about Miami, and if she isn't going to call the police, there's not much else to say anyway. I clear my throat and redirect. "Why did he have that picture? Who *is* that little girl?"

"I don't know. But it's just a picture, Josh. It's not like the child was unclothed, or anything."

"If you won't call about the beating he gave you tonight, call about the picture." I don't want to get into specifics with her as to why, in particular, the picture is concerning. But I don't think she's going to make the call without it. "Chatham's sister ran away and she had a picture of this same little girl in her journal. Something's wrong, Rosie." I fill her in on what she might have missed regarding Rachel Bachton's case, the Baby A buried at the confluence of rivers in Chatham County, Georgia, the rumors about what Savannah and Chatham may or may not have seen in the floorboards of the stables.

"What are you saying? That Damien's involved in Rachel Bachton's kidnapping somehow?"

"Wouldn't put it past him."

"The man who took her is described as five-ten to six-two, and nondescript. Damien stands out in a crowd. He'd be noticed."

"Would a little kid know how tall he is? I'll bet if you ask the girls how tall *you* are, they'd say *you're* six feet. And he hasn't always been as big is he is now. He gets bigger every time I see him."

She considers for a second, then nods. "Maybe."

"Or maybe . . . maybe he didn't take her. Maybe he scouted her out for someone *else* to take her. Maybe he kept her for a while at the cabin."

Again she shrugs and sips her tea. "One of the problems with the case is that they had too many leads in the first few months. *Thousands* of leads. Our police force doesn't have the kind of manpower to work through all those leads, and if we accused Damien just because he has a picture . . . look, he's a lot of things, but he's not capable—"

"Yes, he is."

She shuts up.

"Do you remember that black lab we used to have? Benny? And one day, we came home, and the dog was hanging by the swing from the tree out front. Damien said he must have gotten tangled up with the ropes. Do you remember that?"

I'd always suspected Damien killed the dog, and Rosie probably had thought so, too.

"He kept Benny's collar, remember. To remind us of what he could do. And it's still hanging on the wall. I saw it tonight. He killed our dog, terrified the girls, and he hit both of us tonight."

For the first time, maybe, since she stumbled out of her ex-husband's shack, she looks at me. Maybe it's the first time she sees that I'm wearing the mark of Damien, too.

"He and I got into it earlier," I say. "At the Churchill. And then he had me by the throat when I went in to get the girls. By. The. Throat."

"Josh."

"You call, or I'm going to. And I don't care how many times you lie, I'm going to keep telling the truth. Damien Wick is dangerous, and I can't stay here, Rosie, if you're going to let this happen again and again. If you're planning to keep covering for him, I just might go to the U. I'll *show* you I can do it even if you don't believe I can."

"If you follow that letter all the way to Florida," she says, "I don't know how I'm going to manage. I believe you can do it, Josh—I'm sorry I made you think you couldn't—but I can't do this without you."

I'm sure *some* mothers say things like this all the time, but mine? Not so much.

I could sink into the moment and take stock in this, but that could backfire. It's like telling a girl you like her only after she tells you the same thing . . . and then finding out that she was joking. Can't expose yourself to the vulnerabilities. That nearly happened to me once already today.

Chatham: *I love you.*

Me: *I love you, too.*

Then hours later . . .

Chatham: *This was a mistake.*

My stomach goes hollow with the memory. If I acknowledge Rosie's commentary, next I know, it'll be thrown back in my face. Besides, she's on the defensive. Because I came to her rescue today, I actually have a leg to stand on, so pretty soon, she's going to be scrambling for a way to kick it out from under me. She's always got to have the upper hand.

So I wait it out.

Chatham's voice carries down the hall.

"She seems great," Rosie says.

This might be the only thing we agree on.

She tries again: "The girls really seem to like her."

"They do."

"But someone I've never met shouldn't be sitting with the girls while they're sick."

And there it is. I look at her. "Call the cops." I push back from the table.

"I told *you* to stay home that day."

I turn toward the girls' room.

"Josh."

I wave her off.

I quietly walk into the girls' room, careful not to disturb them. While I'm sure the events of this evening will rear up in their little heads and eventually prove damaging, they're safe and content now, huddled in the same bed, with a book propped between them. They're staring at pictures of Dr. Seuss's fictional creatures.

Chatham is perched on the floor opposite with one of the girls' doodle pads on her lap. She's sketching, and reciting words. Not *reading*. *Reciting* and telling the girls when to turn the page.

This girl is amazing.

Once the story about Sneetches is over, and the girls are all but sleeping, I lead Chatham past my mother, who doesn't even look up to acknowledge us, and to the basement.

I know Rosie's expecting me to take Chatham back to the Churchill, but even if I weren't worried about her being there alone, she and I are not done tonight.

She all-out *flipped out* earlier, and maybe I was wrong to jump to conclusions about her hair, but *there's something she's not telling me.*

"Hey," I say.

"Hey." For all the energy she put into Dr. Seuss, she isn't saying much now. She pulls a few tiles from the Scrabble tray on the side of the table that has become hers over the past weeks.

She places letters A, R, T, and C on the table, and at first she plays *crate*, but then rearranges the letters to play *trace*.

I want to confront her about what happened. I want her to explain what the big fucking deal was that I noticed something about her I hadn't noticed before. I mean, how does a girl have no problem with me kissing her most intimate scars, how does she tell me about her nightmares of little bodies beneath floors of a stable, but not want me to know she's naturally blonde? But I don't know how to ask without sounding pushy, and I don't want to scare her.

So I go with: "You know Dr. Seuss by heart."

"Doesn't everyone?"

"Not like that."

She shrugs a shoulder. "If you memorize a story, you can tell it to yourself even when you don't have the book in front of you."

"I guess you can."

Silence.

I try again: "What happened earlier in the car . . . are you okay?"

"I'm sorry," she finally says. "I don't know why it upset me so much."

"It's all right." I'm sitting on the other side of the table, leaning forward with my elbows on my knees, and I can't help looking at her. It's like I don't want to look away. I want to memorize the way she looks tonight.

Her skin is ivory-white, a stark contrast to her dark hair and dark red dress. Her chameleon eyes are sort of green around the rims tonight.

The longer I look at her, the more easily I can imagine her as a blonde. "For the record, I don't *expect* you to be *anything*. Your hair could be purple for all I care."

"I think, maybe, you're the first person *ever* who could say something like that and I'd actually believe you."

Silence. She starts rearranging the letters on the board again. Pulling letters from words we've already played, and even some from the pool.

C, H, A, T, H . . .

She's spelling out her name. *Fine by me*, I want to tell her. *Label everything in this whole damn place. It's all yours, if you want it. Because I'm yours.*

"It was the way you said it," she says. "Like you thought I was lying to you or something."

. . . A, M, C, L, A . . .

"I didn't mean for it to come across that way. I was just surprised, that's all."

She licks her lips.

. . . I, B, O, R . . .

God, I want to kiss her. "I mean, I feel like I spend most of my free time looking at you, and I'd never noticed. I was excited, and not because you're blonde underneath but because I'm excited *every time* I learn something new about you."

. . . N, E.

"Like your sculpture. I might not understand it," I say, "but you can bet I'm going to be thinking about it for a long time because whatever it is, it's part of *you*."

A hint of a smile appears on her lips, and while it's not much of an invitation, I lean over the table, take her face in my hands, and press my mouth to hers.

"I meant it," she says. "Everything I've told you today, everything I've told you since the caboose park. I mean it all."

The doorbell sounds just as we're about to kiss again.

SIX IMPOSSIBLE THINGS

The whirl of red and blue lights against the side of the house is like a beacon, and some of our neighbors—people I've never spoken to and rarely see—step outside to see what all the commotion is about. What these people must think of us. Cops here all the time, the constant screaming within these walls . . .

I know at any minute that Rosie's going to regret calling. When she appears at the door—I'm already on the front steps—she gives me a panicked look. But this is for the best. The cops need to know what's going on.

"I would've called," she whispers. "You could have given me some time to get myself together."

"Wait. You didn't call?"

She shakes her head.

"Well, *I* didn't call," I say.

"Good evening." An officer approaches. "Joshua Michaels?"

The way he says it, I expect to hear *you're under arrest for* . . .

My heart speeds up. What could this be about?

Did Aiden get pinched? Would he rat me out? Tell the cops I recently made a drop for him? No, he wouldn't . . . But I never paid him for it, never gave him the hundred from that girl with the tattoo. Would that piss him off enough to tell the cops?

Or is this about the rave? I didn't do anything illegal that night, but maybe just *going* to one of those things is illegal.

Or . . . I'll bet Damien called and told them I charged at him earlier today. He probably did it as a precaution, so he could say holding me by the throat against the wall was a practice in self-defense.

I clear my throat. "Yeah, I'm Josh."

"We're responding to a tip that you were assaulted earlier tonight."

When the beam of a flashlight crosses my face, Rosie turns the swollen side of her face away.

The officer turns off and stows the flashlight. "Seems there might be some truth to it."

"My stepfather," I say. "*Ex*-stepfather. Damien Wick."

"Can we come in and talk to you about it, Joshua?"

He keeps calling me *Joshua*. Chatham. She must have been the one to make the phone call.

Of course she did! She's going to tell them about the photographs, too.

Rosie opens the door, and while she doesn't necessarily invite the cops in, she holds the door open just long enough to indicate the two of them can come in.

The girls' rainforest soundtrack filters down to the foyer, a reminder that they're asleep, and after a long, hard day, they need it.

Maybe this is why my mother leads us all down the stairs to my realm of the house, the basement. "Have a seat."

Chatham isn't in the family room, which is dim, lit only by a table lamp in the far corner. I turn on the fireplace and glance down the hallway. The light in my bedroom is on; she must be in there, changing out of her dress.

I sit first, and the cops follow suit, but Rosie lingers in the shadowy outskirts of the room, her arms crossed over her chest.

"We're going to need pictures of the bruises," one of the cops says.

"He hit me in the face, and he had his hands around my throat." I unfasten another button on my shirt. I haven't looked at it yet, but my neck aches, so I'm pretty sure it'll bruise.

Rosie flips the light switch, and the overhead fixture buzzes to life, washing the room in the harsh tint of fluorescent bulbs. "He's going to say my son provoked him. It's what he always says. He's going to tell you I deserved *this*, too"—she drapes her hair aside, allowing a clear view of her shiner—"and this." She twists and lifts the hem of her shirt so we see the bruise I suspected was on her back.

"And this." Then, she turns to reveal a gory splash of black and purple fist-sized contusions on her abdomen. Not one or two. *Several.* Like he pummeled her repeatedly.

"Mom." Instantly, I'm on my feet. Tears cloud my eyes, but I don't care who sees.

"This," she says, "was his reaction when I told him I'm pregnant. I'm not anymore."

Pregnant? The word blows me back, and its shrapnel embeds in my flesh, cutting and burning.

The cops are on her now, asking questions, and she's answering.

The events of the past few weeks come at me like a fast-forward stream of images: the inexplicable bouts of crying, the ring he tried to give her, the incident with the stairs . . . her constantly telling me I don't understand her predicament, insisting he's changed.

The image of her bruised abdomen keeps flashing in my mind. It's now joined the other haunting pictures—Damien coming at me with a knife, Caroline dangling from his hands over the loft, Rosie using Margaret as a human shield—and will I ever forget the fear in Margaret's voice on the other end of the line tonight?

Of course Rosie would insist he'd changed. She's trying to wish it true, trying to convince herself of the impossible.

I keep wiping tears away, but my eyes keep filling up, and I keep playing the scene in my mind: fist after fist after fist pounding into her flesh. And she's so thin . . . there's no protection, no barrier. He probably damaged her insides. Could have broken her bones.

And to think he was doing it with intent! Not only to hurt her, but to kill the mistake they'd made together . . . to kill the baby.

Now, I'm remembering him waling on her when she was pregnant with the twins, and I damn near throw up.

I cover my mouth and breathe through it. It's in the past. It's over.

And maybe it wasn't really over until tonight, but now she's finally breaking. She's finally telling the truth.

"Mom." I want to go to her, but I can't make myself take the necessary steps. I'm angry with her for putting herself in this position, but I know I shouldn't be.

I hear, in the periphery, the cops' questions, my mother's answers—

"How far along were you when Mr. Wick hit you?"

"Have you been to the doctor?"

"Do you have documentation to prove the pregnancy terminated after his assault?"

—but it all seems so far away and distant, like I'm listening from the bottom of the ocean.

I sink back to the sofa, and I drop my head in my hands.

My ears are ringing.

My hands are wet with tears.

My chest is heaving with sobs I'm fighting like hell not to unleash. Have to stay strong. For my mother. For my sisters.

"Mom."

Was the dickweed trying to kill the twins before they were born, too? Is that why he'd walloped her back then? This tremendous sense of loss pours into my heart, and it *hurts*. I can't imagine life without my sisters.

"Mom!"

And the next I know, I'm holding her, and I'm holding her *so tight*, and she's crying on my shoulder.

My mom.

My *mother*. She's so small. Damien could snap her in half, and she stood up to him tonight. She's strong. *So strong*.

She tells the police everything, answers every question.

I fill them in on what happened at the Churchill, about Damien watching Chatham climb in bed with me. I tell them about old shit, too, about how I got the scar on my forearm.

They question Chatham, too, in my bedroom, and for the first time *ever*, Rosie and I have a third party to confirm things happened just the way we said they did.

When they ask for it, Rosie gives the police the photograph Caroline found at Damien's place.

Chatham obviously filled them in about it.

The cops are there for an hour, at least, before Rosie agrees to medical attention, which I turn down. Someone has to stay and watch the girls.

This—when the cops have gotten the last of their statements, the last of their pictures, and when Rosie is on her way to the hospital in a squad car—is when I let loose.

I can't help it. It's like a decade of suppressed frustration and hurt and anger comes pouring out of me all at once. Like the floodgate opened, and I can't close it again.

Chatham emerges from my bedroom, wearing my spare jersey and a pair of my sweats.

I let her watch me fall to pieces. I'm like the tiles on the Scrabble board. Fragments. Impermanent pieces of indeterminate wholes, which could easily dissect and scatter. But somehow I know she's going to scrape it all up and rearrange the letters so they make sense.

Or at least I hope that's what's going to happen.

She's on my lap now, holding my face in her cold hands. "It's over now. Everyone's safe."

It's true. We're safe.

"But we're also changed," I say. "I can't undo what he did to them tonight."

"Is that what you think you're here to do? Sweetheart, no one can do that." Her lips meet mine. "No one expects you to rewind time."

I wrap my arms around her, hold her close, and trace the letters on the back of the jersey.

"This isn't who you are," she whispers between kisses. "It's only where you've been."

Next, I feel her fingers working the buttons on my shirt.

"And we've all been there from time to time. Locked in a closet, scared we're never getting out. But we come out. Stronger."

I nod, and hiccup over tears when I try to verbally agree.

Her hands splay against my chest. "I love you," she whispers against my lips.

I love you, too. I try to form the words, but I can't make it happen. I dip a few fingers into the waistband of the sweats she's wearing and trail my fingertips over the scar on her hip.

P A I N T   I T   B L A C K

"Josh."

I hear my mother's voice through a cloud of static.

She jostles me, and the static breaks for a second.

"I'm home."

I flinch when she speaks this time and bolt upright, and overly aware of the fact that I'm not wearing anything, grip the covers at my waist.

Chatham.

I sense the empty space beside me. She's gone.

I focus on the Rosie-shaped shadow standing over me. "Everything okay?" I ask.

"Yeah."

"What time is it?"

"About five. Just wanted to tell you I'm back from the ER."

"Okay."

"We'll talk later." She's closing the door.

"Mom?"

She pauses at the door.

"I'm glad you're okay."

"Me, too. Go back to sleep."

I lay back down, but only until I hear her footsteps up the

stairs and down the hall. When I hear the click of her bedroom door closing, I get up and shove my legs into boxer shorts.

Did Chatham hear my mother coming and hide? Or did she sneak out of my bed last night to sleep on the couch to ward off an awkward situation? Or is she even here?

God, if my mother had come in and found us together . . .

"Chatham?" I whisper.

I check everywhere I might hide, if the situation were reversed—my closet, the shower, the cubby under the stairs where we store all the Christmas junk—but to no avail. She's nowhere.

Her backpack is gone, too.

She must have walked home.

I'm not crazy about the idea of her trekking across town in the middle of the night, especially after what happened with Damien tonight, even if she is perfectly capable of traveling incognito cross-country to—

Wait.

Incognito.

All the nonsense of last night, with her hair, comes flooding back.

She *did* dye her hair to blend in. And even though she insisted the photograph of the little girl in the purple shorts wasn't her, the shade of blonde is *so similar.* Maybe she didn't want me to notice. Or maybe she didn't even want to admit it to herself: it's a coincidence we can't overlook.

Is that why she was so upset when I mentioned it?

The girl at the rave with the shamrock tattoo . . . *the girl she kissed* but insisted she didn't know.

The mural at the Churchill. The things she drew on that wall . . . She knows things about this town, even if she swears she doesn't remember being here, beyond a vague familiarity about the caboose.

The backpack she never unpacked. The clothes, always shoved into it, as if she'd planned to take off at a moment's notice.

I grab my phone and text her: *Where are you?*

I stare at the screen, waiting for her reply.

When it doesn't come minutes later, I *call* her.

It rings for an eternity, then bottoms out in some generic, panned, computerized indication that the user has not yet set up her voicemail.

My body breaks into a sweat.

I don't feel good about this.

I mean, if she left, that's one thing. But what if someone *found* her?

Wayne and Loretta, her foster parents.

She called the cops with a tip about her foster father and a girl under the floorboards and her sister's memories of being in Sugar Creek, and she was afraid enough to leave home immediately after, even though she originally declined to take the trip when Savannah wanted to bring her along.

She called the cops to tell them she was all right because I insisted on it. Suppose someone found out where she was and came looking for her?

I kick aside last night's khakis to get to the sweats beneath them—the sweats she wore last night—and a key clunks out of my khakis pocket in the process.

The key to the Churchill.

The key to *her place.*

It's on my bedroom floor.

So she didn't go home.

I tear through my room, looking for a note, a clue. *Anything.* She left me nothing.

And after everything that happened last night—and I mean *everything* happened last night—if she'd just leave . . .

I shove my hands through my hair.

It doesn't make sense.

Calm down.

She could've gone back to the Churchill. Maybe she had another key. I shouldn't panic. Not yet.

I grab my keys—and the key on my bedroom floor—and decide to go look for her before I draw conclusions.

On my way out of the bedroom, I catch sight of the Scrabble board.

I scramble toward it.

Who knows? She left a message for me there once before.

I hold my breath as I approach.

But there's nothing written with tiles beyond what's left of our game and her name:

CHATHAM CLAIBORNE

I slowly walk upstairs.

Normally, I'd just take off, but considering what happened last night, I think I owe it to my mom to at least tell her I'm leaving.

So I quietly go up the second half of the stairs, and knock on her door.

After a second, I turn the knob and peek inside to find my mother already asleep. I'll leave her a note.

I look in on Maggie Lee and Miss Lina, who are still asleep, cuddled up together on the twin bed. I let out a slow, deep breath. I hope it's over—all the fear and nervousness and violence. I hope, by the time they're my age, they don't remember living this way.

I go to leave, but at the last second, I spot a piece of paper on the floor, near where Chatham was sitting while reciting *The Sneetches*. She was drawing.

This may be the last piece she'll ever create in my company—a cavern sinks in my chest when I consider it—so I pick it up.

The rendering, in pencil, is of a door. Just a door, with a shadow of a tree cast over it . . . but, no. The shadow of branches, yes, I see that. But really, it's a swing . . . one of those thick boards with coarse, itchy ropes knotted beneath and tethered to a tree branch. And in the midst of the tangles of branches, a closer look reveals the outline of a girl. And she's bound to the swing.

Her arms, like long fingers of branches' offshoots, are tethered, and bent, and limp.

Her hair, tangles of sharp edges, hangs forward over her face.

The tree casts the shadow, but the girl is transparent, as if light is shining through her.

God, the things that must go through her head, the things that might have happened to her, if she's creating things like this!

I don't know if she meant this sketch to terrify whoever saw it, or maybe it was a teaser, one of those optical illusion types to see what the human eye goes to. Do you see a tree? Or a girl? I fold the sketch and pocket it.

I scribble a note on a napkin and leave it on the table for my mother, and hightail it toward the Churchill.

Sugar Creek seems peaceful this morning. I'm the only one on the road, for one thing, but it's more than the sparse population lending to the sleepy atmosphere. It's that I know Damien Wick is getting what's coming to him. He'll be in jail by now. At long last, justice will be served.

I pull up to the room-and-board and don't bother with the buzzer. If Chatham *is* home and asleep, I don't want to wake her. I use the key to gain entry at the front, climb the stairs to #2E, and use the key to enter her room.

It takes a minute for my eyes to adjust to the darkness.

But as soon as I manage to make out shapes, I see the door to the bathroom on the far side of the room hangs askew on its hinges, as if someone barreled into it to break it down. "Chatham?" I flip the light switch.

She's not here.

The place is trashed.

With trembling fingers, I dial the police.

While it's ringing, I take in the sight of the place: the mattress is thrown from the rusting bedframe, and clothes are everywhere—*my clothes*, that is, the ones I brought yesterday when I assumed I'd never go back to Carpenter Street. They're no longer in my duffel bag, but strewn over the floor.

Whoever did this was looking for something.

There's nothing of hers in this place, save the hanger from which her incredible Homecoming dress used to hang, and the artistic creation on the wall.

"I'd like to report a break-in," I say to the dispatcher when he answers. "And my girlfriend . . . she's not here. She's gone. Missing."

Whoever came in did so through the bathroom. Damien was in there; he had access through his girlfriend's place.

Is Chatham gone of her own volition? Or has someone—Damien?—taken her against her will? Numb, I sink to the floor opposite the mural.

"Sir?" The dispatcher.

A guttural noise escapes me, but I can't talk.

My eyes trip from one image to the next. The train. The twins huddled in the corner. The swing alongside the creek.

Wait.

The swing.

It's the same one she drew just last night.

"Sir, I need the name of your girlfriend—"

"Chatham."

"—and her age."

"Sixteen."

"Last name? Her parents?"

He's still talking to me, but I move closer to the mural and study the twins.

Their blonde hair.

Chatham has blonde roots.

The flash of Chatham at the rave, kissing that girl with the tattoo, the blonde girl with the dark blue wig, practically defibrillates me.

And then the images come, one after another, like on a screen in my mind, playing at fast-forward.

The train.

The shamrock she drew in the sand.

The money. God, *the money.* No one travels with that much money unless she's planning to keep on running.

The mysterious blonde toddler in a Polaroid picture, tucked into Savannah's journal, and the picture Caroline found in Damien's closet of the same girl.

The X on Chatham's hip.

The ID she got from Aiden, and the way she'd lied about the reason she needed it.

She said her license was in a box lost in the move.

But there were no boxes.

There was no move.

She came here with only a backpack. To find her sister, she'd said. But I think we found her at the rave, and Chatham pretended not to know her—even after she kissed her.

Dispatch alerts me: "Sir?"

"I'm at the Churchill Room and Board. On the second floor."

"Your girlfriend's last name?"

"Claiborne." I hang up.

She'd dropped clues in my lap all along, even from the very first day I saw her.

The sand castle she'd built . . .

I flip through pictures on my phone until I find one of Margaret and Caroline in front of the very first creation Chatham shared with me. I look from the picture to the mural until I find the same shapes hidden in the swirls and curves she'd sketched on the wall.

It's all there, I'm convinced.

She's hiding in the shadows of a truth she never told me. She said she didn't remember this place, that she didn't remember being here. But she's been remembering. She's been putting pieces of this puzzle together. Maybe she's been recording it in this mural, but she's been keeping it from me.

And Damien's in there somewhere. Always on her heels. Always watching.

I zero in on a creek winding its way through the expanse of

pencil and paint on the wall. Written in the stream, disguised in the waves: **Rachel Bachton was here.**

The way Chatham gripped my arm when we got to Damien's place . . .

The swing she'd later sketched with the girl wound up in it . . . it's like the one hanging from Damien's tree, the one the dog got tangled up in. Only as much as I've ever told her, I can't remember telling her about the dog, so why is the swing here on her wall in her room, before we went to Damien's?

The words she said earlier echo in my brain: *And we've all been there from time to time. Locked in a closet, scared we're never getting out. But we come out. Stronger.*

Is *she* the girl in the photograph Caroline found in Damien's closet? She said it wasn't her, but what if it was? Had she been to Damien's place before?

"It was Damien."

I look up when I hear the voice, and see Damien's too-thin girl-on-the-side standing just beyond the broken bathroom door. Her left eye doesn't look much better than my mother's.

"He was looking for something?"

She nods, but before she can say anything, I probe further.

"What was he looking for? Did he find it?"

Her left shoulder twitches upward, and her fingers move to her temple in a massage. "I guess I asked too many times."

"He did that to you?"

"Guess I was a poor substitute for the one he really wanted."

I'm about to tell her that's how he treats everyone unfortunate enough to cross his path, that my mother could be her twin right now.

"Sweet young thing like her . . ." she says. "Don't know how I didn't see it sooner."

My gaze snaps back to her. "*Chatham?*"

"Is that her name? He looks for her wherever we go."

It hits me, what Chatham said the first night she opened up to me:

It's not like he's following me, but it's weird.

What if Damien hadn't been only following *me* this past month?

What if he'd also been following *my girlfriend?*

T O A D

The owner of the Churchill is pissed about the wall.

"They're not supposed to alter the appearance of the rooms," she says.

The woman in #2F, Damien's extracurricular girlfriend, lingers on the fringes. I volunteer to paint over Chatham's artwork. I figure it's the least I can do. And it'll give me time alone with what she left behind.

"This is a crime scene," a cop says. "No one's changing anything."

I'm not allowed to bring my things back home, either, until the police have determined my clothes aren't evidence.

Now, hours later, back at home, I look at her name, scrawled in Sharpie on my forearm. Proof she was here, like the mural on the walls of the Churchill Room and Board.

The marking is still fresh because I haven't showered yet, but I know eventually, this marker will wear away. It's just another sand castle, waiting to be washed away when the waves roll up on the shore.

The realization needles me like ice-cold rain on the back of my neck.

I don't want to think Chatham just up and left me, although

maybe she was hinting at the possibility last night when she flipped out in the car after the dance. *This was a mistake. I don't even know how long I'm going to be here, and . . . I don't know what we were thinking, getting attached like this.* And if I'm honest, it's preferable to her being stolen away in the still moments of early morning.

If it was Damien who tossed her room at the Churchill, and Damien's in custody at the cop shop, isn't it unlikely anyone else would have access to her while she slept next to me?

So I tell myself she left because she knows I'm safe. She knows my life is about to get better. Like maybe she thinks I don't need her anymore.

Except I'll *always* need her.

I wonder if she went to find the girl with the tattoo, the girl who may be Savannah. I wonder if she's invented a whole new persona by now, if Savannah has, too, and they're continuing their escape of the turmoil of life at the Goudy farm.

But either way, it's like one minute she was here, rearranging the letters in her Scrabble tiles . . . and in a blink, she disappeared.

It fucking *hurts*.

Will I ever stop worrying about her? Will I be forever changed, like Rachel Bachton's parents, and see her face in places she's never been?

I turn on the television, crash onto the sofa, and let it sink in: Chatham Claiborne is gone.

My head hurts, probably from the beating I took yesterday at the Churchill and, later, the blows I took at Damien's place.

". . . And while the bones buried at the confluence of two rivers in rural Savannah—"

I sit up straighter and focus on the television screen for the breaking news.

"—were a negative match to Rachel Bachton's DNA, police officials are not ruling out a connection between the case of the remains known as Baby A, and that of the Bachton kidnapping . . . or between the events in Chatham County and Chicago's far-north suburb Northgate, where sources say recent information has come in that may help to solve the long-cold case of the missing girl."

The anchor cuts to video footage of a policeman, in full regalia, at a podium. "An anonymous tip tied the Bachton case to the Goudy tract in rural Catoosa County, Georgia, some three hundred fifty miles northwest of where Baby A's remains were discovered."

Chatham's tip.

He continues: "Wayne Goudy is currently in custody. At this time, he's being held for questioning. I have no affirmative details to report other than the dogs alerted for human remains at the site in question."

I wonder if "the site" is the stables.

And I wonder if Chatham left Sugar Creek just as this news is breaking because she's afraid of the dominoes she just set in motion.

The police talked to her separately. She was in my bedroom. Mom and I were out by the fireplace. Suppose she told the police about more than what had happened with Damien. Suppose she was afraid. Suppose Damien *had* been following her . . .

And Miss Lina came out of the house with that picture . . .

And then Chatham drew that picture of the swing . . .

What if she was afraid because she suddenly remembered something about what she might have seen as a four-year-old kid the day Rachel Bachton disappeared?

"Yes," the cop on television is saying, "it's true a photograph of a young girl recently turned up, but the family of the missing child denies resemblance."

So the picture at Damien's place, and the picture in Savannah's journal, aren't likely Rachel Bachton. Who else could that photograph resemble?

Considering she's really blonde—as blonde as the girl in the photograph—could it be Chatham?

I try to conjure her smile, try to remember the feeling of her body against mine, and fresh as it is, the sensation is already fading.

It's not fair. Why do I remember so accurately the way Damien's knife felt the moment it sliced into my skin? But I can't remember what it felt like to kiss her?

This fear I feel—the fear of never seeing her again—has been with me, I now realize, since the first second I saw her. Like an omen of what eventually was going to happen.

I have to make her stay.

Have to make her permanent.

I know only one way to do that.

I grab my keys.

A few minutes later, I'm at the Temple Tattoo Shop on Hauser Street, sitting in a black pleather chair across from some guy who looks like he once belonged on the cover of '80s-metal-band vinyl. Slight build, wiry. Like everything and everyone in this place, he's clad in black. He wears his long, scraggly hair loosely pulled back and secured at the back of his neck.

Imagine this guy, Toad, scratching at a mostly gray beard he maybe hadn't intended to grow, so much as he'd passively allowed it to appear, millimeter by millimeter, through neglect.

Too many late nights. Too much bourbon and not enough razor blades.

"So. Josh. How old are you?"

"Twenty-two." So I lied. It's the age on the fake ID Aiden made for me, so I suppose it's true from a certain point of view—the point of view of the illusion. And that's all life's been since Chatham Claiborne arrived. Illusion. I realize I don't know anything about her.

"You drunk?"

"No, sir. Just . . . got a lot on my mind."

"Never"—Toad points an inking tool at me—"*ever* put a chick's name on your body unless you're ready to explain it for the rest of your life."

He's prepping his tools with focused attention, as if he's threading a needle fit to sew all the continents on the globe back together.

"You ready to do that? To explain it to every other girl that crosses your path?"

"It's not her name." I roll up my sleeve and reveal Chatham's drawing in Sharpie. "It's her signature."

A clue is more like it. Someone she was for a brief moment in time. Just a page in her history book.

"All right. Give me two good reasons to put her name on your body."

"It's the way she wrote it." I glance at her signature—all artsy, with a pronounced scroll on the C, the loop in her Hs, the upstroke on the M. "She's an artist." Pointing out the obvious seems to be a talent of mine lately. I wonder, and not for the first time since I walked into the Temple, if Toad remembers seeing her. She said she'd dropped into this place looking for Savannah. Maybe she would've shown some of her work to this guy/amphibian (if you look him in the eyes, you'll see that he has traits of both). Or maybe she would've just felt at home here, among people who see things the rest of us don't see: the colors reflecting off the lighthouse at the brink of twilight, the splash of red veins in a fallen yellow leaf, the crack in the pavement on Second Street, which oddly resembles the coastal border of Texas. She'd pointed out all those things to me. I don't look at the world the way I used to . . . before.

"And the second reason?"

I don't want to say it. Saying it might make it true. I swallow hard, like forcing down a mouthful of mushy, canned peas. Always overcooked. "She's dead."

And I suppose it is true, one way or another. Dead to me, or dead to the world, is still dead.

"That, my friend, is maybe the best reason I can think of." Latex gloves slap against his wrists as he yanks them over his talented hands. He looks at me over the rectangular spectacles he must've slipped on while I was pondering Texas-on-Second-Street. "I'm sorry to say it," Toad says, although I don't think he's sorry to say anything. "But it's a damn fine reason to put her name on your body."

He explains he has to recreate the signature, has to clean the Sharpie from my skin and prep it to ward off infection, but it'll look the same when it's done. Only it'll be permanent.

"Last chance to change your mind," he says.

"Not gonna happen, brother."

It's not really about her name, just like the number on my chest isn't really about football. It's about a turning point in my life.

I was fourteen when Damien's knife pierced my left arm. Fourteen when I realized it was time to be a man. I had that number inked into my skin, and I wear that number on my back, to remind myself of victory, of survival.

And that's the same reason I'm sitting at the Temple now.

This, too, will strengthen and harden me. This hurt, too, will pass. But that doesn't mean I ever want to forget her.

I watch as his needle drags through my skin on one of the places her lips often landed, over the scars Damien left there. Bubbles of blood boil up in the wake of Toad's instrument, reminding me of the day it happened: my mother's glass-shattering shriek, my sisters huddled behind the sofa, their tiny arms fixed around each other as if the world was about to implode.

"Your body's a temple, man." Toad periodically wipes my flesh clean of blood, demonstrating the ink remains. Proof that what he's doing is permanent, sure, though not as permanent as death by knife would've been. "I'm just here to paint the walls."

The buzz of his tools makes my teeth vibrate. I watch the outline of her signature appear, letter by letter: C, H, A . . .

It's what you do when you don't want to forget. You make things permanent.

"Why didn't you just write her name in Sharpie?" Aiden says later, when I peel away the tape and wrap.

"Funny you should say that," I say. "That's why it's here now. She wrote it in Sharpie first."

He hits his pipe, and because my world is empty now without the girl I fell hard for, I might partake, too.

"You want?" Aiden offers me the pipe.

There's a certain poetic symmetry in the prospect of getting absolutely blotto tonight, the first night without Chatham Claiborne, as I was undeniably inebriated my first night with her, too. I could handle sinking into the comfortable numbness of an organic high tonight, if only to stop the emptiness stabbing at my soul every waking second of the day.

Except that my sisters are asleep upstairs, and my mother, with her black eye fading already to purplish blue, is working at the hospital, and I can't imagine how it might go if Margaret or Caroline happens to wake up and I'm semi-high.

My sisters are another problem altogether. How do you explain to four-year-old girls that Chatham's not coming back? That you don't know where she went? That you don't know why?

Aiden's phone chirps, and he offers his pipe and a lighter.

Just one hit won't impale me, but I responsibly wave it off. Can't handle the paranoia of the random drug tests in the locker room so close to playoffs anyway.

He's dealing with his phone, shrugs, and places the still-smoldering bowl on the table. "So where'd she go?"

"Don't know."

I wish the cops would say what's up with Damien and the photograph. I wish they'd tell me if there's any connection between the swing in Damien's yard and the swing Chatham repeatedly drew. I mean, I can't ignore the coincidence of her leaving the same night all this bullshit with Damien comes to light.

"One thing I know about girls," Aiden says.

"You don't know anything about girls."

His phone chirps again, and instantly he's texting back. "I know *one thing*. They say shit like 'don't follow me,' but they *want* to be followed. They *want* you to ask what's wrong, even after they tell you *nothing* is wrong."

"Not this time. Not her. She's just . . . gone."

"And what do you do, when you can't find something?"

I follow, with my gaze, the letters scrolled over the scar marring my arm. "There's nothing *to* do."

"You retrace your steps. You stumble over things you maybe overlooked before."

Easy for Aiden to say. What's he lost? A dollar bill, here and there? A bag of pretzel M&M's? "The problem is that she didn't leave anything behind."

"She'll turn up," he says.

That's what everyone said about Rachel Bachton. And it's been twelve years since anyone saw her.

Chirp, chirp. "Girls don't just let you have your way with them and take off."

I think it was just the opposite, actually. I think she had it all planned. I think *she* had her way with *me*. And I think she did it because she *knew* she was leaving. I'm already regretting telling Aiden about what happened last night, and I didn't tell him because I think it's his business. I told him because it confuses the hell out of me. I mean, why close the gap between us, why bring us as close as two people can ever be, if you're only going to take off a few hours later?

"Before you know it, she'll be back in the palm of your hand."

She already slipped through my fingers.

Chirp, chirp. "Fucking Kai. I'm starting to remember why we broke up in the first place."

While he's dead-on right on the Kai front—she's too clingy, he's too aloof—Aiden doesn't get my dilemma. He doesn't know about Chatham's backpack, or the things she kept in it. He doesn't know about the scar on her hip, or the horror she endured in that barn with the cattle brand when she was a kid—or even before, in that hot car, surviving while her baby brother slowly drifted off to a sleep from which he never awoke.

He doesn't know what I know: that she and her runaway sister may have witnessed Rachel Bachton's kidnapping. Why would Wayne disappear when bones turned up at the rivers, if he had nothing to do with their being there? And why wouldn't there be a report for two runaway girls from Georgia unless the parents don't want the girls to be found?

Posting them missing would mean police interaction. And that might equal enlightening the cops to family secrets.

Aiden never saw the girl at the rave draw her lips over my girlfriend's in a way that was more familiar than sexy, now that I think about it. Was it a sisterly kiss, more than a prelude to two hot chicks making out? Which, of course, Chatham didn't let happen.

But if so, why didn't Chatham own it? Why did she lie to me? *Did* she lie to me?

I don't kiss girls, or strangers.

Yes, she said *specifically* that it wasn't Savannah.

And why can't I find any reference to Chatham Claiborne online? No Facebook, no Instagram. I wonder if her Snapchat is even receiving the messages I'm still sending.

She had to get a phone hooked up when she got here. Why? Wouldn't her old phone work just as well here as it did in Georgia?

Unless she didn't want anyone to track her by the calls she was making, it doesn't make sense.

And if she's a ward of the state of Georgia, in the foster care system, even if she wasn't adopted like her sister Savannah, wouldn't the officials there be checking up on the family? Wouldn't *they* report her missing?

I wonder again if Chatham Claiborne is even her real name.

"She'll turn up, man."

Aiden's clueless.

He's never lost something that can't afford to be found. If I can find her, Wayne can find her. Damien can find her. And so can anyone else. Aiden doesn't get that she doesn't *want* to be found.

But maybe he can help me.

"Do you still have the pictures of Chatham? The ones you took for her ID?"

PLATINUM

If Sugar Creek High officials knew their netbooks could be used for such devious deeds, I wonder if they'd force us to purchase them.

Aiden's got his school-issued hardware up and running, connected to an online program the school sponsors for the graphic design classes.

Between texts to Kai, he flips through logos for Motor Oil Hum and Mindjam, the two strains of weed he hopes to market legally someday. At least the guy's got ambition.

Finally, he stops at a picture of Chatham, and my breath catches in my throat when I lock my gaze on her. Even in a two-dimensional image, nestled neatly into an Illinois state driver's license, she draws me in with her eyes.

"Can you make her blonde?"

Aiden looks at me. "Dude. You aren't going to ask me to hook up a Barbie doll at the end of this. 'Cause I gotta be honest with you, man. I don't think it'll be quite the same as the real thing."

He's referencing the mid-'80s John Hughes movie where two schmucks make a girl on a computer.

"Really? I had my heart *set* on the Veterinarian Barbie."

That's me on sarcasm. "I just want to see what she looks like blonde."

"Whatever," he mutters, but he gets to work on it. "How blonde?"

"I don't know. Fucking blonde."

"Golden blonde? Dirty blonde?"

"Lighter than that."

"Platinum?"

"It's a place to start."

My laptop is open, too, and I'm searching everything I can think of—even outlandish possibilities that never crossed my mind before. If Savannah came here because she was present at the Northgate farmers' market when Rachel was taken, it makes sense to come here and revisit the facts of Rachel Bachton's kidnapping, in hopes of gleaning some sort of information about the child witness who's never been named. Especially if Chatham happens to be that witness.

For the hundredth time, I go back to Savannah's Instagram—I remember her username, *Farmgirl1004*, from the night Chatham and I went to the rave—and look through the photos allowed to the public.

I compare the few to the picture in my mind of the girl with the shamrock tattoo.

I wonder if tattoo girl is still around, if she'd mind answering my questions.

I arrive at a picture of the tattoo itself. Is this the same tat I saw on that girl's ankle? I stare at it, willing myself to remember, as if I can conjure the image of something I know is lost. I stare at it—its scrolls and loops—until it goes blurry.

It's familiar, as if I've seen it before.

But that makes sense because I *have* seen it. Chatham

drew it in the sand, and I got a good look at the girl at the rave's tattoo.

I flip through other pictures on my phone. She incorporated those rolls and curls into the mural on the wall at the Churchill, into the clay relief hanging in the showcase at Sugar Creek High.

Wait.

I blink away from the picture on the screen and look at the signature Toad inked onto my arm.

The flourish before the *C*s on my arm . . . the same scroll-like loops . . . so similar to the leaves on the shamrock.

"Aiden . . ."

"Huh?"

"Look at this." I point to a detail on my newest tattoo.

"Yeah, I've seen it, numb-nuts." He clips me upside the head.

"No, *this*." I zero in on the identical scroll on Savannah's tattoo. "And this." I point out the same details in the Churchill mural, in the clay relief.

I can tell by the way he looks at me: he sees the similarities, too. "What's it mean?"

I'm pretty much convinced: if there are similar elements in all of Chatham's works, and the tattoo on the girl at the rave shares those attributes, Chatham could have designed that girl's tattoo. Which is more proof that she lied to me. The girl who kissed her must have been Savannah.

"That guy I dropped for a while back," I say.

"Yeah. Don't worry about the coin, man. Consider it payment for services rendered."

"No, I mean . . . thanks." I spent what was left of it on my new tat, but I can pay him back. "Do you know him personally? I mean, he places a lot of orders?"

"Pretty regularly."

"There was a girl there."

He glances up at me. "Yeah?"

"She has a tattoo like this."

"Fuck, man."

"I think she knows Chatham. You ever see a girl with him before?"

"Which girl is more the question."

"Oh." I think of the way she flirted with me, the invitation to the rave . . . Maybe it's naïve to think she might still be there with Aiden's customer after all this time. Still, I wonder if it's worth a try.

Suddenly, the need to drive out to Sheridan Road seems crazy-urgent. I can't go now, obviously. Rosie's at work, and the twins are asleep. Maybe I can send Aiden. He might have an in with the guy I won't have. But if she's there, *I* need to be the one to talk to her, to look at that tat, see if it's Chatham's work. Besides, he's blitzed and shouldn't drive. And because he's blitzed, I can't very well ask him to stay here with the girls. But I feel like if I don't go now, she'll be gone tomorrow . . . if she's not gone already.

Aiden's phone chirps again. "God."

I have to go out there. I have to know what that girl with the tattoo knows. Even if she doesn't know anything, even if the tattoo is a coincidence, it'll tell me something about the girl I thought I knew.

"You think it's all right if Kai comes over for a bit?" Aiden says. "I mean, tell a girl I gotta be here for a brother, but she won't let up."

Lightbulb.

"Yeah, that's fine."

"Cool." He offers a fist for a bump.

I go in. "You think Kai'd mind sitting with the girls? As a special favor to me?"

"Maybe. When?"

"You and I have to head out to Sheridan Road."

He turns his screen toward me. I stare at the image of my girlfriend as a platinum blonde.

I try to see her as a scared little girl in purple shorts.

Even if she didn't believe she was the child in the photograph, I can't rule it out. Particularly with the blonde hair Aiden's drawn on her fake ID, there are definite similarities.

I can't take my eyes off Aiden's screen.

I wonder if that's what she'll look like next time I see her.

I wonder if I'll see her again at all.

MINDJAM

The old Josh wouldn't have said anything to his mother about leaving Kai with the twins. But I'm not the old Josh and Rosie isn't the old Rosie.

I dial her on the way out to Sheridan Road: "I know you're not going to like this, but I've got a line on Chatham." I go through the whole rigmarole, Kai is certified in CPR, the twins are in good hands, all that bullshit, then get to the meat of it.

"You think her sister is there?" Rosie asks.

"Good chance." So I bluff that part of it. "I *know* I said I'd be there for the girls, and I *wish to God* Chatham hadn't taken off just now, but please understand. And trust me when I say I've left Margaret and Caroline with someone so qualified that—"

"You're already on your way out there." There's a slight edge to her tone now. "You're calling me on the way."

My first instinct is to lie to her, then fight it out later. But I bite the bullet and tell the truth: "Yes."

A beat of silence answers me.

"Rosie?"

"We'll talk about this later." She sighs, but not in the way she usually does, like I'm the biggest disappointment in her life. "Just text me when you're home safe."

And that's *it*. No drama. I wonder if it's because I took the initiative to be honest with her, or because she's just exhausted. Either way, I know she wouldn't have been so complacent, had she known there's another shrink-wrapped book in Aiden's bag.

I drive down Washington, then hook a left onto Sheridan.

Aiden's busy texting the guy, telling him we're in the neighborhood with a frequent-buyers' gift, whatever.

I glance down the street where Rachel Bachton used to live, and nearly slow to a stop when I see the news vans. Someone's taping a story. "There's news about the case."

"Huh?" Aiden looks up from his phone to see what I'm talking about.

It probably has to do with the photograph the Bachtons have denied has anything to do with their daughter. But I wonder why the crew is taping in front of the house that hasn't belonged to the Bachtons in years.

I inch forward, but keep glancing in my rearview mirror, as if I expect to see all the answers to all my dilemmas unfolding on the road behind me. Eventually, I pull up to the enormous house with all the stairs, and we start to climb.

After all the formalities, which include the enormous guy who lives here—he's got to be about six-four, two-seventy-five—patting me down to ensure his safety, and asking me all the typical questions to convince himself I'm not a cop, I enter. Aiden waits on the front porch with his shrink-wrapped book.

"So," the guy says. "What can I do for you?" He's led me to a formal room with an elegant couch, the back of which is shaped like a camel's hump. It's hard to believe he would've chosen this furniture, and I instantly assume this place belongs to a grandmother or a great-aunt. Nearest to us is a pair of dainty chairs I can't believe will hold his weight. But he sinks onto one, and offers its twin to me.

I sit. "There was a girl here last time I came."

"Usually is."

"This one's blonde, with a shamrock tattoo on her ankle. You took her to a rave."

"*Rave?* I don't do that shit. Alana goes where she wants to go."

My heart sinks a little in my chest. *Alana.* "That's her name?"

"It's the name she gave me. What about her?"

"Is she still here?"

He shakes his head. "Took off."

"Can you tell me . . ." I flip through my phone for the screenshots of Savannah's Instagram and present him with a close-up of the tattoo. "Is this the same tattoo?"

Dude takes my phone. "Could be. To be honest, her ankles weren't what I was interested in." He hands back the phone.

"Did she, by any chance, ever wear a dark blue wig?"

"How the fuck should I know?"

"You didn't know her too well?"

He looks down at me, with his lips pressed into a thin, white line.

I twist in my seat.

"What," he says. "You want to know if she's a *natural* blonde? Do your own dirty work."

"What I mean is . . . was she new in town?"

"Yeah."

"Did she stay here with you?"

"What's it to you?" His skin's a little redder than it used to be. "You know, when I told Aid I'd talk to you, I didn't think I'd be under a fucking firing squad."

"My girlfriend's gone. And I think she knew yours. I'm just trying to find—"

"Let's get something straight. She's not my girlfriend."

"Okay."

"So whatever she's mixed up in, I don't know about it."

"Okay."

"And I don't care about it, either." The guy stands up, signaling our conversation is over. "What do I care that she took off yesterday?"

"Yesterday?"

He's almost back to the front door.

"Wait." I offer my phone again. "Is this Alana? Is this the girl I saw here that day?"

Just when I think he's going to squash me into oblivion, if only with his hard-ass stare, his shoulders relax a little. He takes the phone.

"Farmgirl." He reads the username and, this time, takes it upon himself to flip through the pictures on my phone. "Yeah, that's Alana."

"My girlfriend calls her Savannah," I say. "Says she left Moon River a few months ago."

"Moon River?"

"Georgia."

"Alana was from Georgia. I saw her license once." He sort of smiles a little. "And on certain words . . . she had a cute twang after she'd had a couple drinks."

I know the twang to which he refers.

"She's underage. She lied and told me she was eighteen, can you believe that?"

"Yeah."

"That's what I thought this was about. I mean, I met her

in a *club*. I'm twenty-two years old. I wouldn't normally . . . you know. But what do you do if the girl lies, right? I put an end to it as soon as I found out, but—"

"Yeah."

"Sixteen. Christ."

"Chatham—my girlfriend—she came here, to Sugar Creek, looking for her. Says she's her sister. And now they're both gone. Both left last night. Would you happen to know Alana's last name?"

"I was too focused on her birthday to notice."

"Yeah."

"Well." He hands back my phone. "*If* Alana's your girlfriend's sister, I hope you do find them. And if you don't mind, tell her she can keep the watch if it'll ward off any legal fallout from the time we spent together."

"Yeah."

"Good luck. Wish I knew more." He opens the door. "*Then,* and now."

"We brought a little something for your trouble." I don't want to make eye contact—he might then notice that I'm close to falling to pieces—but I force myself to look him square in the face because he's been walloped, too, in his own way. "I'll let her know about the watch, if I find her. Thanks again."

I go back to the car, while Aiden and this guy chat it up on the front porch.

If that girl—Alana—is Chatham's sister, it means Chatham lied to me. About her sister's name, about knowing her at the rave. About everything.

God, I wish Aiden would hurry the fuck up. I just want to go home.

If you've ever had something precious in your sights, and

come *this close* to grasping it before it's out of reach, you understand: I could scream right now. It's like surviving a shipwreck in the middle of the ocean, only to die by whale bite at Sea World.

I roll down the window. "C-caw!"

Aiden takes the hint and finally joins me in the car and makes some statement like *we'll find her, man,* and other bullshit he means to be encouraging. And it's not that I don't appreciate it—I do—it's that I'd rather face facts than believe in a fairy tale.

We swing past the spectacle at Rachel Bachton's old house, but we can't tell what's going on. There are only two crews, which is strange. In the early days of the investigation, even up until about five years ago, the road would be so crowded you couldn't turn onto it. I wonder if other crews are set up at the lighthouse, on the boardwalk, or other places Rachel Bachton was known to be way back when.

I'll turn on the news at home.

Once we get home, Aiden and Kai head out, I text my mother, and I'm sort of relieved to be alone. Aiden left his netbook—what's he going to do with it when he's high anyway?—so I know I'll see him tomorrow when he comes to get it.

For a few seconds after I sit down, I'm locked in a staring contest with blonde Chatham on Aiden's screen. Then I look at the Scrabble tiles that spell out her name, as if waiting for them to move. I consider keeping them, framing them. Her fingers touched them, laid them out in this display.

I snap out of it and turn on the television, and find a channel covering the Rachel Bachton story.

I'm trying to listen to everything being said, but my mind is tripping back and forth, trying to put pieces into the puzzle, trying to decide why Chatham would lie to me about knowing the girl at the rave.

Alana-slash-Savannah.

Why would Chatham lie about her name?

Wait.

If her name is really Alana . . . her license could be a fake, after all.

I open my laptop and type *Alana Goudy* into a search engine.

"Holy fuck."

Within the past couple of hours, it's official: the foster girls entrusted to Wayne and Loretta's care have been declared missing and endangered. I'm staring at a picture of two girls. Two girls I've seen before. But they're not who I thought they were. Savannah is the girl at the rave, no doubt about it. But Alana—Alana Goudy is Chatham Claiborne, with blonde hair.

DRINK ME

So why did Chatham/Alana concoct a whole new identity? Why give herself a whole new name? And why did Savannah assume Alana's name?

Chatham asked for an ID.

I helped her get it.

What if Chatham didn't have ID when she arrived in Sugar Creek because Savannah had taken Alana's license with her when she left? Because Chatham had refused to run away with Savannah, Savannah could have swiped the driver's license to avoid leaving a trail. If Savannah was approached, she could pretend to be Alana—whom no one would be looking for because she opted to stay on the farm. Being Alana would have raised fewer flags than being Savannah on the run.

I think back to the day Chatham told me about what Savannah had said about the stables at the Goudys' farm. She'd been convinced Savannah was in danger because she'd found Savannah's money, and her license, under the floorboards of the stables. She realized then, she should have gone with Savannah.

Either way, what do these sisters have to do with Rachel Bachton? Have they come all this way, to this has-been town, to convince the police their foster parents are involved in Rachel Bachton's disappearance?

I look up at the television, where a reporter is discussing the case in front of Rachel's old house:

". . . despite sightings at train stations along the East Coast, despite *thousands* of tips, and despite the recent surfacing of a photograph, and the testimony of a man currently in custody on charges of domestic violence who may or may not be involved . . ."

Damien!

". . . police are no closer to solving the case than they were a decade ago. The missing girl's family holds out hope that even though this lead did not pan out, others will. Police continue to cite a possible connection between Rachel Bachton and the case of Baby A, whose remains were found earlier this year in rural Chatham County, Georgia."

She goes on, but I'm distracted by the reporter's backdrop: Rachel's old house; more specifically, a leaded glass window in the door, just beyond the gate the reporter is standing in front of, the gate against which sympathizers tied ribbons and left flowers and teddy bears.

I hear the echo of my sisters' voices on the beach on the last day of summer: *criss-cross windows!*

I practically bounce off the sofa cushions. The house!

Of course!

It's the house Chatham sculpted on the beach! The turret, the wrap-around porch. The criss-cross windows!

By the time I get the picture up on my phone to compare, the camera cuts to Rachel's parents, who are thanking the public for their continued concern, awareness, and support. "We've been through this before. Some young woman insisting she's our daughter, some Good Samaritan thinking he's seen our Rachel. But even every negative result, every lead that doesn't pan out, puts us one step closer to knowing the truth."

There's a photo-montage of their precious daughter on the screen now. In some pictures, she's posing with her little brother.

I snap a picture of one in particular—Rachel on Northgate Beach. The lighthouse is in the background. She's wearing a two-piece swimsuit with wide ruffles; it coordinates with her brother's stars-and-stripes trunks.

But it's not really about the beach. And it doesn't matter that it must be the last summer she spent with her family before someone grabbed her.

It's what I see that a lot of people might not notice.

I enlarge the picture and study what I think I saw:

Rachel has a birthmark on her left hip—an oval patch of dark against her ivory skin.

I flash back to the day Chatham unbuttoned those amazing cut-offs and revealed the X on her hip, and I hear the words she said to me in the back of my mind: *It makes sense, based on what Savannah remembers. She says it wasn't an accident. She says Loretta held me down and Wayne branded me. Like, some sort of punishment. She saw it, she says.*

Ohmygod ohmygod ohmygod.

My fingertips are tingling, and it's getting hard to breathe.

"Here is an age-progressed image of what Rachel Bachton may look like today."

I snap a picture of that, too, because I'm on overload. I can't process.

"If anyone has any information . . ."

I take a deep breath and compare the age-progression of little Rachel to the teenage blonde Rachel. She's not identical to the Chatham Aiden's doctored on his screen, but there are definite similarities.

Is the scar on Chatham's hip a coincidence? Or did the Goudys purposefully burn her to get rid of an obvious connection between her and a missing girl from northern Illinois?

It's possible. Chatham had a vague recollection of being at the farmers' market, and she assumed it was because she might've witnessed Rachel's abduction.

Could it be she was wrong?

Could it be *she* was the one who was abducted?

"Someone saw something," Rachel's mother is saying on camera. "It's been long enough. Tell us what you know. Put us—put *yourself*—at ease, and tell us. And, Rachel, if you're out there, and we believe you are, all you have to do is tell someone. Tell someone about the charm on your necklace. Even if you don't have it anymore, it's all right. Tell someone."

FEED YOUR HEAD

"What's all this?"

I look up from the coffee table in the basement.

Rosie's standing at the stairs.

"Hi, Mom."

"What are you doing, Josh?"

I've taped news stories to the walls—stories about children fatally left in cars on hot days, stories about Rachel Bachton sightings.

I've drawn a rudimentary map of the eastern coast of the United States and pinpointed where the sightings were in relation to Northgate, Sugar Creek, the confluence of the Vernon and Moon Rivers, and the Goudy tract. And I've printed out sections of map to supplement and see these locations and the roads, and railways, that connect them.

I've written a timeline of Damien's life since he arrived in Sugar Creek, noting the years we were living with him and highlighting all the terrible things he did that we can either prove or suspect.

I've printed out pictures of Chatham (both brunette and blonde versions), pictures of Chatham and Savannah, and pictures of Rachel, and I've taped those to the wall, too.

I've printed pictures of the mural Chatham started at the Churchill.

And last, I've printed a picture of Chatham's relief and cut out each square of it individually. I'm moving the pieces around on the coffee table over the Scrabble board to see if they make up a picture that makes sense when rearranged. "I'm analyzing and resynthesizing," I say.

"Okay."

"Taking apart the relief Chatham made and putting it back together in a new form."

"Why?"

"Chatham liked to rearrange the Scrabble tiles before she played them."

My mother takes a few steps closer.

"I think she likes puzzles. Anagrams. Like you'd think she was going to lay out *rats*, but she ends up playing *star* instead."

"Are you all right, Josh?"

I glance up at her. "Yeah."

"Have you slept?" She's practically right next to me now. "At all?"

"No."

She grabs my wrist; her fingers land on the scab of my new tattoo. "You tattooed her *name* on your *body*?"

"It's not her name," I say.

"What do you mean it's not—"

"Her name is Alana Goudy. So this signature is a clue."

"Oh, God." A whimper laces through her words. "Joshua, go to sleep."

"Okay, Mom. You have to hear me out."

She covers her mouth with a hand to muffle a sob.

"I'm okay," I say.

She's shaking her head. "This"—she indicates toward all my clippings—"is not okay. *This* borders on obsession. And I know you liked this girl, but this . . . It's not okay."

"It's not just about Chatham." I take her hand and give it a squeeze. I show her the squares I've rearranged on the table. "She made this clay relief in sixteen different sections. Each square could potentially belong in any of the sixteen slots," I explain. "Each square has four potential edges that could be its top. So if I move the squares around, that's over a thousand possibilities as to what she really wanted us to see in this relief, right? And that's only if we're assuming its final shape is a square."

"What's all this about, Josh?" My mother is looking at me, not the rearranged squares. She reaches out to feel my forehead, like she did when I was a little kid running a fever.

"I'm *fine. Look.* I figured out if I took each square, shifted it once to the right, and flipped it to the left . . . we get a totally different picture."

After a few seconds, she looks at what I've done.

"This looks like the house Rachel Bachton used to live in," I say.

She nods.

"And this—" I show her a picture of the sand castle Chatham built for the twins. "She sculpted this house in September. And it looks like Rachel's old house, too."

"It does."

"I couldn't find a record of Chatham Claiborne online. And it's because it isn't actually her name. She's Alana Goudy."

"Who's Chatham Claiborne, then?"

I pull out a map I've yet to pin to the wall. "This is the grid of a city map. And this part here? See that?"

My mother is still nodding, her brows slanting downward in concern. Maybe she thinks I've lost it.

"Look at this." I point to a picture I taped to the wall; it's the bird's-eye view of a borough in New Jersey. "This is one of the train stations Rachel Bachton was seen at just after she was taken. *Chatham* Station, New Jersey. And the little girl's bones were discovered in *Chatham* County, Georgia. And this . . ." I point to the next picture. "This is the town closest to where Chatham grew up. The street closest to the station there is *Claiborne* Street."

My mother is staring at me like I'm crazy.

"This train station is a few miles from where the dogs alerted on the Goudy tract of land."

"The Goudy tract? Isn't that where they're looking for Rachel Bachton?"

"Don't you get it? Mom, Chatham doesn't remember her childhood. But she has this scar." I fill her in on the cattle brand "accident" and show her the picture of Rachel just before her abduction and point out the birthmark. I tell her about Savannah, the little girl under the floorboards in the stables, the shamrock pin that was red and gold . . . and could have been strung on a gold necklace Rachel was reportedly wearing, or even made to incorporate the heart-shaped charm on Rachel's necklace. "Chatham drew this swing, too, and she was terrified the moment we pulled up to Damien's place. It's possible she'd been there before. She drew these things on the wall at the Churchill . . . Look." I show her pictures of Chatham's mural. "There's shades of Damien in there. Am I right? And that photograph Caroline found . . ."

"What are you saying? That Chatham has something to do with Rachel Bachton's kidnapping?"

"No. Mom, I think Chatham *is* Rachel Bachton."

At last, my mother sighs. "You might be onto something."

My shoulders, which I didn't even realize were tense, fall in relief.

"I think we should call the police, Josh." My mother believes me. She's going to stand behind me.

CHESHIRE GRIN

The department sends two plain-clothes detectives to our house in an unmarked car, which relieves Rosie, given we're probably getting a reputation with the neighbors with all the recent police visits.

I've never seen either of these guys before. They tell me they're from the county force, that they've worked missing persons before. The older one—Guidry's his name—has been on the Bachton case since she disappeared. His sidekick, Hinkley, is new to the game, relatively speaking, and just made detective last year, but he's had some success in the field.

It's interesting, their giving me their résumés, as if they want to boost my confidence in their ability to find my girlfriend—and solve the mystery of Rachel Bachton's disappearance at the same time.

Rosie is upstairs with the girls, who are busy with breakfast and Sunday kid shows. It's also interesting that she trusts me to convey what I think I know to the police. She's not hovering over me, implying I should leave Damien out of my story, or attempting to persuade me to put a spin on the facts or my opinions to save him. I feel a shift in the universe this morning because of it.

Hinkley's the one studying my work, my maps, my pictures, while Guidry asks specific questions and takes notes about my theory, about hints Chatham left in the clay relief, in the sketch, in the mural, and in the sand castle.

"We gave the police a picture of a little girl. We found it at my stepfather's place, and Chatham had a picture of the same girl. What did Damien say about it?" I ask.

"Nothing," Guidry says. "He's not talking. Denies any knowledge."

"That's bullshit," I say. "Why else would my sister find the photo in his closet?"

"You may be right."

I do a double take. "Really?"

"Gotta hand it to you, kid." Hinkley turns from the wall to look at me. "You've drawn a lot of parallels."

"But none of this matters if we can't find her," I say. "This . . . it's all fine and good in *theory*, but what matters is finding out if I'm right. We have to know if the girl I know as Chatham Claiborne—who's really Alana Goudy—is also Rachel Bachton." I think about how finding Chatham would be the best thing I can imagine, but that if finding Chatham meant finding Rachel . . . God, could anything compare? "Damien's been following her," I continue. "Since before he possibly could have known she was special to me. And he tossed her room at the Churchill the other night."

"Yeah, I have that report here," Hinkley interjects.

"I think he knows who she is. I think that's why he's been following her . . . maybe why he tore through her room . . . to see if she is who he thinks she is. Why would he do these things if he didn't have something to do with why she's gone?" I ask.

"That's what we're going to find out," Guidry says. "Also, we have a link to your phone number. You called in a tip about a red and gold charm?"

"It wasn't a charm. It's a pin. But Chatham and I guessed you could put it on a chain . . . or maybe the stone in it was from the charm Rachel's mother references."

"Can you describe it?"

"It's a gold shamrock. About the size of a nickel. With a red heart in the center of it."

He's writing down everything I say.

"Was the stone in the middle—the heart—was it one piece? Or made up of two?"

"One," I say.

"One solid piece?"

"Yeah. Is it the charm on Rachel's necklace?" I ask. "The one her mom keeps talking about on television?"

"We'll let you know if what you describe bears resemblance."

Hinkley steps in again. "Did Chatham use your phone to call in a tip, too?"

"I know she called the tip line in Georgia."

"This would have been recently."

"She called the police in *Moon River*, but not the . . ." I shut up. Maybe she *did* call the tip line from my phone *instead* of calling the police in Moon River. I'd insisted she call to report she was safe—but that was when I thought she was the foster child of the Goudys. When she'd called, she'd said *My name is Chatham Claiborne. I'm calling to tell you I'm okay.* "She could have called anyone, I suppose. Now that I know the name Chatham Claiborne wouldn't mean anything to anyone, I understand why no one came looking for her."

What if, instead, she'd called the Rachel Bachton hotline to connect the dots between Rachel and Chatham? With that call, she could have both appeased me, and led the Rachel Bachton investigation full circle to where it began—here, in Sugar Creek.

"Wait," I continue. "There's something else." I go to the wall and pull down the article that references Chatham and her brother in the hot car. "This woman was on television, talking about how the state of Georgia trusted the Goudys to raise her daughter. As fosters, you know. And that she hadn't seen her kid in years. She said it like the Goudys kept her from her daughter or something. Only, if you ask Chatham, she says this woman basically decided to stop seeing her a couple years ago."

Hinkley raises a brow. "But if the girl you know as Chatham is actually Alana Goudy—which is apparent with what you've found on social media . . . the woman's not credible."

"Right. But there was another girl. Under the floorboards of the stables."

The cops share a look, like what I'm saying is crazy. "Under the *floor*?"

"Savannah used to talk about her," I explain. "Chatham thought it was to scare her into being good. So I'm thinking, if I'm right, and Chatham is Rachel—"

"This woman's daughter could have been Alana Goudy, and she could have been the girl in the stables," Guidry says. "If the Goudys got their hands on Rachel and tried to pass her off as Alana . . ."

"A mother would know her own kid," Hinkley says. "She'd know what kid wasn't hers."

"Right. And Wayne could have moved Alana's body to the rivers. Is there a way to match the DNA of Baby A . . ." I trail off, when I realize the cops might have already matched the

DNA to Alana Goudy. *Baby A* could have been a reference to Baby Alana. She would have been little when she died. *When Wayne killed her.*

Guidry's nodding.

"Or could they match the photograph Damien had in his closet to pictures of Alana Goudy when she first arrived at the Goudy farm?"

Guidry: "Devil's advocate: if what you're saying about Alana Goudy is true, it happened in Georgia. What role would Damien play?"

"I don't know. But I think he knows something," I say.

"And he's clammed up." Guidry perches on the edge of the sofa arm and looks to his partner. "Let's see if we can find a connection between Goudy and Wick."

"Why else would he have a picture of the girl?" I ask.

"And you're certain the picture wasn't Chatham as a little girl?" Hinkley asks. "Or Savannah?"

"Chatham said it wasn't her, and it wasn't Savannah."

"And you're thinking it might be Alana."

"Yeah." My head is spinning with the web these sisters have woven. Savannah posing as Alana. Alana posing as Chatham. I wonder . . . "Did Savannah know Chatham might be Rachel all along? Is that why she wanted to bring her here? Did Chatham know? Or did she start to suspect it when we started learning more? Like maybe when she came face-to-face with Damien's house . . . and she realized she might have been there before."

"We still don't know, beyond a doubt, if Chatham *is* Rachel," Hinkley reminds me.

"And you said Chatham took everything with her when she left," Guidry says. "Nothing lying around we could send to the lab for testing."

"We could dust the whole place." Hinkley shrugs a shoulder. "Things she likely touched. Get the kid's prints"—he nods in my direction—"compare to the prints at the Churchill to determine which are hers."

"Not a bad idea," Guidry says. "We have the Bachton girl's prints on file."

"Fingerprints?" I start gathering all the papers I've strewn over the coffee table, and finally reveal the Scrabble tiles she put in place to spell her alias. "You can start with these. Chatham's prints are all over them."

Hinkley and Guidry look at each other. They grin.

"What do you say?" Hinkley says. "Offer this kid a job."

They phone in for an evidence tech.

"That'll take care of whether or not this girl is who you think she is, as long as we can get some clear, definitive prints." Guidry turns to Hinkley. "But at the end of the day, no matter who she is, she's still gone. And it doesn't solve the issue of getting Damien to tell what he knows. Obviously, he didn't keep the girl. So what was his role? What can we use?"

"We have the domestic battery," Hinkley says. "He had a productive Saturday in that department."

"Yeah," Guidry says, "but he'll be out on that charge in a day's time with bail and fines paid. We need something more. Something with more meat on the bone."

"Possession of child porn? Think we could hedge it?"

"Won't stick. What we have hardly constitutes porn."

Guidry turns to me. "That photograph your sister found . . . it's enough just cause for a search warrant. Maybe something will turn up at his place."

"Look." I meet his stare. "If Rachel was there, it was so long ago. There's nothing left in that shack that'll prove it."

"Then why'd he keep the photograph?"

"I don't know. But if you killed a dog—if you *hanged* a dog by the ropes of your stepson's swing because he barked when you were hung over—would you keep the collar? Would you hang the collar *on the living room wall* to remind your stepson of what you'd done? Of what you *could* do? If he dared to step out of line?"

"Huh."

My eyes start to tear up. I can't help it. It's not just about the dog, but about everything I've been through, about the thought of a little girl falling prey to all of this. I cough and try to hold back.

"I'll bet he kept that photograph just so he could remind himself he got away with it." I swipe at my eyes, hopefully before the cops notice. "He's capable. You both know he is."

"He's a big guy," Guidry says. "Taller than the description."

"Yeah, but who gave the description?" Hinkley says. "A little kid."

ON THE BRINK

I've Snapchatted Chatham a dozen times.

But I know I won't hear from her. I can only hope it's because she doesn't want to be found, as opposed to can't be found.

Laundry.

Homework.

Dishes.

Rosie's phone starts to buzz, just when I hear a car door slam outside.

Rosie darts to the living room window.

I answer the phone. It's Guidry.

"Girls, go to Joshy's room," my mother says.

The fear in her voice is all too familiar. I know Damien's here.

"Some rookie prick let him out on bail," Guidry's saying. "Listen to me!"

The doors are locked, but I've recently seen what Damien can do with a locked door in his path.

"Hurry, girls." Rosie's rushing my sisters down the stairs. "Hide in the closet, okay? Don't come out."

Guidry's telling me there are units on the way.

To sit tight.

I can't focus.

Too much is happening.

The whole house shakes when Damien's fist meets the front door.

He pounds a solid three times.

"Don't answer that door," Guidry says. "We're en route."

But we still need to know what he knows. I grab my phone from the counter and start an audio recording, just in case we need it later as evidence.

"Fucking let me in!" Damien yells from the other side of the door.

"He's going to break down the door." Rosie's trembling, and I see it come over her: the paralyzing fear that lets him win every time. "I have to let him in. He's coming in anyway. It'll be better for all of us if I just—"

Guidry: "Don't let her open that door!"

"He'll be angrier if I don't let him in."

"Rosie, don't."

But she's already halfway down the stairs.

It happens in slow motion:

The life drains from her face.

Her body goes flaccid against the door.

Wait a minute, Damien. Just a second. I see her lips moving, and I sort of hear her, but the words are cloudy; my ears are ringing.

She frees the deadbolt on the door.

Flips open the lock on the knob.

I drop my mother's phone to the counter.

He bursts through the door like a hurricane and grasps my mother just under the elbow and forces her up the stairs.

I swallow over the lump in my throat and blink hard to focus.

"I don't know what he told you." Damien's pulling the belt from his jeans. "But the boy has to be dealt with."

"I'll talk to him," Rosie says. "Please. Just let me talk to him. He's sorry—we both are—for what happened last night."

"What happens between us is *family business*." He shoves my mother aside and snaps his belt; the leather claps together. "No one has a right to tell a man how to deal with his family, and we have a lot to deal with these days, don't we? You"—his finger is in my face—"you have something that belongs to me. Did you give it to your piece of ass?"

Rosie: "Damien."

I have something that belongs to him? What do I have?

Is that why he trashed Chatham's room at the Churchill? Because he thinks I took something of his?

In a split second, the hundred pieces of this puzzle I've been juggling suddenly start to fall into place. I practically hear them click together.

"I don't know what you're talking about," I say. Except I do.

"I gave it to your mother."

"The unicorn? That broke. I don't know what happened that day, but—"

"Not the fucking unicorn." He rhythmically slaps the belt against the table, slow and steady. *Slap, slap, slap.* "It's important, so I want you to think long and hard about it."

"If I knew, I'd tell you," I lie.

He stares me down.

"Caroline found a picture in your closet," I say. "Is there something you want to tell *me*?"

"I don't know where that came from, and that's none of your fucking business anyway."

"Except it is," I bluff. "Does the name Alana mean anything to you?"

Rosie: "Josh."

"Shut your fucking mouth, you disrespectful punk."

"Alana Goudy." I take a step back.

He takes a step toward me, but I don't care, as long as I draw him far away from my mother.

"She was at your place, wasn't she?" I continue with slow words, so he's sure to process and understand. "A long time ago? Except that's not the only name she goes by anymore. You were following her. On the beach. At the diner."

"Just give him the ring, Josh," my mother says. "Damien, we can sort through everything. Start over. Start fresh, and we'll figure things out, okay?"

"I don't know what ring you're talking about." I keep walking slowly backward. He keeps in close pursuit. "But I do know you've been following my girlfriend. Chatham Claiborne. The girl with the X on her hip. That's what you wanted to see the other day, isn't it? When you were spying on us at the Churchill? You wanted to see if she had a scar where a birthmark used to be. You thought you recognized her when she came back to town. Maybe you followed the twins and me to Northgate Point Beach that day, and you saw her. You started following *her* after that."

"What's it to you?"

"Josh," Rosie says.

"What were you going to do once you figured out who she was?"

"Shut your fucking mouth."

"Josh," Rosie says. "You *know* the ring. Just give it back to him."

"I *don't* know the ring, Rosie! I don't have it! I don't even know what it looks like!"

"Gold," Damien says. "Dark red stone. Shaped like a teardrop."

A teardrop that is half of a heart-shaped charm on Rachel Bachton's necklace. No wonder the cops asked if the center stone of Savannah's brooch was one piece or two. No wonder they weren't fazed when I mentioned it. If I'm right, the heart-shaped charm on Rachel's necklace was actually two tear-drop stones fashioned together to make a heart. And one of those stones is in the ring Damien threw at my mother.

Savannah's brooch has nothing to do with Rachel, but this ring *does*.

"Dark red." I start to nod. "Maybe I've seen it. Maybe I *did* give it to Chatham. You wouldn't happen to know where she is, would you?"

Rosie approaches. "Josh, just give it to him!"

"Maybe I'll beat it out of you." Damien lashes with the belt, but not at me. It cuts across my mother's thighs.

"Mom!"

She recoils, but swallows her scream.

"There's no need for that, Damien." My words are coming more quickly now, but I try to keep my voice even, so as not to give away my fear. "I know the ring."

"I'll teach your ass for lying to me."

"I'll tell you where it is. But you have to promise not to hit my mother again."

"Oh, I've got other plans for her." He cups his cock through his jeans.

"It's in this room." I only hope it's still where it landed, under the breakfront. I can't let him leave with it. "It's in this room."

"Yeah, and I might fuck her in this room, too."

Keep him focused, keep him wanting.

"It's in the flour," I say. "At the bottom of the canister. It's where she keeps the cash."

Rosie hiccups over a sob.

"I'll get it," I say.

"And so will I." He pops the button on his fly just to irk me.

I inch my way to the pantry, where we keep the canisters. I pull the top off the largest one, and just as I'm about to toss a handful of flour into Damien's face, if only to buy my mother time to get out of the room, I hear the front door whip open.

Damien throws his belt around my neck and yanks me back to his chest.

The belt is tighter around my throat now, and he's lifting me off my feet by my neck.

I manage to get a few fingers under the leather strap, and I'm wriggling to get free when I hear:

"County PD."

"Lose the weapon, Mr. Wick."

In seconds, I'm free, on my knees, coughing to draw breath.

"You talking about my belt, or my dick?"

I take to the floor, lying on my back, breathing through the panic. If Guidry's guys hadn't come in when they did, would he have killed me?

My mother is at my side now.

"Go to the girls," I manage to say. "I'm fine."

And I see out of the corner of my eye that Damien's in cuffs. "Forced entry," Guidry's saying.

"She fucking let me in."

"Yes, she did. Under threat. I think I heard another threat to rape your ex-wife in front of her son. That's potentially two counts of sexual abuse—one against her, one against him. Another rap for domestic battery, Damien." Guidry clucks his tongue. "Damn, you're getting notorious for that these days. Not to mention the attempted murder we just interrupted."

I wheeze when I sit up.

"I think at least one of those is going to stick, boss," Hinkley says.

I nudge my way through the sea of people crowding this room, toward the breakfront. I reach beneath it and feel the square box at my fingertips. I grasp it, then think to get up, but I can't. I'm just too tired. Exhausted is more like it. I stay on the floor, sitting, and leaning against the wall.

Within minutes, after the uniformed officers have removed my mother's ex-husband from the house, Rosie returns with the twins, who are still crying.

They dart to me, and I take them in my lap and wrap my arms around them. "It's okay, sisters. I'm okay."

"Joshy's okay?" Margaret sniffles over her words.

"Love you," Caroline says.

"Love you, too," I tell them. "But I have to get up. Have to talk to the police now, okay?"

Rosie sits at the table with her head in her hands. "Nothing. We got him to admit *nothing.*"

"Not quite, ma'am," Hinkley says. "We got him on—"

"Nothing at *all* about that little girl, though, and now—"

"No, Mom. You don't understand. He just admitted *everything.* And I recorded it on my phone." I drop the ring on the table and say to Guidry, "Show this to Rachel Bachton's mother."

"I'll be damned," Guidry says as he studies it.

Rosie looks up. "What?" Caroline crawls onto her lap, and Margaret snuggles in close to me.

"A while back," Guidry says, "I closed a case on a kid missing over two decades. She had a rosary on her when she was snatched—she hid it from her abductor—and years later, she pulled a stone out of the rosary and made it into a ring for her daughter. It was in all the papers. I wonder if Damien might have done the same thing—pulled a stone out of the charm on Rachel's necklace and made it into a ring for you."

"But why?" Rosie asks. "Knowing what's at stake, knowing he could be found out . . . why would he risk it?"

"Well." Hinkley sits down next to my mother. "Think about it like a stolen car. It's harder to salvage what's lost, if all the parts are scattered in different places. So *if* the stone in this ring *used to be* part of Rachel's necklace . . ."

She nods. "Okay. *If.*"

"I'm pretty sure Mrs. Bachton will tell you," I say. "The stone in this ring is half of the red and gold heart charm Rachel had on her necklace when she disappeared."

H O L L O W

"Breaking news: Wayne and Loretta Goudy, residents of rural Catoosa County, Georgia, have been arrested for the murder of their foster daughter, known only as Alana."

I drop my cereal bowl in the sink—I think it cracks and breaks—and glue my eyes to the television, while I try to swallow a mouthful of cornflakes, mushy and sticky in my throat. Tears well in my eyes.

She's dead. Just like I told Toad at the Temple Tattoo.

I conjured her at the beach that first night, and I erased her from existence just as easily—with just a spoken thought.

I think I'm going to throw up.

"The remains of the child, Baby A—"

"What?" I breathe through the nausea. And although I'm confused, I know one thing for certain: "It's not Chatham. Not Chatham."

"—were buried at the confluence of the Vernon and Moon Rivers, in Chatham County, some three hundred fifty miles south of the Goudy tract. Originally thought to be those of missing Rachel Bachton, the remains were discovered in late summer. It is estimated the murder occurred nine to twelve years ago."

"Police sought Wayne Goudy for questioning for months before tracking him down in relation to the Bachton kidnapping, which police say is closely linked to Alana's murder. No details yet as to how these cases are linked, but the timeline proves it's possible. Rachel Bachton disappeared—"

"You can get the girls to school today?" Rosie breezes into the kitchen and dumps a few items into her bag for lunch: an orange, an apple, a few stalks of celery.

"Yeah." I sniff over my emotions. "Yeah, I got it."

I look up at the television again to see a picture of Wayne Goudy today alongside a composite sketch of Rachel's kidnapper. There's no resemblance. ". . . leaving the media puzzled as to what the connection may be."

"Josh." My mother touches me on the arm and looks at me. Really *looks* at me. "You okay?"

"Yeah. There was a bulletin about a murder, and I thought it was Chatham."

"But it wasn't."

I shake my head. "I broke a bowl."

"That's okay."

For a second, we stand there in silence.

"Maybe you shouldn't watch the news for a while."

"I can handle it." I think not knowing would be worse than knowing too much.

"We'll talk later? After school?"

"Sure."

I drop the girls at Peppermint Swirl Pre-K, and I'm on track to hit Sugar Creek High fifteen minutes before breakfast club starts, but instead, I wheel down Washington and head to Northgate Beach.

It's only fitting. It's the first place I saw her, the first place I went when I realized I needed to see her again. And that night, I imagined she was here, and then she materialized. If only I could do that again.

I pinch my eyes shut and imagine her casually strolling down the shore.

Hey, cute boy. She'd kiss me, instantly warming me, and maybe she'd laugh at the idiocy of it all—how, despite withstanding the attacks of our perpetrators, losing track of someone who makes you feel whole can rip your heart out and leave you hollow.

By now, everyone on the team must know what happened with Chatham, and they'll have to forgive me for being a bit late to the weight deck. I text Coach Baldecki for the fiftieth time since everything went down, tell him I'm going for a run on the beach this morning. Clear my head. Get ready for Friday night. All the stuff he wants to hear, sure, but it's also the truth.

There's a nip in the air, but I'm layered in a T-shirt, a waffle-knit, and a hoodie. I park at the gate and climb over the rails to the boardwalk. I lean against the railing and watch the waves, silvery and already smelling of impending winter, roll up on the shore. Winter always comes to the lake first. We won't see snow for a month or two, but here on the beach, everything is gray, as if the great artist upstairs is readying this canvas before all others.

My gaze draws from the horizon, near the lighthouse, down the shore to the patch of sand where I first saw Chatham Claiborne create.

A line of footprints mars the smooth, wet sand high at the shoreline, where the early morning waves break against the bluffs.

I picture her at the end of that line of footprints, lifting her chin confidently, hands on hips. *It's been days. What took you so long?*

I hurdle the boardwalk railing and land in the sand below, and beeline toward the footprints in the sand.

With every footfall, I acclimate to the terrain and become more focused.

I know I won't find her, trailing these prints, but not finding her is not an option. I just have to go about it another way, stick to it until I figure it all out. Here are the facts:

Damien had Rachel's necklace.

On it was a charm—two red, teardrop-shaped stones pieced together to look like a heart.

He broke the stones out of the charm and used one of them in a ring he had made for my mother.

The other stone is likely still at his place, and maybe the police have even found it by now. But it's not information they're sharing with the public.

When Damien realized Chatham was special to me, and when Rosie failed to wear the ring he threw at her, he thought I'd stolen it and given it to Chatham. That's why he tossed her room at the Churchill. It was imperative that ring not fall into the hands of those who could connect it to Rachel Bachton.

Twelve years ago, he did, in fact, bear resemblance to the longhaired man who snatched Rachel, as long as you forgive a few inches in height discrepancy.

If that were all there was to it, okay. He'd be a suspect in Rachel's kidnapping. Why would he have taken her? What would he have done with her? The police would form theories, bring the dogs in, maybe dig up the land around his creek-side shack, and maybe demolish the shack itself, in search of bones.

But there's more to it than that. The case is complicated . . . because of Chatham Claiborne.

If I'm right, Chatham Claiborne followed her sister's trail here after the discovery of bones at the confluence, when Wayne was already gone.

Savannah came here because she remembered witnessing the kidnapping of Rachel Bachton. Maybe she, like the media, assumed the bones at the confluence were Rachel's remains, given the rumors about the girl in the floor of the stables. She'd wanted Chatham to come along. Maybe she knew Chatham would come eventually, which could be the reason she'd left her journal under Chatham's pillow. They'd be here, then, far away from the Goudy tract, when the police identified Baby A, and she'd be able to tell the police what she knew. She'd be able to incriminate her abusive parents before they realized she knew too much to let her live.

Chatham, remembering nothing, came in pursuit of her sister, following clues Savannah purposely left behind in a journal, when Chatham realized her life might be in jeopardy, too.

So who did the clothes beneath the floorboards belong to? Were they Rachel's? Were they the clothes Alana was wearing when she died?

The Bachtons had denied the photograph Savannah found there was Rachel.

My guess is those clothes were Alana's.

And given the scar on Chatham's hip, the house she continued to sculpt and draw, and the images of Damien's swing she'd included in her works of art, my guess is that Rachel Bachton is alive and well.

My guess is the child beneath the floorboards was the Goudys' foster daughter, Alana. She died, maybe before they put her under the stables, or maybe *because* they put her there. Wayne buried her at the rivers. And if she'd been dead twelve years, and Rachel's been missing twelve years . . .

What if Damien took Rachel to give to the Goudys? He would keep the necklace and the charm as a memento of what he did, of course.

But what's the connection between Damien and the Goudys?

"He scouted her," I say aloud. "Goudy sent a picture. The child had to pass for Alana, the child they'd killed. When he'd found the perfect target, the Goudys came to town. Went to the farmers' market that day, used Savannah to lure Rachel, and Damien snatched Rachel and handed her over later at Damien's house."

It would explain how the same picture of Alana ended up in two places with a stretch of America between them. The Goudys had taken the picture, and sent a copy to Damien.

It would explain why the Goudys had to remove Rachel's birthmark—Alana didn't have one.

But what's the motivation to replace a child who's died or who you've killed?

Maybe they just thought the state wouldn't know the difference between two blonde preschoolers. And they took Rachel to get away with murder.

Maybe that's why the Goudys never adopted her. Adoption would call attention to the child.

But the question remains . . .

If all of this is true, or even if it isn't, where is Chatham Claiborne now?

I'm nearing the lighthouse.

I should turn back.

But there's something up the shore . . .

I keep running.

As I approach, I see a sand castle, worn by wind and water, but its remains are no less elaborate than the one Chatham sculpted weeks ago on this very same beach, complete with the criss-cross windows that delighted my sisters.

After the rave, Chatham said she'd keep building castles so Savannah would know she'd been there, so Savannah would know she's still looking for her.

I catch my breath for a few seconds, then pull my phone from my pocket.

I take a picture of the sand sculpture and send it in a snap to Chatham.

Then I call Detective Guidry: "It's Josh Michaels. This might be out there, but I've been mulling over some things Chatham told me over the past month or so, and I've got a theory."

I tell him what I've been thinking about during my run.

He doesn't give my theory affirmation, but he doesn't tell me I'm nuts, either.

"So no word from her," he says at the end of it all.

"No, sir."

"You'll let me know if you hear from her."

"Yes, sir."

I look at the sand castle one last time before I start my run back down the shore.

There's no way to know for sure, but I prefer to believe:

She was here.

DISSIPATE

Even when I close my eyes, I see her—Chatham Claiborne—and all she created and conjured.

Right now, she's sixteen squares of clay relief, arranged in a mosaic of four by four.

Sort of like the tattoo of her name on the inside of my left arm, and the scars it covers: permanent in this form.

It's ironic, in a way, her creating something I can describe with such a word. But that's the way I see her now. Molded, glazed, and fired. Permanent.

Every artist leaves her signature on her work, and Chatham's may as well be art itself: each letter of her name is tucked away in the relief—one letter per tile.

Sixteen squares make up a whole, but each square is its own sliver of beauty, its own window into a world that is distinctly—solely?—Chatham's, a corridor into the heart of the girl I've come to crave, the girl I've come to believe is as necessary to my survival as air or water, the girl I'll forever search for.

She's sand on a beach.

The flame licking at the wax of a birthday candle.

It's Friday.

It's been six days since the best and worst night of my life.

No one's seen Chatham Claiborne since.

Guidry called to tell me what I already knew: that the prints on the Scrabble tiles were consistent with Rachel Bachton's, and furthermore that the ring Damien gave to my mother did, in fact, include a stone which used to comprise half a heart, nestled in a charm on Rachel's necklace. The police found the charm, with one-half of the heart missing, amongst other things in Damien's closet.

But he's not telling me the one thing I desperately need to know: where the hell is she?

Like I said before: knowing what happened won't bring her home.

This morning, an Amber Alert was issued for Rachel Bachton, and a picture Aiden took of us at the Homecoming dance is circulating the press. I'm blurred out, as if I'm an inconsequential casualty in this whole mess.

I wonder if I'll ever see her again. God, I *need* to see her again.

But that wonder and need will be here a good, long time, and I can't focus on it tonight because tonight, I have a job to do out on the field.

"You good?" Jensen, all suited up, with his helmet at his hip, pauses in front of my locker, where I'm sitting on a bench, pulling at the shoestrings in my cleats.

I've yet to pull my jersey over my pads. "Yeah. Stellar."

"You know, after the week you've had, no one's going to blame you if you're not up for this."

"I'm up for it."

"Robinson's been throwing pretty well, you know. He's not as fast as you are, doesn't have instincts like yours, but if you feel you can't—"

"I *can*." I yank my jersey over my pads and give him a nod. "I got this."

And I'm dedicating this game to Chatham Claiborne.

It's the last game of the season.

"I can do it," I assure him one more time. I didn't come this far, or garner this much attention from college scouts, because I *can't*. Word's not even in my vocabulary right now. So I was dealt another shitty hand, played another shitty card. What else is new? Still, I'm here. I'm surviving.

On the field, I'm firing away with all the anger, all the frustration, all the hurt channeled into the cannon my right arm has become.

Connecting.

Boom, boom, boom. Touchdown.

Boom, boom, boom. Touchdown.

My name echoes through the speaker:

"Number fourteen, Michaels! With a twelve-yard sneak."

"Michaels! With a fifty-five-yard pass to twenty-six, Novak!"

"Michaels . . . Michaels . . . Michaels!"

"And the Sugar Creek Cavs are *going* to the *playoffs* . . ."

The D-line hoists me on their shoulders. The O-line carries Novak off the field in the same fashion. Dude deserves it. He caught everything I fucking threw at him, and even some I placed just out of reach.

And as much as I appreciate Rosie bringing Maggie Lee and Miss Lina to see me play tonight—the first time *ever*—I wish Chatham were here to see it, too.

I go through the motions.

High fives in the locker room.

Chocolate cake at the Tiny Elvis.

Someone carved **Rachel Bachton was here** into all the tables. No one knows as intimately as I do how very true that sentiment is.

I stay at the diner past close, with the rest of the team, till they kick us out.

And when I leave, I can't help glancing back at the second floor of the Churchill, where I'm sure Chatham's mural is already scheduled for a fresh coat of paint.

"Hey there. Joshua."

I stop in my tracks when I hear the voice, the slight lilt in her words. Pure Georgia. I smile. "Chatham." I spin around to face her.

"Sorry to disappoint."

"Savannah." I'm standing face-to-face, for the third time, with Chatham's sister. She's dressed more conservatively today, in shin-length jeans and a baggy, black hoodie. Her toenails, which I see only because she's wearing a pair of worn flip-flops, are painted a glittery purple. Her blonde hair is pulled back into a messy ponytail, and she isn't wearing any makeup today. A watch is wrapped around her ankle, like it's a piece of jewelry.

I can't read her expression. Her casually turning up here could mean good things, or bad.

"She's okay," Savannah says.

A sense of relief flits through my system—Chatham's okay—but instantly, knowing *she's okay* isn't enough. "Where is she?"

Savannah opens her mouth, almost like she's going to tell me, but then she clams up.

I look at her hard. "You expect me to believe you don't know? I'm pretty sure she met you after she left my place that night."

Her nod is so minute that I would've missed it, had I not been paying close attention.

"People are looking for you, you know," I say.

"Yeah. Don't tell, okay?"

"God, do you know what I go through? Wondering where she is . . . hoping she's alive . . . Come to think of it, it's exactly what *you* put *her* through when you took off."

This pisses her off. She sort of stiffens, and frowns at me.

"When you didn't show at the beach on the last day of summer, like you said. What happened, Savannah? Why weren't you there?"

"I saw someone I thought I recognized."

"Damien? Chatham said she saw a man following her that day, too."

"I was scared, so I had to leave. I found a place to stay."

"On Sheridan Road."

"Yeah."

"Where are you staying now?"

She answers me with a silent stare. She isn't going to tell me.

"This man . . ." I pull my phone out of my pocket and scroll to the pictures of Damien feeding his girlfriend at the Tiny E. "This him?"

She studies the picture. "Yeah. He was there that day. At the farmers' market. I think he knows Wayne."

"How?"

"I don't know. He was at the farm once or twice. But when I saw him, I got scared. I thought maybe Wayne told him I ran away and sent him to look for me. I didn't know he *lived* here until my sister said she saw his cabin."

"Yeah. He's local."

"Can we go somewhere else to talk?" she asks.

"Nowhere really *to* go to talk this time of night." I cop a squat on the sidewalk, near the coastal-border-of-Texas crack. "Have a seat."

She sits next to me. "Listen. She's sort of overwhelmed with all this, you know?"

I can imagine.

"She's sorry she misled you, but it wasn't like she planned it. She never really was on board with my theory, and didn't want to believe she was Rachel. She even thought for a while that *I* was the one who was kidnapped because she didn't remember anything. She *just couldn't face it.* But then you took her to the train car in that park. She started to remember. And when you took her to the cabin by the creek . . . Joshua, she thinks she might have been there before."

"Why didn't she tell me? Or at least tell the cops? She talked with them later that night, at my house. She *called* them. Why wouldn't she have said anything?"

"You have to understand. She doesn't even know who she is anymore."

"I need to see her. Where is she?"

"She thinks you won't forgive her."

"What's to forgive?"

"She's afraid you can't possibly love her after—"

"After what?"

"Well, after she lied about knowing me. At the rave. It was my idea, not hers. I told her to pretend. To stay anonymous until we knew what was going to happen in Moon River. Can you imagine what would have happened if Wayne's friend found us together? If anything, you should be mad at *me.*"

"I'm not mad at anyone. Christ, look at this." I yank up my

sleeve and display my tattoo. "Whenever she questions the way I feel, tell her what I've done to remember her."

Savannah stares at the tattoo. "I can't believe you did that."

"Well, I did. Tell her about it."

"I will."

"None of this is her fault. Savannah, if you love your sister—"

"Of *course* I love my sister."

"—you'll turn yourself over and tell us where to find her so she can start again. So she can reconnect with the family that's been missing her for *twelve years*."

"I took beatings for her. Did she tell you that?" She glances at me, but quickly averts her teary eyes, and continues staring out over Second Street. "I'd provoke him so he'd come after me instead. I made sure that asshole *never laid a hand on her*."

"He shouldn't have touched either of you."

"I stole their money so I could come here. For *four years* I've been taking everything Wayne left around the house from quarters to twenties. But I paid for every cent in punishments. Whippings. Extra chores. *Other things.* They thought I stole the money for drugs, and sometimes I did. But most of it, I kept. I left her all of my money with practically a treasure map for her to find it."

"In the stables."

"I left her all my notes so she could follow when she'd finally realize I was telling the truth. I suspected for a long time where she came from, even if she didn't believe me, and I wanted to bring her back here, so don't you dare accuse me of not loving my sister."

"I'm sorry. I didn't mean it that way."

"I had to get her away from him."

"Away from Wayne?"

She nods and wipes away tears.

"Alana . . . my first sister. She just didn't get up one day. He hit us both, but she didn't get up. Loretta wasn't there to stop him that day, and once he got started . . ."

My heart aches for what I know she's going to say next.

"He just couldn't stop once he got started. He wouldn't let up. He had her by the hair, and just kept pounding on her."

I feel dizzy and lost, hearing all this.

"He told me she was sleeping. He told me if I wasn't good, I'd be sleeping in the stables, too. Under the floorboards."

"Jesus."

"And then he had me convinced that the new girl we brought home was the same Alana. Only this time, she was good."

I'm sick to my stomach. To think Chatham and Savannah had to live with that man . . .

"He preferred me blonde."

"Blonde?"

"And not just any blonde. *White* blonde. Just like the new Alana. Loretta's been bleaching my hair since I was about five."

I understand a little better now why Chatham freaked out when I commented on her hair Homecoming night.

"Guy was sick," she continues. "Wanted us to look a certain way while we mucked the stables and delivered calves."

"She was good at delivering cows?"

"We were *both* good at delivering cows. Both hated it."

For the space of a few minutes, we're sitting there in silence. She shivers. Like her sister, she doesn't dress for the weather. I put my arm around her and let her rest her head on my chest while she cries. I have sisters. I know how to deal with tears.

"I know she has to start being Rachel again," Savannah says. "But what happens to me? Everything I do—everything I've done since she came to me—is for her."

"Believe it or not, I'm in touch with that sort of burden."

"So if she goes on with life, what happens to me?" she repeats.

For the first time, I realize this might be the reason Chatham took off that night, the reason she's hiding from a truth she must have realized by now. That she'll have to leave Savannah.

"Loretta and Wayne won't get you back," I say. "You know they're in custody."

"So I'll be chucked back into the system for my remaining year-and-a-half before I'm legally declared an adult, in Georgia, away from my sister."

"Do you think they'd do that?" I briskly rub her arm. She's so cold. "Or do you think they'd try to accommodate what's best for you and your sister? You're both victims."

"There's an obvious solution for my sister. There's no clear-cut path for me. She's here, so I want to be here. But who's going to take me in? You think I'm going to have a multitude of options?"

"Maybe not *multitudes*, but options? Yes."

She pulls out of my grasp. "No *nice* family is going to take in a girl like me."

"You don't know that. It happens."

She rolls her eyes. "I've been taking care of myself for a long time. I'm not good at rules of the household."

"Tell you what." I reach into my pocket for my phone and cue up Guidry's number. "If you agree to call the detective, and tell him where to find your sister, I'll get you a place to crash for the night. You can explore your options in the morning. I'm talking a nice place, great view of the lake. All you have to do is hit the call button."

Hesitantly, she eyes my phone.

"You know Chatham won't move on until you do," I say. "And I know it sucks, having to be the responsible one, always having to think about her before you make a move yourself. But you and I both know: it's just part of having little sisters. And would you trade being her sister for anything in the world?"

She takes the phone.

Makes the call.

Then I call and arrange her accommodations for the night.

I think Aiden's going to like her.

JABBERWOCKY SLAIN

With tiles scattered about its perimeter, my Scrabble board still sits on the table untouched, as if waiting for closure.

And while I think I might never find it, Rachel Bachton's family finally has the closure they've been seeking since they opted to go to the farmers' market that morning—the morning Rachel was kidnapped.

I watched her reunion with her family from afar, just like everyone else. There was a parade of celebration, but she wasn't in it. There were statements to the press, but she didn't make them. Her parents have spoken on the news, and while they mention her slow reintegration process, and its successes, the world has yet to see her smile, hear her voice, or feel her contentment.

But whatever name she's going by—Rachel, Alana, Chatham—I'm confident when I say that I do know her . . . possibly better than anyone. I memorized her smile long ago, and I can see it if I close my eyes and concentrate.

The police still have the tiles that used to occupy this game board. They're in an evidence locker somewhere, bearing the fingerprints of Chatham Claiborne/Rachel Bachton. Maybe someday the police will bring them back. I've already decided that if they do, I'm going to shellac them together, make them as permanent as the clay relief Chatham designed and created, which still hangs in the art showcase at Sugar Creek High, like a memorial.

Chatham Claiborne was here.

I pull new Scrabble tiles from the sea of overturned squares and lay out sixteen of them one by one:

CHATHAM CLAIBORNE

I wonder when, exactly, Chatham realized who she was. If she'd known the moment she saw Savannah at the rave, if she'd pieced things together slowly, or if it all came flooding back like a tidal wave at the caboose or at Damien's cabin.

It all happened, more or less, the way I'd sorted things out during my run along the beach. When Goudy cracked, and admitted Damien Wick was his cousin—*kinfolk* is the word he used—and that Damien had helped secure a girl to replace the foster girl Wayne had killed in a fit of rage, the trial was over within a week. The police department gave me some bogus award I'm pretty sure they invented, and publicly thanked me for my part in bringing Rachel Bachton home. Rosie was so proud, and so happy, that she kissed Hinkley square on the mouth. Maggie Lee and Miss Lina were over-the-moon happy for me, too.

But just as I told the cops, I didn't do anything but love Chatham Claiborne. She chose to trust me with her memories. She chose to share with me details of her life, of her body . . . details that ultimately saved her. She's the real hero here, not me.

My phone buzzes with a text. It's from Savannah: *Saw her today. She's good.*

Savannah texts every now and then, from her bunk at Winston Hall for Teens in a suburb, just south of Sugar Creek.

Aiden hears from her more often than I do—I think they're secretly getting it on—but that's no surprise. I knew he'd like her. He's even taking her to winter formal next month.

But Savannah assures me that Chatham is adjusting to life as Rachel. I imagine the transition was much like the confluence at which Alana Goudy's remains were uncovered—choppy at the intersection, but finding a new, unique current once the waters blended and calmed.

We're all like river rocks at the bottom of that confluence. We all bear the marks of the waters that wear us down, but it's also the waters that contour and smooth our exteriors. It's the turbulence that makes us what we are, inside and out.

And so the Bachton family blinked out of the media eye as abruptly as it emerged twelve years ago, a testament to the saying *life goes on.*

The Sugar Creek Cavaliers lost in the second round of state football playoffs, but the appropriate statement was made. College coaches abound; they all know we're a budding force no one wants to fuck with. College is no longer a pipe dream for me, but an eventuality I look forward to.

I've texted Chatham, but she doesn't reply. Detective Hinkley recently told me Chatham has a new phone, and a new number, so I shouldn't read into it, that she'd get in touch with me when she's ready. He delivered a letter I wrote her months ago, and another one I wrote last week. But so far, she hasn't replied. I try to understand, try to remember what the cops tell me: give her time.

But how much time is enough time?

How much time does she need to reconcile her life before with life now?

Do I even fit into her life now?

I push a few Scrabble tiles out of line:

CHATH_ _ CLA_BORNE
AMI
I AM

I suspect she's making a clean break from the chaos she knew when she was with me, and I can't say I blame her.

_ _ _TH_ _ C_A_BO_N_
CHAAMLIRE
I AM RACHEL

But still . . . I hope she remembers that whatever her name is, or was, I'm part of her, just as she's part of me.

"Oh my God," I whisper as I look down at the board.

_ _ _ _ _ _ _ _ _ _ _ _ _ _ _ _ _
CHATHAM CLAIBORNE
I AM RACHEL BACHTON

. . . Because even if she wasn't ready to tell me her name, she's always known, on some level, who she is. You don't need to know your name to know who you are.

TIME

It's January now—going on three months without Chatham—and I'm shoveling snow, while my sisters watch with their hands pressed against the picture window in the living room. They stick their tongues out at me. I stick mine out at them.

I'd often tried to imagine this town without Damien in it.

Life without the threat of him.

A mother and sisters without the fear of him.

And this is it. He's behind bars, and he'll be there for a long time.

"Need some help out here, Josh?"

I turn to face my mother's latest flame, who just pulled up a few minutes ago. "Sure."

Hinkley hasn't even been into the house to greet my mother, but he's already armed with a shovel, and he's already clearing the sidewalk of snow. "Some of the guys on the force are taking their families sledding this afternoon. Thinking of taking the girls."

"They'll love it."

"You want to come along?"

I glance up at my sisters, who are giggling and happy, like normal almost-five-year-olds. "Wouldn't miss it."

"If you have other things to do, if you wouldn't mind just driving the sled out there, or loaning me your Explorer—"

"No, I'll go. I'll load up the toboggan, take the girls. You and Rosie can have a few minutes of peace to yourselves on the drive out."

"If this works out between your mom and me, we'll have to think about buying a car we can all fit into."

"Yeah." I laugh. After tossing a few more shovels full of snow, I admit, "It's something I wanted to do with Chatham. Take them all sledding." I know I've said it before in his company—I've been thinking a lot lately about the things Chatham and I never got around to doing—but Hinkley's gracious about my repetition.

He shrugs a shoulder. "Well, you never know. It could happen someday."

Hinkley's like that. Optimistic. Believes in positive reinforcement. He's a pillar of the community, makes his own money, has his own place, and has a daughter from a previous marriage *for whom he pays child support.*

And *this* is the guy Rosie decides to take things slow with. Drunk and abusive she falls for within minutes. Upstanding guy? Let's give it some time. Ironic. But actually smart, too.

"Why don't you go in," Hinkley says. "I'll finish up out here. You've done most of it."

"No, I can—"

"Josh, go ahead. I have a feeling your mom's going to need help wrangling those little monkeys into snowsuits."

He has a point.

When I walk in, Rosie's stirring the contents of the crockpot so we'll have a warm dinner when we get home.

"Hinkley's finishing up." I put on a pot of coffee, because

he's gonna need it. He has no idea the energy required to repeatedly climb the toboggan hill with my sisters in tow.

"You know, you can call him Steve."

"No I can't." After a second, I add, "Mom."

"We're good, right? Steve, you, the girls . . ."

"Yeah." And I actually believe it.

■ ■ ■

"Stay close," Rosie calls to the twins, who are falling into the snow on purpose, amazed it doesn't hurt. She and Hinkley each have a hand on the toboggan tow, and I smile to see their fingers playing with each other when they think no one's looking. "We have to walk up the hill," she tells my sisters.

"Joshy!" Margaret squeals.

"Joshy!" Caroline parrots. She jumps at me and I lift her in my arms. "It's so fun!"

"Yeah, you're about to have the best fun in the world," I assure her.

"Best fun," she says.

"Best fun," I say.

Once we're waiting in line at the top of the hill, I gaze out at the horizon. I see the Northgate Lighthouse to the right. I see the abandoned caboose to the left.

Rachel Bachton was here.

My phone buzzes with a text.

It's from a number I don't recognize, but I open it anyway:

It's a picture of a snow castle, which could only be a creation by the best artist I know: *Chatham.*

I smile, and laugh, and wipe tears from my eyes.

Another message comes through: *Hi.*

I reply: *Hi.*

She returns: *Tiny Elvis sometime?*

A sense of relief and excitement flows through me. She wants to see me.

I type: *Chocolate cake's on me this time.*

ACKNOWLEDGMENTS

Special thanks to my second family, the Coverts—Chris, Mary, Margaret, Jonathon, and Caroline—who always welcome us with open arms. It's no secret you are the example I strive to follow. I thank you for the Tupperware reference—always—and for "Annoy Them With Music." You are true treasures for all of us. Thanks, by the way, for lending me a couple of names for this manuscript. Where would this story be without Maggie Lee and Miss Lina?

To Alix Reid: Another excellent collaboration! And to think it all began as a conversation at Counter Coffee Shop in Forest Park—I feel cooler just saying I've been there (snap, snap, snap)! Thank you for believing in this concept, and for helping me rearrange the structure. Again and again and again. I love working with you.

Andrea Somberg, I'm forever grateful for your guidance. You're the best agent EVER! Thank you for taking the time, and paying attention . . . and for putting up with my often long-winded emails. Commiserate with Alix. I'm not known for my brevity.

To my kindred spirits at David Heigl Design Group: thanks for understanding when the words take precedence over Vintage Blue Toile and Caesarstone.

Aiden: I enjoyed meeting you on the Jersey Shore years ago when you were a little boy. I named Aiden for you, although he grew to be nothing like you. Say hello to your cousins, your grandma Sue, and your Auntie Dom and Uncle Jason for me. The next time I'm in Jersey, I'd appreciate hearing another of your ghost stories.

Samantha, there's a little of you in every heroine I write. Chatham Claiborne stole your seat at open studio. Thanks for sharing it with her. It was through your intense study of art this past year that I was able to channel the artist Chatham Claiborne came to be. She Snapchats in your fashion, she's incredibly thoughtful, and she shares your ambitions and your lively spirit of survival. By the way, does Chatham's Homecoming dress sound familiar?

Madelaine, my every heroine has attributes of yours, too. Chatham Claiborne borrowed your wardrobe—and your haircut! You gave her such style that I often envisioned you as I wrote her. She's a born leader, a survivor, and a giver beyond reason. She wouldn't hesitate to help her friends, and neither do you. Your talent with pencil rendering definitely influenced Chatham's. I'm sure she's listening to twenty one pilots as she's sketching.

Joshua, your triumphs fleshed out a character who's been throwing ropes in my brain since before you dropped your call with Bruce in San Antonio. Your sense of responsibility, as well as your recklessness, filled the lungs of these pages, and they're now breathing. You never quit, and your history proves it. I appreciate all our Q&As about high school football, and I hope I've done the sport decent justice. I appreciate your dimples and take pride in seeing them more often now that we've found our forever.

To my readers:

See you next time **IN WICKER PARK**.

ABOUT THE AUTHOR

Sasha Dawn creates tales of survival and error, disasters and dreams. She has degrees in both history and writing, and loves old buildings and new ideas. A warrior, she fights traffic daily in the north suburbs of Chicago, where she lives with her husband, daughters, and puppies. Sasha is the author of the critically acclaimed *Oblivion* and *Splinter*.

UNEXPECTED.
ECLECTIC.
ADVENTUROUS.

For more distinctive and award-winning YA titles, reader guides, book excerpts, and more, visit *CarolrhodaLab.com*.